I0768727

GARROTED IN THE GALLERY

A BREEZE VILLAGE COZY MYSTERY

KATE MACLEAN

Copyright © 2024 by Kate Maclean

All rights reserved.

No part of this book may be reproduced in any form or by any electronic or mechanical means, including information storage and retrieval systems, without written permission from the author, except for the use of brief quotations in a book review.

This is a work of fiction. The names, settings, places, and characters are fictitious and not intended to represent specific places or persons, living or dead. Any resemblance to actual events or persons is entirely coincidental.

Book cover design by ebooklaunch.com

This book is dedicated to my mother; to Shelley, who also mothered me; and to all of the mothers who would believe their daughters and fight for them.

GARROTED IN THE GALLERY

CHAPTER 1

Virginia barely saw the lights of Seaview fly by outside the car window as she sped down the street. She didn't see the red light in front of her at all, blowing through it, a lightning bolt of adrenaline surging through her as she realized her mistake too late to stop. It was three blocks before her breathing slowed, before she stopped waiting for the flash of blue and red to activate behind her. That was the last thing she needed—not with where she was headed, what she was doing.

Lucy's words sounded repeatedly in her mind, layering over themselves as the surroundings blurred in her vision. "Mom," her daughter had said, her usually self-assured voice sounding small and afraid instead. "I need your help."

Virginia muttered under her breath as she drove. "I'm coming, honey. I'm coming."

She tried to convince herself she'd misheard the rest of the phone call—the part where Lucy said she'd been arrested for murder.

An hour ago, Virginia had been happily conversing with Sam, her daughter-in-law's mother, who had, until recently, been something of a nemesis of Virginia's. Now, since they had both become grandparents for the first time with the birth of Jack's and Stephanie's baby girl, a new bond seemed to be forming between them.

Virginia's heart pounded as she remembered that soft bundle in her arms, the one she'd handed back to Stephanie when Lucy had called. That wriggling mass of warmth and love that was so like Lucy herself had once been. One second, Virginia wanted to press harder on the gas and fly faster toward the police station where she was sure her daughter was being wrongfully held for something she didn't do. She wanted to rescue that baby girl and cradle her close. The next second, she wanted to throttle Lucy for missing her niece's birth and for pulling Virginia away from her newborn granddaughter. And then she wanted to protect her again.

A sob slipped from Virginia's lips, the dueling emotions overwhelming.

At a stoplight, Virginia checked her phone again. Nothing new from Jack or Stephanie. Nothing from Lucy. No word, no text saying *It was all a misunderstanding! They let me out, and I'll head straight to the hospital to meet up with you all!*

A car horn sliced through Virginia's disappointment, and she jumped, registering that the light had turned green and pressing on the gas. Her car lurched forward, sending her stomach churning inside her, and the car behind honked again for good measure as it sped around her.

Alone again, with no cars behind her, Virginia felt the shock dissipate and her mind clear. For the first time, she let it wander to the possibility she hadn't allowed herself to consider before: what if Lucy really had done something terrible?

She forcibly shook the thought from her head and pressed on.

Virginia hadn't been to the Seaview Police Station many times in her life, even though her best friend's daughter, whom Virginia had helped raise, had worked there for over twenty years. Dylan had climbed the ranks, eventually becoming Assistant Chief of Police, only stepping down to pursue a relationship with another officer at the start of the year just weeks earlier.

The first time Virginia had set foot in the building was less than a year earlier. She was hoping to glean information to help her solve the murder of Ruth Beaumont, one of Breeze Village's residents, but she was ignored and dismissed. The next time, she'd been under questioning as a suspect in another murder investigation after the owner of Breeze Village was killed. Now, her body responded to her pulling into the parking lot by tensing, ready for a fight. Her pulse raced and her hands shook on the steering wheel. Her thoughts swirled, garbled together unintelligibly while every instinct in her screamed to get away from that place, and as her thoughts became less and less discernible, sheer panic rose.

It was the memory of her daughter's voice that pierced the fog and brought her back to reality. Back to what she'd come here to do. *I've been arrested for murder.*

The inside of the police station was unchanged. The

small lobby's scuffed floors held the same benches where Virginia had first waited to see Dylan when she'd come to ask for information on Ruth's murder. They were all unoccupied now, and through the entry into the main office space, Virginia could tell that the activity level in the station was low. It was late. Most officers were home with their families, and the ones working the night shift were mostly out on patrol. Virginia's stomach hurt with how badly she wanted to be back in that hospital room, cradling her granddaughter and sharing the joy with the rest of her family.

"Can I help you?" The middle-aged woman behind the front desk put down the book in her hands, and through the plexiglass separating them, Virginia could see it was a book of puzzles. The woman was working crosswords in hot pink ink. For a stunned moment, Virginia found herself unable to respond, intimidated by a woman with that level of confidence.

"Ma'am?" the woman asked again.

"I'm sorry. I—err—I got a call from my daughter. She's been arrested. I'm supposed to bail her out. At least, I think that's right?"

"Hang on." The woman turned back to her puzzle, filled in another answer, then set the pen down and turned back to where Virginia stood, stunned, on the other side of the divider. "When was your daughter arrested?"

"Today," Virginia said. "A few hours ago, I think. She just called me."

"We don't have night court here. You can't bail her out until after she's arraigned. That'll be tomorrow. They do arraignments at eight-thirty in the courthouse next door."

Virginia looked at her dimly. Finally, she formed the questions, "How can I see her before then? What can I do now?"

Unsympathetically, the woman smacked her gum and rifled through papers in a desk organizer. She pulled one out and set it in front of her. "If they let her out without bail, you just pick her up after the arraignment. If she gets bail, you're going to want to be there at the arraignment to pay it right away. Makes things quicker."

Lucy's voice played in Virginia's head again. *I've been arrested for murder.* "I don't think they'll release her without bail." It occurred to her that it wasn't guaranteed they'd release her at all—not with a murder charge. Her hands shook, and she clenched them into fists by her sides.

The woman nodded and smacked her gum again, unfazed. She slid the paper she'd pulled out under the plexiglass divider and across the desk to Virginia. "This is our bonding procedure. There's a list of approved bonding companies." She poked at it with a finger. "They're open late." She swiveled her chair and picked her hot pink pen up, returning to her crossword, and Virginia took that as a dismissal and an indication that she shouldn't wait until morning to give one of those companies a call.

She muttered a thank you and turned, unsure where to go. She could sit on one of the benches in the empty waiting area, but despite the receptionist not showing any judgment, Virginia didn't want to talk with the bondsman in front of her. So, she returned to her car, her breath forming little clouds in the cold night air, and called the first company on the list.

* * *

VIRGINIA DIDN'T SLEEP that night. She slunk through the doors of Breeze Village and went straight up to her room, but spent the hours between arranging Lucy's bail with the bonding company and going to the courthouse lying in bed with her eyes open, staring at the ceiling. With the sky outside just barely turning from gray to light blue, a pale band of pink visible on the horizon when she looked out her window, she gave up any attempt at sleep, changed clothes, splashed water on her face, and then slipped out of the building.

Lucy's arraignment was both boring and confusing. It was the first moment since the phone call where Virginia nearly fell asleep, but then Lucy was standing up and everything was happening and Virginia wasn't sure what it all meant, and then it was over. The bondsman paid the bail, and Lucy was a free woman until her trial date nearly two months later. They didn't talk about the astronomical figure. The bonding company set Virginia up on a payment plan for the less-astronomical-but-still-eye-boggling fee. They didn't talk about the trial or anything that would come next. Lucy let her mother hug her, but where Virginia expected a tight, warm reception, instead she got a quick embrace, which Lucy immediately pulled away from.

As she pulled back, Virginia caught sight of the black

ink smudges on her fingertips. Lucy's face went red as she noticed the direction of Virginia's gaze. She didn't make eye contact, just led them both out of the building and into the parking lot.

Stung, Virginia held out her keys for Lucy to take. Both understood without speaking that they'd be safer after the night they'd been through if Lucy drove, and they climbed into Virginia's sedan. Wordlessly, Lucy started the car and pulled out of the parking lot. Virginia found the sting and confusion morphing into anger and frustration with each mile they drove, until she could hardly hold it in by the time they reached Lucy's apartment.

No sooner had they stepped inside than Virginia dropped her bag to the floor and turned her exhausted form on her daughter, unwilling to wait any longer for an explanation.

"Talk."

CHAPTER 2

*L*ucy didn't talk. At least not at first.

Still in a skirt suit and heels, though looking more disheveled than Virginia had ever seen her daughter as an adult, Lucy started a pot of coffee and spent the time it took to brew scrubbing at her fingers in the kitchen sink. Not until she was seated, heels removed and legs folded under her, on her pristine white couch with a steaming cup did she look to her mother and take a deep breath.

"Dax is doing something shady." Her voice was shaky, and she spoke quickly, as if in a rush to get the words out. "And I've gotten myself involved. I didn't kill anyone, though." The last declaration came out even faster, a forceful assertion.

She searched Virginia's face, whether for forgiveness, condemnation, or an assurance that she could fix this, Virginia wasn't sure.

"What do you mean, *shady?*" Virginia poured herself a

cup of coffee, figuring that, at this point, it wasn't going to wreck her sleep any more than staying up all night getting her daughter out of jail already had. "And what do you mean, *involved? And who is Dax?"*

Lucy glared at her through squinted eyelids, then pointed at a framed photo on the side table that Virginia hadn't noticed. "My boyfriend," she scoffed as if she'd told Virginia about him a dozen times before. Virginia wondered if maybe Lucy had, and she'd just forgotten. She leaned in to look at the photo.

In it, Lucy was dressed in a baby blue pencil skirt and heels, the very image of prim and proper, but she was looking at the man next to her and laughing, a candid vitality on her face that Virginia had never seen. The man was devilishly handsome, dark eyes fixed directly on the camera. He had a thick beard, cropped short and square over a strong jawline, and the hem of his jeans was rolled up over the tops of black boots.

Lucy went on, snatching Virginia's attention back, "And I mean *shady* as in *probably not above board. And involved* as in *I've been exchanging briefcases with one of his associates for him and not looking inside."*

"You've what?" Lucy flinched, and Virginia set her coffee down to avoid spilling it. Her hands were shaking as she struggled to process the scraps of information Lucy doled out. She looked across the couch at her daughter, the put-together marketing professional who hadn't caused a lick of trouble since she'd snuck out of the house once at seventeen and then felt so guilty she confessed it all over breakfast the next morning.

Virginia's heart snagged on the scared look Lucy was giving her. "I didn't mean to yell. I'm just… surprised. And confused."

Lucy nodded, her eyes softening and her body relaxing. "At first, I just offered to help him put together a website—he does furniture restoration, and I knew an online presence would help his business—and help out with all the business marketing stuff that small business owners hate doing. It's up my alley, and I love him, you know?"

Virginia didn't know. She still didn't recall ever hearing Dax's name. Not wanting to derail the story, she nodded anyway.

"So, I made him a website, and business picked up. I did a few ad campaigns and things picked up even more. Things were booming with my help, and he got busier trying to keep up with the demand." She took a sip of her coffee, blond curls falling in front of her face as she bent her head. Virginia could see she was straining not to cry. "There was this meeting he said he couldn't make. At the art gallery."

The words were almost a whisper on Lucy's tongue, and Virginia found herself leaning in closer, straining to hear.

"He was so stressed that week, in over his head with the work. I was only supposed to make the trade that one time."

"A briefcase?" Virginia asked.

Lucy nodded. "He gave me a briefcase, and I took it to the art gallery, unsure what to expect. A man with an identical briefcase came in and set his down. I started to talk to him, but then he just picked up my briefcase and walked out, so I took his briefcase to Dax. I demanded to know what the hell I had just been a part of, but he shut me down. Turned the whole thing around on me. And then, later, he was sweet to me. Apologetic and grateful that I'd helped him out.

"The next week, Dax was busy again, and he asked me to 'take the meeting,' as he called it. I didn't want to, but I did. And then the week after that, and the week after that..." She took a shuddering breath. "I felt like I couldn't say no, since I'd agreed that first time."

Virginia tried to make sense of it, to picture her daughter trading briefcases with seedy men. It sounded like something out of a movie, and not a very good one. She hesitated, then asked, "What's in the briefcases?"

Lucy looked embarrassed. "I don't know. I didn't look inside. I run the marketing, but if I try to ask about the books or any of the actual *business* side of the business, he shuts down. It's shady, right?"

"Oh, it's shady," Virginia agreed.

The two sipped their coffee in silence. Virginia didn't want to come right out and ask her daughter to explain what happened at the gallery the day before but was running out of patience. Finally, Lucy drained her mug and set it down, a tiny quarter-ring forming where coffee had dripped down the side. It looked out of place on the otherwise spotless acrylic coffee table, the only imperfection in the impeccably curated space.

"I was at the art gallery to exchange briefcases yesterday when..."

Virginia nodded. She didn't need Lucy to say it. She

knew how the rest of that sentence went. *When I was arrested for murder.*

"I went, as always, with a briefcase. I admired the art, or pretended to, inconspicuously making my way to our meeting point in one of the back rooms." She frowned. "Who do I think I am, acting like some sort of spy?"

This jab at herself sent Lucy into hysterics. She threw her head back and let out a primal wail, then shook with silent sobs. Virginia reached out and touched her daughter's leg, then withdrew her hand, uncertain. *Do mothers and daughters touch each other's legs?*

Trying again, she reached, this time for her daughter's shoulder, and rubbed her hand along the top of Lucy's arm. The motion felt stiff, and shame flushed Virginia's face while regret twisted her gut. She didn't even know how to comfort her own child properly. Her child who had been arrested for murder. If she'd ever wondered whether she'd failed as a parent, in that moment, she knew it for a fact. Tears stung her own eyes, and she wiped them away as discreetly as she could.

"I showed up at three o'clock on the dot, just like always. We meet all the way in the back of the gallery in this tiny, cramped room. When I stepped through the doorway, at first, I thought he hadn't shown up yet, but then when I looked down, I… He… He was lying on the ground, dead."

Lucy dissolved into sobs once more, this time putting her face in Virginia's chest, and Virginia rocked her, rubbing her back, remembering the ways she used to soothe her children without even thinking about it. How easy and uncomplicated motherhood felt then before she'd had decades to muck it up.

"I ran out screaming and called 9-1-1. The people on the street must have thought I was crazy, running in circles in high heels and a suit, absolutely losing my mind." She let out a bitter laugh.

"Was anyone else at the gallery?" Virginia wanted to know. "I just don't understand why the police think you did it."

"The gallery owner was there. He was on his way out when I went in. I didn't see anyone else, but I think some artists work in a studio space upstairs sometimes. There could have been people there I didn't see."

"What about the briefcase? Was it there next to the man when you found him?"

Lucy frowned, her brows knitting together. "I don't know. I don't remember seeing it, but the whole moment is pretty hazy."

"And the briefcase you brought? What happened to it?"

Lucy shook her head. "I don't know," she repeated. "I'm sure I dropped it when I saw the man laid out on the floor and started screaming for help."

"Did any of those artists who work upstairs come to help?"

Lucy's voice got shorter as she said again, "I don't know. I told you, as soon as I found him, I freaked out and ran outside into the street. I didn't go back inside until after the police had arrived, and then the only people around were police setting up crime scene tape and collecting evidence."

"When you went back inside with the police, your briefcase was gone?" Virginia asked again. "Did the police have it? Did they ask you about it?"

Lucy stood, jerking herself out of Virginia's embrace. "Look, Mom, I've told you what I know. I went in with a briefcase and found a dead guy. I ran out screaming, and when I went back inside with the cops to show them where I found him, they arrested me for killing him. I didn't see anyone else besides the gallery owner, like I already told you. I don't know what happened with the briefcases. I don't remember anything else."

She leaned heavily against the marble island separating the living room from the kitchen and turned to look at Virginia over her shoulder.

"Did the police ask you about the briefcase when you were arrested?" If Lucy's briefcase had still been there for them to find when they went into the gallery, Virginia imagined they would have questioned her about it and its contents.

Lucy turned back around, her shoulders curved forward. She shook her head. "They didn't ask, and I didn't leap at the chance to tell them about it. I told them I was just at the gallery to kill time between appointments in the area."

A piece of Virginia recoiled. Her daughter was good. Her daughter wasn't someone who lied to the police.

Except, here she was saying that's exactly who she was now. Someone who fell in love with a dirty man, traded cash or drugs or weapons in an art gallery, and then when it landed her in a room with a dead body, lied to the police about it.

Virginia drained her cup of coffee in one gulp and set it down decisively. Lucy raised an eyebrow in question. "It sounds like there's one person who might have some information to help piece this all together. You need to call that boyfriend of yours."

Lucy might have become reckless and even a liar, but she wasn't a murderer. The easiest way to prove that, Virginia knew, was to uncover who was. And that would be easier if they knew what business Lucy and the deceased were involved in—what they'd been trading, who else knew about it, and who might have wanted the contents of those briefcases.

"There's no way he's awake now." Lucy spun, leaning her back against the island. "He's not a morning person."

Virginia thought there wasn't much morning left, but said nothing.

Lucy cleared her throat, and Virginia looked up to find her nervously biting her lip. "If you feel half as bad as I do after last night, I'm sure you'll want to get back to Breeze Village and rest, but there's one thing I think might actually turn this day around. I'd like to go meet my niece."

* * *

"WHAT'S SHE LIKE?" Lucy asked tentatively, not looking away from the road as she drove them across town in Virginia's car. "The baby?"

Virginia considered for a moment. She'd only seen her for a few minutes before getting Lucy's call and leaving the hospital. And really, what could she be *like*, having barely been on this earth twelve hours? "She's perfect," she said anyway, and meant it.

Despite sporting three-inch heels, Lucy left her mother in the dust on their way to the elevators. By the time Virginia entered Stephanie's hospital room, Lucy was already inside holding her niece. She looked as comfortable as if she did this every day, impossibly normal given the previous twenty-four hours. She cradled the infant, swaying and bobbing ever so slightly, cooing at Emily between talking with the other adults.

"You're right," Lucy said, smiling at her mother when Virginia came into the room. "She is perfect."

Stephanie beamed up from the hospital bed and reached out her arms, desperate to be reunited with her child after a moment apart.

"I'm just happy you were able to come," Jack said from his place beside Stephanie's bed. Virginia's stomach tightened. She wondered if the others knew about Lucy's arrest. She didn't know how they would. She hadn't told them when she left the hospital, not wanting to worry the new parents when there wasn't anything they could do. Still, it seemed wrong that her world could have just tilted on its axis, but everything in this room continued on exactly as it was.

Wriggling against her mother, Emily opened her tiny mouth and let out a sharp cry. The whole room turned their attention to her, rapt. Just when it looked like she was ready to let out another wail, she sucked in a deep breath and fell right back asleep. The room let out a collective sigh of relief, then a shared laugh.

The peace that came over Virginia as she watched her

son look down at his newborn child settled deep in her core where it could not be shaken. Not even when that child opened her mouth again moments later and began to shriek in earnest. Not even when the door burst open and Sam surged into the room, cardboard coffee carrier in hand. Not until Sam's eyes went wide at seeing Lucy, and Virginia knew that she knew. Somehow, she knew.

Sam's gaze met Virginia's and hardened. "Virginia, Lucy, can I speak with you two outside?"

In the hallway, the three of them shot furtive looks up and down the hall to ensure they were alone. Then, Stephanie's mother spoke in a low voice. "I have it on good intelligence that Lucy was just arrested for murder. What is she doing here with my granddaughter instead of in jail?"

Lucy sputtered, trying to formulate a response. Virginia was indignant. "*Your* granddaughter? That baby is *my* granddaughter, too, and Lucy's niece. And I'll have you know that Lucy didn't murder anybody. So, your 'intelligence,'" she said, making air quotes with her fingers, "must not be as good as you thought."

Sam pursed her lips, unconvinced. "Hmph. When I went to get coffee, a pair of police officers ahead of me in line were talking shop. I'm certain they said 'Lucy Walker.' One of them even joked about wearing a skirt suit to commit a felony." Her eyes raked down Lucy's body, and Lucy's face went beet-red as her arms unconsciously hugged herself.

"Everything okay?" Jack stuck his head out of the door, and the three of them jumped before immediately attempting casual body language.

"All good," Lucy assured him. Before Jack could return to the room, however, the double doors at the end of the hallway swung wide and Virginia's best friend Marney flew in.

"Virginia, Lucy! You're here! I didn't expect—I mean, I just thought—Oh, I was so worried!" Marney wrapped Lucy in a hug, then stood back and held her at arm's length, assessing her. A sequined shawl dripped from her shoulders. "I knew Dylan had to be mistaken, but it's still such a relief seeing you both."

Dylan. Virginia hadn't called Marney yet to tell her about Lucy's arrest. In the chaos, it hadn't even crossed her mind. Even though she'd stepped down as Assistant Chief, Marney's daughter still had police connections. Connections who knew Dylan was close to the Walker family and would care about Lucy's arrest. Connections like Dylan's new beau, Officer McNeil. Even off the Force, Dylan would have heard the news and told Marney straight away.

Jack's shoes squeaked on the gleaming linoleum, and they turned their heads to see him leaving the doorway and heading toward them. Virginia's stomach sank at the sight of his face. "What's going on?" Jack's voice was icy cold. Virginia knew that lying to him would be a mistake, not to mention futile. But when she opened her mouth to tell him the truth, nothing came out.

Sam and Marney looked from Jack to Virginia to Lucy and back, waiting for someone to explain. Virginia's mouth just opened and closed stupidly.

Lucy finally spewed the words, "I was arrested last

night, but it was all a mistake and I'm out now, so *do not worry.*"

Jack's eyes looked ready to pop out of his face with worry, never mind Lucy's assurances. "You *what?* For what?"

"It was all a misunderstanding. Mom came and got me." Sidestepping her brother's question, Lucy raised her hands, then pulsed them away from each other a few times as if to emphasize the lack of handcuffs. "See? Everything is fine. Like I said, don't worry."

A little triumphant sound came from Sam's throat. "I knew it! I knew I'd heard right." She whirled on Virginia. "You lied to me?"

Marney twisted to put herself between the two new grandmothers, but Virginia stepped out from behind her to face Sam down. "I didn't lie." She looked over to her daughter, whose face was flushed bright red with embarrassment. "Lucy hasn't murdered anybody, exactly like I told you."

"*Murder?*" Jack threw his hands up in the air, brought them down on the top of his head, and tugged at his dark hair. The harsh lighting accentuated the growing number of silver streaks through it. He paced with his eyes closed, muttering unintelligibly, before turning to Virginia and Lucy. "Whatever this 'misunderstanding' is, take care of it. But keep this mess away from me and my family. We don't need this right now."

Virginia tried not to react physically to the blow that was hearing her son refer to his family as a unit that didn't include her, even if she understood. His wife and child were his priority.

"Make up an excuse," Jack continued. "I won't say anything to Stephanie, at least not until we're home and settled in a bit. The stress she's been under... Argh, I can't believe this!" He shot an anxious glance toward the room before turning back to the others and repeating his orders. "Make up an excuse to leave. Keep this whole situation away from Stephanie. She can't handle something like this dropped on her right now."

After Jack's outburst, Sam left with a smug look of satisfaction on her face, slipping into the hospital room to cradle baby Emily while Virginia and Lucy stood shell-shocked. Marney apologized profusely, beside herself with guilt. "I should have just kept my dang mouth shut! It's all my fault he found out in the first place." But Virginia couldn't fault Marney for failing to keep a secret she didn't know was secret.

Marney dropped off the blanket and hat she'd crocheted for the baby, then left with Virginia and Lucy. When they reached the sun-drenched lobby, Marney asked, "So, what's the plan? Whatever mistake led to your arrest, do you need any help clearing it up? Because I can make Dylan step in. She's still got contacts on the Force, and she can—"

Lucy cut in. "It's under control."

The look she cut her mother indicated with little room for misinterpretation that she didn't want to share any more information with Marney, and she didn't want Marney's or Dylan's help. "Like I said to Jack, it was a misunderstanding. It'll all be cleared up soon."

On the drive from the hospital to the art gallery, where Lucy's car was still parked on the street, Virginia listened to the dial tone while Lucy tried to call her boyfriend over and over. After the fifth unanswered call, she said gently, "Maybe he's busy. You said he restores furniture, right? Some of those tools can be awfully loud. He probably can't hear his phone." She didn't believe a word coming out of her own mouth, of course, and was silently considering how she might get the address of this man whose name she'd already forgotten so she could ambush him at home. But the desperation in Lucy's eyes compounded with each call, and Virginia would have said anything to try and allay that despair.

"I couldn't reach him last night, either." Lucy's voice was a whimper. "I tried to call him from the police station, but he didn't answer."

Anger rose up in Virginia. Her daughter's freedom was threatened by the actions of this man who had lured her into loving him, thrown her into a dangerous situation, and now wouldn't even take her calls.

"What's his name, again?" Virginia fought to keep her voice steady, hoping it didn't betray her seething rage. When Lucy repeated his name—*what kind of a name is Dax?*—she pretended to feel around in her purse for a piece of hard candy but instead scribbled it on one of the small notepads she kept to augment her memory.

"Don't worry too much," she told Lucy when they reached her car and she got out. Virginia couldn't help but look at the gallery only a few yards up the street. "I'm sure he's just busy." Lucy gave a stiff smile, pretending to believe the assurances Virginia herself didn't believe. "He'll call back, and then whatever he knows about the briefcases or who else might have been doing business with the man you found will lead the police to the real killer."

Lucy squeezed her mother's hand, then kissed the top of her head before climbing into her own car and driving off. Alone in her car, Virginia pulled out the notepad where she'd scrawled the name. "Now, Dax, where the hell are you hiding?"

CHAPTER 3

$\mathcal{B}$reeze Village was bustling when Virginia climbed the front steps with a Publix sandwich nestled in a plastic grocery bag, ready to retreat to her room, refuel, and sleep for days. Before she could make a beeline for the elevator, a familiar voice called out from the dining room, "Is that Breeze Village's newest grandma?"

Virginia turned to see Ronald smiling broadly over a hand of cards and a glass of iced tea, his grin showcasing his many missing teeth. She couldn't help but smile at the sight of her friend and the reminder of her new title: Grandma.

"How'd you know?" she asked, changing course and taking a seat at the round table where he and Patricia were playing their card game. Her mouth watered as she pulled her sandwich from its bag.

"You were out until all hours last night." Ronald lowered his head in a chastising look. Since a serial killer had set her sights first on Colleen, Breeze Village's resident psychic, and then on Virginia, Ronald had taken up the mantel of protecting the residents. It had been Ronald who had charged into her room when Virginia found herself staring down the barrel of the killer's gun, Ronald who had thrown her to the ground and protected her. And after that incident, he'd taken his role as Breeze Village's protector very seriously, keeping an eye out for suspicious characters. And, apparently, keeping tabs on the residents' comings and goings. "When I went to bed, your car wasn't in the lot. When I got up to pee, it was. You snuck in at midnight and then back out again this morning before breakfast. There's only one reason I could think of for that."

Across from Ronald, Patricia set her cards down in front of her. "That, and Colleen made a whole grand announcement at breakfast this morning."

Virginia didn't know whether the grin that spread across her face was from the first bite of solid food she'd had in eighteen hours or the image of Colleen standing up in the packed dining room to make an announcement. She was sure it was grand; Colleen didn't do things any other way. Whether or not the rest of Breeze Village wanted to enjoy the fruits of her psychic powers, Colleen would share them. Since narrowly avoiding death, she'd taken on a more fervent stance that gifts were meant to be shared, and she owed it to the world to share her visions whether the world wanted them or not.

Patricia turned her face skyward and closed her eyes, assuming a rigid posture and opening her mouth wide. In her best imitation of Colleen's voice, she quoted, "'A new soul has joined us in the plane of the living. Let us welcome Amelia Walker on this journey we call life.'"

Virginia guffawed. "She wasn't too far off! They named the baby Emily."

A handful of residents entered the dining room and paraded in a single-file line of walkers past the beverage dispensers, taking glasses of tea before filing into one of Breeze Village's two activity rooms.

"Oh, it's time for book club!" Patricia stood in a hurry, flipping her cards face up in front of her. "I win," she told Ronald before shuffling off to join the group.

Alone in the dining room, Virginia asked Ronald, "If you wanted to find someone but only knew their first name, how would you go about it?"

Concern immediately spread across his face, and Virginia rushed to assure him it wasn't anyone dangerous. "Just a friend of my daughter's."

"Well, in that case, I imagine I'd just ask my daughter."

But Virginia had a feeling Lucy wouldn't want her poking around, showing up at her boyfriend's house. Meddling was nothing new in their family—Jack and Lucy pushing her to move into a place like Breeze Village before she was ready, and Virginia taking up this new identity as a private investigator after practically running the neighborhood gossip mill for decades—but it wasn't received well by any of the Walkers. She could imagine Lucy's face when she found out her mother had ambushed her boyfriend to demand he give her information on his shady business dealings so she might clear her daughter's name in this murder case.

Virginia hemmed. "What if that's not an option? What

if it's… It's for a surprise party! So Lucy can't know I'm talking to her friend or she'll get suspicious."

"I don't believe you for a second, but what does that matter? If you want to find this person, you'll keep digging until you figure out a way." He took a deep breath, absently shuffling his deck of cards while considering the question. "I guess under those circumstances, I'd take a leaf out of my ex-wife's book and just follow Lucy around. Wait until she goes to visit her friend, and then you've found them."

"You had a wife?" Virginia asked.

Ronald just shrugged. "In another life."

Crumpling up the paper wrapping from her sandwich, Virginia stood to leave but was interrupted by a muffled voice calling her name. "Virginia! Ronald! Open the door!" She turned to see a large Black woman in emerald green pants and a cyber yellow sweater standing outside the French doors leading from the dining room outside to the courtyard. She was holding a plastic cake carrier with both hands, and Virginia's stomach churned in protest at the sight of it.

Virginia pulled the door open, and Gemma squealed, leaning in for a one-armed hug while the cake carrier teetered precariously. "Congratulations, Grandma!" She looked around at the nearly empty dining room and frowned. "I was hoping there'd be a few more folks here, but you and Ronald will do just fine. I need you to taste this cake I made."

Ronald's chair squealed beneath him as he abruptly stood from the table. "I was actually on my way out. I'm awfully late for—err—for a doctor's appointment!"

"I didn't realize you had an appointment today." Virginia narrowed her eyes at Ronald, a wry smirk on her face. "Which doctor is this?"

Caught in a lie or not, Ronald wasn't sticking around. "Who knows? You know how it is at our age—doctor's appointments practically every other day. I can't ever keep them straight. Anyway, I'm real sorry I couldn't try your cake, Gemma. I'll be sure to taste the next one!"

Gemma had recently learned that Jimmy, her new "not my boyfriend" with whom she spent almost every night, had a birthday in February. Despite her insistence that *It's not like that between us!* and *We're both free to do whatever we choose!*, Gemma was taking Jimmy's birthday very seriously and was determined to learn to bake in time to bake him a cake. Luckily for her, Jimmy rarely left his room except for the dates he and Gemma went on to steal pudding cups from the second-floor fridge. When she brought her practice cakes into the main building from her Independent Living cottage around back, Jimmy, holed up in his room, was none the wiser.

"I went with a lemon and blueberry sponge this time," Gemma said. Before Virginia could mutter something about being full after her sandwich or trying to cut back on sweets, Gemma removed the top from the cake carrier and cut Virginia a full, thick slice.

The cake didn't very much resemble a sponge. It seemed more like a cross between a brick and a sandcastle. Virginia took a bite and let out an exaggerated *Mmm!*

"You're getting so much better!" she enthused. It was the truth. This attempt was markedly more edible than the last attempt, a double-chocolate monstrosity in which she was pretty sure Gemma had lost count when measuring the cups of flour and sugar.

Gemma beamed. "Jimmy said the other day that he's not a big fan of chocolate, so I had to go in a new direction with this one."

"Definitely the right direction," Virginia said, swallowing another bite and trying not to wince. The texture, though not what the recipe creator likely had in mind, wasn't the main problem. The problem was that Gemma seemed to have added at least three times the recommended amount of lemon juice, and every bite made Virginia pucker, a sting jolting the back of her jaw. "How much lemon is in this thing?"

A horrified look came over Gemma's features, her hot pink lipstick emphasizing the expression. "Oh, no! Did I forget the lemon?"

"No, you definitely did not."

One bite of her own creation, and Gemma took Virginia's plate away from her. "Don't you dare eat another bite of this just to humor me." The pair dissolved into giggles, Gemma exaggeratedly dabbing at her tongue with a napkin, and when they recovered, Gemma asked how Jack and Stephanie were doing after Emily's arrival.

No questions about Lucy. Virginia breathed a sigh of relief that at least word of Lucy's arrest didn't seem to have made it to Breeze Village, though she knew it was only a matter of time.

Virginia had left the dining room and made it halfway across the lobby toward the elevators when Gemma called out, "Oh, did you hear about the murder downtown yesterday?"

* * *

A GOOD GAUGE for how thoroughly some piece of news had spread through Seaview was who was talking about it at the Piggly Wiggly. When friends saw each other in the dairy aisle, did they stop and speculate? Did they bring it up while unloading their groceries onto the conveyor belt in Virginia's checkout line? If, when asked how she was doing, Virginia said she was hoping to check out a new exhibit at the art gallery after work, did the patrons grimace and lean in to tell her in a low voice about this awful piece of news they'd heard?

On this particular Friday, the answers were no, no, and no. With a cold and bitter wind pushing through town, the fine citizens of Seaview were cocooned in their homes as much as could be, and the spread of gossip was slow. The spread of relief through Virginia's veins was slower, but it spread nonetheless as each customer passed through the sliding doors without mentioning the murder.

By the time Soccer Mom Carole, as Virginia thought of the woman whose hair and makeup somehow remained impeccably in place while she wrangled three dirt-covered children in soccer uniforms through the lane at least twice a week, turned into her checkout line, Virginia's guard had come down. Though Carole was well-connected when it came to Seaview's hottest stories and always had some piece of gossip to share, either with Virginia or with a friend loudly over the phone, impervious to the looks other grocery store patrons were giving her, Virginia was still surprised when Carole leaned in.

"Did you hear?"

Virginia's stomach dropped at her furtive tone. Carole didn't even notice her cleat-clad sons grabbing candy bars from the aisle display and loading them onto the conveyor belt; she was poised in wait for Virginia to respond, eager to deliver a particularly juicy piece of news.

With a smirk, Soccer Mom Carole looked around and then revealed, "That Italian restaurant over on Third Street doesn't make their own pasta like they claim. A friend of mine saw it online—some food blogger with a crusade to bust restaurants that pretend to make everything from scratch when it's really just a sea of microwaves in the back posted about it."

She tossed two packages of tortellini onto the belt, followed by two different brands of jarred tomato sauce. "That's their secret," she continued. "The two brands of sauce. They just mix them together and put it on ready-made pasta. And no one can tell!"

Virginia approximated a noise of surprise and intrigue as she scanned the groceries, when in reality she felt like the world had just tilted on its axis. Luigi's? She couldn't be talking about Luigi's. But Virginia knew for a fact there wasn't another Italian restaurant on Third.

How many times had Virginia visited Luigi's with her own casserole dish and slipped Luigi himself—and his father Marco before him, and his father Luigi before him —a few bills to fill it up so she could present something "homemade" when she didn't have time to cook? All those years, all those conspiratorial glances…

"It says it's waiting for the cashier." Virginia started

and looked up to see Soccer Mom Carole gesturing at the card reader, evidently pleased with herself at how hard her revelation had rattled Virginia.

With a hasty apology, Virginia finished the transaction, handed the woman her receipt, and shut off the light above her register. It was time for her break, and not a moment too soon.

THE FACT that no one at the grocery store was talking about the murder at the art gallery—or any arrests or suspects in connection with the case—was but a small consolation when news of the crime had already reached the senior living centers. If Gemma had heard the news, it was only a matter of time before the story reached other residents, and theories and rumors about suspects wouldn't be too far behind news of the event itself. If Sam had heard Lucy's name in connection with the case out in the wild, there was no telling who else might know and who they might be whispering to, setting off the game of telephone of Virginia's nightmares. She spent the remainder of her shift at the grocery store feeling sick to her stomach, her mind leaping from thoughts of how they could clear Lucy's name before gossip spread to visions of what she would say to Luigi next time she paid his restaurant a visit.

By the time she clocked out that afternoon, she was itching for a confrontation. She weighed her options—surprise Lucy at home and demand they pay Dax a visit, or show up at Luigi's and demand an explanation for his betrayal—but was stopped in her tracks by a message from Sam before she reached her car.

If you're going to pull another Senior Sherlock, you'd better get to it. I can't take this much longer!

Virginia turned her phone over in her hand once, so baffled by the message she wondered if she'd somehow grabbed someone else's. But no, it was hers. Confused, she typed out a response.

Did you send this to me by mistake?

Your son is RUINING my life!

Three dots popped up, and dread pooled in Virginia's stomach while she waited for Sam to elaborate.

CLEAR UP THIS CASE!!!!! ASAP!!!!!

A coffin emoji followed by an emoji face with glasses followed.

Virginia made up her mind and turned around, heading back into the grocery store and picking up a pack of disposable aluminum baking pans before jetting off downtown. When she thrust one of the pans into Luigi's hands without the usual folded-up bills, she stared him down despite his raised brow and smirk.

"Where's the—?"

Virginia cut him off, her voice low and firm. "Two brands of jarred sauce mixed together. Ready-made pasta."

Luigi's eyebrows shot further up, nearly entirely hidden behind the thinning hair that flopped over his forehead, and he took the pan from her without another word.

Having now avoided the Southern woman's mortal sin of turning up empty-handed, Virginia pulled up in front of Jack's house, ready for a second confrontation. She could practically feel the heat of Sam's angry messages radiating from her phone, even as it sat nestled in the bottom of her purse. She swayed unsteadily crossing the yard, the wind beating against her as she navigated the uneven grass, still in her grocery store cashier uniform and without her cane for stability. She'd left it propped in her room at Breeze Village when she'd left for work.

Before she knocked on the door, Virginia could hear crying inside. She hesitated, fist raised, unsure whether she should call Jack instead of disturbing the whole family by knocking, but the door opened before she could decide.

"Mom?" Jack wore slacks and a button-down, and for a moment, Virginia marveled that she'd somehow raised two children who wore business professional attire even in their own homes, when Virginia would wear stretchy pants day in and day out if she didn't have places to be. At the moment, Jack's business professional attire bore more than one spit-up stain, and his dress shoes were two different colors, clearly put on in haste while his focus was elsewhere. One hand carried a reeking trash bag, and he stood totally bewildered to see her in the doorway.

Virginia, equally bewildered to have had the door open unexpectedly before her, suddenly felt ridiculous. "I brought, err…" She lifted the tray in explanation and trailed off, embarrassed.

"What are you doing here?" Jack demanded.

Without waiting for a response, he stepped out of the house and closed the door behind him, striding quickly toward the trash bin around the side of the house.

Virginia didn't respond. It wasn't until he'd dropped the stinking bag into the bin that he whirled on her and said, "I told you to stay away from us as long as Lucy and you are involved in this… whatever it is. I don't want any of this mess near Stephanie." He waved his hand in disgust and started to walk past her, back to the front door.

"Sam sent me a message." Virginia waited for Jack to stop and turn back to her before continuing. "She said you're, and I quote, 'ruining her life.' There were a lot of exclamation points."

Jack scoffed. "If being in the room when she's with Stephanie to make sure Sam doesn't accidentally reveal to my wife that her sister-in-law is currently a murder suspect means I'm ruining her life, then her life was more fragile than I'd realized."

"This has nothing to do with Sam."

"Have you spent any amount of time around the woman? She can't keep her mouth shut for anything, and she's even worse around Steph!" Jack let out a furious huff. "She may not be involved, but she knows about Lucy's arrest, and if she's alone with Stephanie and accidentally says something… I told you Steph isn't in a position to handle anything like that right now."

Virginia's head spun.

"How long are you going to keep this from your wife?" she asked.

Jack looked perplexed. "Until the charges against Lucy are dropped. Look, right now, Lucy's future is entirely up in the air. I'm not letting Stephanie take on the stress of worrying about Lucy while we've got a shrieking newborn who won't sleep. And, until she's cleared, I can't let a murder suspect around that shrieking newborn, even if she's my sister."

"You know Lucy didn't kill anyone!"

"Do I?"

"If you don't, then I don't know where I went wrong," Virginia said. "But *I* know Lucy didn't kill anyone, and I expect Stephanie will, too."

Jack turned, shaking his head and dismissing the conversation. Virginia stopped him in his tracks. "What about after? When the police catch whoever actually killed that man in the gallery and Lucy is cleared of any involvement, what then? Someday, someone will mention the time Lucy got arrested for a murder she didn't commit, and Stephanie is going to know you kept it from her."

Her son stood completely still for a minute, considering, then said, "That sounds like a fight we'll have down the road. But right now, I have to protect my wife." He walked back to the front of the house. "When this is cleared up when Lucy's not on trial anymore, and it's all in the past, then you're more than welcome here, and Sam can have all the unsupervised visitation she wants."

He turned and took the hot pan from Virginia. "I'll tell

Steph you dropped this off, and that you're sorry you couldn't stay but that you had other obligations."

* * *

TRUDGING through the doors of Breeze Village, still in her cashier's uniform and with her conversation with Jack playing on a loop in her mind, Virginia started for the elevators but heard a familiar laugh coming from the dining room that made her look. She was surprised to find that, in addition to Ronald and Patricia and the unlucky residents who thought they stood a chance against Ronald at poker, Dorothea and Gemma were sipping tea and having cake. From the way they were enjoying it, it didn't seem to be one that Gemma had made.

Dorothea, one of Virginia's former neighbors and the reason Virginia had taken on her first investigation, when she'd discovered Ruth Beaumont dead the year before, waved Virginia over to join them.

"Gemma asked me to bring her my recipe for my famous coconut cake. I'm pretty sure it's what finally got Jason to propose."

Virginia reeled. "You're engaged?"

Dorothea had been seeing her much younger boyfriend longer than any of the neighborhood ladies guessed it would last, but Virginia hadn't expected a wedding.

"I'm manifesting it," Dorothea said, moving her hands in a rainbow motion above her head and wiggling her fingers. "You have to talk like it's already happened.

Anyway, I'm pretty sure it's this coconut cake that finally does the trick, and I figured instead of just sharing the recipe, I could bring a whole cake."

Gemma moaned in pleasure around a mouthful of cake. "This is it. This is the one. Jimmy is going to go nuts over this."

"Maybe he'll propose." Dorothea wiggled her eyebrows, but Gemma shook her head.

"We don't like labels," she insisted. "Who needs them at our age? Besides, there's nothing less romantic I can think of than getting the government involved in what we've got."

Dorothea looked baffled, like this was beyond comprehension, and Virginia gave her a shrug.

"I'm just getting home from a long shift at work, but it's good to see you." She started to head upstairs, but behind her, she heard the conversation start up again.

"Are you sure he was strangled to death?" Dorothea asked Gemma. "I heard he was shot."

Gemma shook her head, a smug smile on her face. She had the look of a cat with a mouse, relishing being the one with the best information. "Nope, strangled."

Virginia turned on her heel so fast she nearly lost her balance. "What are you talking about?"

"There was a murder at the art gallery earlier this week," Gemma said. "Chloe from yoga knows someone at the morgue, so I got the inside scoop. I haven't even seen it in the paper yet."

"Are you going to investigate?" Dorothea wanted to know. She looked up at Virginia eagerly, and Virginia took a step back.

"Why would I do that?" *Did they know?* The desperation gave an acidic edge to her question.

Taken aback, Dorothea said, "Well, it's just what you do."

Gemma cut in. "Virginia's been a little busy, what with welcoming a new granddaughter."

The two squealed, and Virginia breathed a sigh of relief, her face flushed.

"Yep," she said feebly. "Too busy for investigating right now. Anyway, I've got to run."

The moment she was gone, Virginia dialed Lucy's number. People in town knew about the murder. They were speculating about the means over cake. They may not yet know that a suspect—Lucy—had been arrested, but it wouldn't be long. Jack was right: Sam couldn't keep her mouth shut to save her life, and if she let it slip to someone that Lucy was arrested in connection with the case, it was only a matter of time before that bit of information snaked its way through town. And if that rumor snaked its way to Stephanie, Virginia could imagine Jack's fury.

"Mom? What's going on?" Lucy's voice was a mix of groggy and panicked, which sent Virginia's heart racing.

"Are you okay? What's wrong? Why do you sound like that?"

"I was napping."

"People are starting to talk," Virginia hissed. Even in her room, alone, surrounded by solid walls, she looked around anxiously and kept her voice low. "About the murder."

"And later, they'll talk about my wrongful arrest once

the police investigation uncovers the truth and proves my innocence."

Lucy's dismissiveness rendered Virginia speechless.

Lucy clucked her tongue, then asked impatiently, "Is that all you wanted to tell me?"

Virginia sat on the edge of her bed, head in her hand. "We have to clear this up! We can't wait for the police to take care of it."

"How exactly do you expect me to clear this up? I get to plead 'not guilty' when we go to court. That's my opportunity to give my side of the story. I've got a lawyer."

"A lawyer?"

"Jack sent me his information. Mr. Murphy."

Virginia's stomach roiled. She felt like vomiting. She'd sat in the office of Mr. Murphy, Esquire, last summer when she was suspected of killing Michelle Martin, the former owner of Breeze Village. He was awful.

Virginia knew they couldn't let this go to trial. That was months away, and she would be kept away from sweet Emily, unable to be there for Stephanie when she most needed support. And she couldn't let Lucy's freedom depend on the police alone, or on the testimonial powers of a lawyer who had bragged about defending guilty people.

"We need to talk to that boyfriend of yours. Dexter?" Virginia reached into her bag for the note with his name on it. "Then go to the police with whatever information he gives us. If you want the police to stand a chance at finding the killer, they need to know about his shady business dealings and who else is involved."

"Dax. And I told you, he's not answering his phone."

Virginia let out a frustrated huff. "So, we go to his house. We didn't always have phones, you know. They're not the only way to get in touch with people."

Lucy was quiet. "Mom, it's been a hard couple of days. Can we talk about this later? I just want to sleep."

Lucy was nearly fifty and Virginia eighty, but one conflict threw them right back into the parent-child dynamic they'd had when Lucy was a teen. Virginia opened her mouth to tell her that no, it couldn't wait, that she didn't want all of Seaview mistakenly believing her daughter was a murderer when they could be doing something to straighten things out themselves. But before she could say any of this, Lucy said a rushed goodbye, assuring her mother they'd talk later, and hung up.

Later, my ass. Virginia checked the clock on her bedside table. She had an hour and a half before her American Sign Language class at the community college. After the day she'd had, she wanted to skip it and curl up in bed. Instead, she quickly changed clothes, grabbed her car keys, and headed back downstairs, then outside to the parking lot.

Virginia didn't believe for a second that Lucy would sit idly by, waiting for her boyfriend to pick up the phone. In high school, when a boy had stood Lucy up for a date, Lucy had waited outside his house for hours to confront him in the front yard. But if she wasn't going to play ball and let Virginia in when it came to Dax, Virginia would take Ronald's suggestion and stake her out until she led Virginia to him.

CHAPTER 4

It took Virginia all of fifteen minutes to modify her opinion on stakeouts. They weren't glamorous or exciting like on TV; they were boring.

After five minutes of staring at the door to Lucy's apartment complex and no one going in or out, Virginia found herself rummaging through her purse, looking for anything that might entertain her. After ten minutes, she'd eaten all the emergency snacks she carried in her bag and was still bored but now also uncomfortably full. And after fifteen minutes, she was thinking she should have brought a book. The radio host's voice was grating on her, so she turned it off and sat in silence. After another minute of that, she turned it back on.

Half an hour after beginning her stakeout, Virginia shifted in her seat and groaned. Her back was stiff, and a lightning bolt of pain shot through her left leg when she moved. She climbed out of the car, leaning against the cold metal body while slowly flexing and stretching. If she was going to continue with this stakeout business, she needed to figure out a more ergonomic way to go about it.

Her phone rang with a call from Marney. They hadn't seen each other since the disastrous hospital visit where Marney had accidentally revealed Lucy's situation to Jack and Sam. When her friend insisted she come by her cottage to fill her in, Virginia jumped at the opportunity to abandon her post.

"Why are you walking like that?" Marney asked when Virginia entered her cottage, one of the Independent Living residences at Breeze Village.

"Attempted stakeout gone wrong," Virginia said, sinking into Marney's couch with a sigh of relief.

"Care to elaborate?"

Marney poured iced tea and stirred a pot of chili on the stove while Virginia recounted the events of the past forty-eight hours, from the call she received from Lucy at the hospital through her miserable first stakeout attempt. "I just don't believe Lucy is going to sit around and let this boyfriend disappear on her. Even if he didn't have information that might help clear her name, he's her boyfriend, and she's just been through one of the most traumatic events of her life. And it's his fault she was there in the first place! He should be falling all over himself to comfort her right now."

Marney offered a bowl to Virginia, but she shook her head. "I'm full of stakeout snacks. Does Lawrence know you made chili without him?" Lawrence had been Virginia's neighbor for decades and was the third member of their friendship triumvirate. When Bellemeade Property Developers bought up the Grove Park neighborhood the previous year, he'd moved to a beachside condo, and Virginia still missed seeing him every day.

"He does," Marney said, slathering butter on a piece of cornbread. "And he's devastated to miss it, but he had a date last night that went so well he's going on a second date tonight."

Virginia raised her eyebrows suggestively but inwardly felt a pinch of guilt. His last beau had been using Lawrence for a place to live, which Lawrence seemed not to mind—he'd enjoyed the man's company enough that he thought it a fair trade until he learned his beau was also in the business of scamming grocery store cashiers. It had been Virginia who had uncovered this last piece of information, shattering the first relationship Lawrence had had since his partner Ben died decades earlier. She hadn't gotten over the regret at being the one to break that news.

"Anyway, I've got my ASL class at the community college tonight," she said, "so I can't stay. And Lucy is free of me trying to tail her until tomorrow, at least."

"That's probably best," Marney said brightly. "Good for the whole *mother-daughter trust* thing, you know, not to be following her around."

* * *

THE MAN next to Virginia tapped his fingers together, then pointed to her, all with his eyebrows furrowed to indicate he was asking a question.

NAME YOU?

During their first class, and once again since then, their professor had given an impassioned lecture on the importance of facial expressions and body positioning in addition to the actual hand movements in American Sign Language. Her partner had taken the professor's lecture to heart, furrowing his brows like his life depended on it.

Virginia peered down at the printed ASL alphabet on the desk in front of her, twisting her fingers into the shapes to spell out V-I-R-G-I-N-I-A. The class was partnered up, practicing asking each other their names, fingerspelling their own names, and querying whether their partner was deaf or hearing, whether they had siblings, children, or grandchildren, and most importantly, signing that they couldn't understand and to please repeat the question. Of all the signs they'd learned so far, AGAIN was the one Virginia had most mastered.

I B-I-L-L.

Virginia had to refer to the printed alphabet again to make out her partner's name.

She turned to him with an apologetic grimace. AGAIN?

Slower this time, he fingerspelled his name and beamed when Virginia repeated it correctly, spelling it back to him to indicate she'd understood. Bill.

HEARING YOU? *Are you Hearing?*

Virginia was so taken in by his smile that she nearly missed the question, but she surprised herself when she understood it. She made the sign for yes, a motion like knocking at a door, then asked him the same.

Bill signed his response. HARD-OF-HEARING.

It wasn't until this admission that Virginia noticed the hearing aids in his ears. He asked another question. CHILDREN YOU?

She blinked, then asked, AGAIN PLEASE?

CHILDREN YOU?

She tried to answer that she had two children, one boy and one girl, but she messed up and got flustered, then ended up just nodding.

GRANDCHILDREN? Bill signed, undeterred.

Virginia nodded again, this time with enthusiasm. GIRL. Unable to resist using her voice to speak the words she couldn't sign, she said, "Just born two days ago! My first grandchild."

"Voices off," the instructor reminded the class, and Virginia's cheeks burned. Bill didn't look concerned, though. He brought his hands together and shook them firmly in front of him in a sign Virginia took as congratulations.

When the class was over, Bill followed her out, then caught her elbow just as she was about to pass through the glass double doors out into the dark parking lot.

"It was nice to meet you, Virginia."

Bill's voice was deep and smooth, and hearing it for the first time made Virginia's throat catch. She choked out, "You, too."

"I'll see you on Monday, then?" Bill's eyebrows raised, an eagerness to the question that made Virginia's cheeks flush.

"See you Monday." Her voice cracked as she spoke, and she cleared her throat after, but he just turned that breathtaking smile on her again and waved goodbye.

Virginia crossed the parking lot, streetlights spilling pools of yellow light on the dark asphalt. She looked down at her feet, watching her steps and wishing she'd brought her cane. It had been a long day, and she was spent. Her mind kept returning to Bill's face, how keen he'd seemed to see her again the next week. Lost in thought, she didn't notice until she was mere feet away from her car that someone was leaning against it, waiting for her.

"It's about time."

Virginia leapt back, hand flying to her heart. Her pulse swelled in her ears, drowning out any other sound. She stumbled backward, landing hard against the next car over and setting off its alarm. Frantically, she whirled to face the wailing car, arms outstretched as if she could stop the car alarm with her mind.

To her great surprise, the alarm did stop, and the voice behind her said, "I didn't mean to scare you."

In the fresh panic over the car alarm, Virginia had already forgotten the figure waiting at her car, and she spun again to face them.

"It's me." Marney's eyes were wide with horror at the scene she'd caused, and she extended a hand hesitantly toward Virginia after tucking her own car keys back into her bag. Virginia looked from her friend to the car behind her, putting together that it was Marney's car she'd fallen into, setting off the alarm.

As the adrenaline faded, cold anger and embarrassment coursed through Virginia's veins.

"If you were trying to give me a heart attack, I think you might have been successful." She pushed past Marney to open her car door, then sank into the driver's seat, leaned her head back against the headrest, and laid her hand across her chest, feeling the quick drum within.

She looked up from the seat toward Marney, expecting an apology, but instead, Marney thrust an envelope toward her.

"What's this?" Virginia turned it over in her hands. It was thin, and printed neatly across the front was the name *BIANCA*.

"A letter from Lucy's boyfriend to his wife, if I'm not mistaken."

CHAPTER 5

*V*irginia flipped the envelope back over. "Where did you get this? What do you mean, *wife?*" She slashed it open with a fingernail without waiting for Marney's response.

"I got it from a scary-looking man in front of what I think is Dax's apartment."

Before she could answer any further questions, Virginia had unfolded the single sheet of paper inside the envelope, and both women scanned it hungrily.

Bianca,

Something's happened, and I've got to leave Seaview. Don't look for me. When things calm down, I'll find you.

Dax

"That's it?" Virginia read the short note over and over, flipping the paper in her hands and searching for more. "Why do you think this Bianca woman is his wife?"

Marney peered over Virginia's shoulder at the letter with a deep frown. Evidently, she'd been expecting more, too. She took a deep breath and shifted her weight on her feet.

"How about I tell you all about it over a glass of something strong on my couch instead of in this parking lot?"

Marney mixed drinks while Virginia eased her body down onto the couch. Marney's small gray tabby cat, Pancake, leapt up onto the couch just as Virginia lowered herself, then let out a yelp when she nearly sat on him.

"Get out of here, you little pest!" Virginia swatted at him, then bent to kiss his head when he crawled into her lap.

"Always underfoot." Marney carried the drinks in from the kitchen, handed one to Virginia, then said, "Don't be mad, but I followed your daughter around after you left. You were right that stakeouts are a total bore."

Virginia's eyebrows flew up. If Marney had asked her to guess what she'd been up to for the past two hours, following Lucy wouldn't have made the top one hundred guesses.

"You *what?*"

"I followed Lucy, just like you already did today, so you can't be mad that I violated your daughter's privacy." Marney took another sip, allowing Virginia to object, but she didn't. "It was lucky timing. She led me to Dax, just like you were hoping she might."

Virginia took a long glug from her drink before setting the glass down, her mind reeling. The excitement of having a new lead combined with the self-satisfaction at having predicted that Lucy would seek out Dax set her body itching to move and release some of the emotion.

She stood and gripped the arm of the couch for stability, sending Pancake from her lap to the floor.

As she paced across the room, holding on to furniture as she went, she told Marney, "Tell me more."

"You left, and Lawerence was busy on his date, and I was thinking of what to do with myself on a Friday night alone. I figured if Virginia thinks Lucy is going to lead us to this guy, we don't want to miss that. And what else did I have going on? So, I headed over to her apartment. I nearly missed her, actually. Like I said, lucky timing. She was leaving right as I pulled up, and she wasn't dressed like her usual self. For one, she didn't have high heels on. I don't actually know if I've ever seen her without high heels on before today—"

"Anyway," Virginia cut Marney off, making an impatient gesture with her hands.

Marney cleared her throat and pursed her lips.

"Anyway," she said, "she left, and I followed her. She went to the bank first, to the drive-thru ATM. Between the sneakers—honestly, did you know Lucy owned sneakers?—and the trip to the bank, I was a little afraid she was about to skip town."

Virginia stopped in her tracks, immediately deflated. Lucy wouldn't skip town. Innocent people didn't skip down, and Lucy was innocent.

Marney continued, "So, I'm looking at the dashboard thinking I should have gotten gas before the stakeout, because if she skips town, she's probably got a full tank of gas, and I don't want to lose her on the highway because I had to get off and fill up."

Another biting glance from Virginia compelled

Marney to skip ahead past the bits of the story where she thought Lucy was about to leave town like a guilty woman.

"But then after the bank, Lucy led me to an apartment complex north of town. It's pretty far out—almost to Chester. I thought for sure—" She stopped herself and cleared her throat. "Anyway, she pulled into this apartment complex and drove past the front. It's one of those where the stairs are outside, and you can see the individual apartment doors. This big guy in a tight shirt was standing in front of one of the stairwells. He had a box next to him—oh, I forgot the box!"

"What box?" Virginia looked around but didn't see anything in the small living room.

Marney stood and headed toward the door. "I left it in my trunk."

"How did you end up with the box?"

"Well, that's the part of the story I was about to tell."

Virginia gestured for Marney to come back to the couch and finish the story before going to fetch the box, and Marney obliged.

"Lucy drove past twice, and from what I could tell—I parked kind of in the back of the lot to watch her, but it was tough to see in the dark—she was looking at the guy by the staircase. I thought maybe that was Dax, but then Lucy left without getting out of her car to talk to him. Instead of following her, I decided to talk to the man. I figured either he was Dax and he and Lucy were fighting because of him bringing her into his shady business, and that's why she didn't get out and talk to him, or he wasn't Dax but might know where Dax is."

"And?"

"Not Dax," Marney said. "I marched up to him and, Virginia, this man was big. I know I already said he was big, but I didn't realize how big until I was right up on him. Anyway, just as I was realizing both how big this man was and that I hadn't planned out what to say to him, he talked to me like he was expecting me. Well, expecting someone."

"What do you mean?"

"He asked if I was the mother-in-law." Marney puffed out her chest and, in a New Jersey accent, quoted, "'You the motha-in-law?' I assume he meant Dax's mother-in-law, and I figured that was you. The modern youth don't always want to get married, you know, but sometimes still call each other's families in-laws. Either way, the man didn't even wait for me to confirm who I was. He said Dax wasn't available this week, handed me the box of things, then got in a car and drove off. The letter was sitting on top of the box."

"What did he mean, not available this week?" Virginia wanted to know.

Marney shrugged. "He wasn't particularly verbose. The box was full of women's stuff—a bra, a pair of high heels, a couple jackets, some CDs..."

"Lucy's?"

"I don't think so." Marney went to retrieve the box from her car, then set it on the coffee table where the two could peer into it from their seats on the couch.

Virginia picked up the bra with two fingers, dangling the lacy, leopard-print number in the air. It certainly didn't seem like something of Lucy's.

Any anger Virginia had held at Lucy for getting mixed up in this mess was immediately replaced with blind fury at Dax. He'd corrupted her daughter, leading Lucy down a path that involved a shady business and ended in her wrongful arrest for murder, and he was cheating on her to boot?

"Lucy's boyfriend is seeing another woman. Is married to her, if he has a mother-in-law."

"Like I said, in these modern times, he might—"

"Where'd you say this apartment was? Near Chester?" Virginia's voice came out thin, stretched with rage as she interrupted, and Marney grimaced like she was debating how to respond.

"He won't be there," she finally said, glancing over to where they'd laid the letter on the kitchen counter. "He said he was leaving town, and this seems like he was giving this Bianca woman back whatever she'd left at his place…"

Marney was right, of course. Dax wasn't in that apartment. And in his short letter to Bianca, he hadn't given Virginia a location to find him to… What did she want to do to him, anyway? The answer, of course, was that she wanted to kill him. She wanted to look at him with a stare so piercing he withered on the spot, never to hurt Lucy again.

But without superpowers, what did she want to do? Virginia refilled her glass and drained it. She wanted to drag him by the collar into the Seaview Police Station and see him thrown behind bars. She wanted to twist his ear until he yelped out an apology to Lucy for betraying her trust and putting her through hell. And then she wanted to kick him in the shins for good measure.

"Do you think Lucy knows where he went?" Marney asked. She'd unconsciously stepped back from Virginia, giving her a wider berth. "Maybe he sent her a letter, too?"

"I can think of two ways to find out," Virginia said. "One: we follow her around and apologize to our spines later for all the time spent sitting in our cars."

"Or two," Marney said grimly. "We ask her."

* * *

THE KEY JAMMED in the lock, and try as Virginia might, she couldn't get it to turn.

"I'm not so sure about this." Marney stood behind her, on her tiptoes to peer over Virginia's shoulders.

"She gave me the key for emergencies," Virginia huffed, giving the key another violent jiggle. "She was recently arrested for murder and her maybe-the-actual-murderer boyfriend is missing. Given the situation, I'd say her not answering the door or my phone calls qualifies as an emergency."

"Maybe the murderer? That's quite the leap, from being involved in suspicious activity and having informa-tion that could help close the case to being a killer!"

Virginia whirled, leaving her key jammed in the lock. She stood only a few inches taller than Marney but drew herself up in frustration.

"Do I need to tick off all the reasons for concern? This boy strings along my daughter, all the while married to someone else, and gets her involved in his business that is almost certainly illegal. Then, at the handoff for the illegal activity that *he* orchestrated, someone is killed. Dax—and I will never get over what a silly name that is—doesn't answer his phone. My daughter gets arrested because of him, and he doesn't even answer his phone when she tries to call him.

"And then, as if we need more, he goes missing, leaving a note for his *wife* saying he'll find her 'when things calm down.' Doesn't that seem like something a killer would do —get rid of his phone and skip town? And have a secret wife?"

Marney started to retort, but Virginia turned her back to her friend and gave the key a good, hard yank. It came loose, sending Virginia sprawling backward and knocking into Marney so they both fell hard against the wall.

Sputtering apologies, Virginia clambered up and offered Marney her hand. They were both assessing themselves when Lucy's door swung opened and her blond head poked out.

"What the hell are you two doing here?" she hissed. She leveled a glare at her mother and her friend as they straightened themselves, then sighed. "Given that you've tried calling a half dozen times and are now breaking into my apartment, I assume that if I told you to go away, you wouldn't listen?"

"You know what happens when you assume," Marney said, at the same time as Virginia said, "You're exactly right."

"How'd you even get in here?" Lucy asked, looking up and down the hallway. "This building is supposed to be secure."

"We came in the front."

"The security guard at the front desk didn't stop you? You don't live here."

Virginia shrugged. "I guess we don't look like burglars."

Marney giggled. With another deeply aggrieved sigh, Lucy pulled the door back farther and beckoned them inside, casting a withering glance at the clock by the door.

"Coffee? Tea?" Lucy stood behind the island that separated the small kitchen from the living room, hair neatly curled and outfit put together, but her makeup didn't hide the dark circles under her eyes, and her shoulders sagged as she leaned against the countertop. Virginia almost laughed out loud. Here they were, showing up unannounced and unwanted, and Lucy was surely about to tear into them for coming at all, but she wouldn't dare neglect to offer a guest refreshment, no matter how unwelcome they may be.

Virginia shook her head, eager to get on with the conversation, but Marney took Lucy up on the offer and sipped appreciatively at the glass of sweet tea.

"You didn't answer my calls!" Virginia tried to keep her voice level, but the moment she started talking, it rose to hysteria. Tears welled up, and her throat burned as she continued. "You didn't answer the door! I thought—I didn't know—"

Lucy wasn't having it. She turned her furious eyes on her mother.

"I—an adult woman—didn't respond to your messages for a single morning, and you thought a reasonable response was to try to *break into my home?*"

"We knocked first!"

Lucy threw her hands up. "I wanted to be alone!"

Virginia opened her mouth to yell some more, but Marney placed a hand on her knee to stop her. She looked at Lucy with compassion.

"I'm sorry, Lucy," she began softly.

Lucy seemed to consider whether she was going to accept the apology or continue yelling, then finally nodded, giving Marney tacit permission to continue.

"We shouldn't have shown up unannounced. And we certainly shouldn't have tried to let ourselves in. That was a breach of your privacy and a violation of your trust."

Again, Lucy nodded silently.

"When your child is in a scary situation, well, your wits sometimes desert you. You do foolish things. But that doesn't excuse our behavior."

Virginia watched to see how this would go over with Lucy. Sometimes, the mention of a mother's love made her stiffen; she took it as an insinuation that Virginia resented her for not having children of her own or that Virginia saw her as a burden or source of stress. But this time, coming from Marney, it seemed to soften her.

"I appreciate the apology," she said, her voice soft but still firm. "But I really would prefer to be alone. I am safe. I just need some time to myself." She turned her gaze to her mother and waited defiantly to see whether Virginia would accept the dismissal.

Marney patted Virginia's knee, encouraging her to agree. With a harumph, Virginia inclined her head in a tiny nod and stood, face drawn.

On their way out, Virginia held up her keys. "You did

give me a key for emergencies. So, I don't think characterizing our entrance as a break-in is entirely accurate." She picked out Lucy's key from the few keys on the chain and waved it in the air.

"That's not my key," Lucy said with some amusement.

Virginia looked from her daughter to the key and back. "What do you mean?"

Lucy took the keychain from her mother and picked out a different key. "This one's mine."

Marney let out a guffaw, doubling over to brace her hands against her knees. "That would explain the trouble," she wheezed through her laughter.

The mix-up seemed to loosen Lucy a bit as well, and she cracked a smile.

Seeing her daughter let her guard down a hair, Virginia weighed her options. "Lucy," she began with a speck of hesitation. "About Dax..."

To her surprise, Lucy didn't cut her off immediately. She just stood, wary but listening.

"Marney followed you to his apartment." If they were invading Lucy's privacy and overstepping boundaries, better to spread the blame between the two of them. And besides, it was the truth. "There was a man outside. You drove off without getting out of your car."

Lucy's eyes were wide, her mouth hanging open just a fraction at the surprise. She blinked, then nodded, and in a frosty voice, said, "Dax's cousin Charlie. I didn't have anything to say to him."

"You didn't think he might have a message for you from Dax?"

"Dax knows how Charlie and I feel about each other. If

he wanted to pass me a message, he wouldn't use Charlie to do it." The disdain dripping from her voice told Virginia and Marney all they needed to know about how Lucy felt about Charlie.

"Well, Marney did talk to him. He gave her a box of another woman's belongings on Dax's behalf." Virginia paused, gathering herself before delivering the final blow. "Lucy, Dax is married."

Virginia waited for Lucy's eruption, but it didn't come. Her stony face gave nothing away, and the pair waited in silence.

"You tried to break into my home so you could tell me you stalked me across town and found out my boyfriend is married?"

Virginia and Marney exchanged glances, and Marney gave a shrug. This was not the explosive reaction they were expecting.

"Err, yes."

"I know about Bianca," she said, and both Virginia's and Marney's eyebrows shot up immediately.

"What do you mean, you know about her?" Virginia demanded. All hesitation left her in an instant. "You *knowingly* dated a married man?"

When Lucy didn't deny it or immediately offer an explanation, Virginia barreled on. "I don't believe this. How could you have so little self-respect?"

Lucy moved to the window, talking but looking away from her mother. "The marriage was just... It was an agreement of sorts."

Virginia snorted. "Yes, that's what marriage usually is."

Lucy turned and shot her a scornful look. "Not an

agreement between Dax and Bianca. An agreement between Dax and Bianca's father."

Marney looked as curious as Virginia felt, confused by this disclosure. Lucy took her sweet time before continuing, seemingly enjoying having the upper hand.

"Dax and Bianca's father worked together. Frank was ill, and he wanted to ensure his daughter was cared for after he was gone. So, Dax agreed to marry her and take care of her, and in return, Frank set Dax up with his business contacts or something like that. Dax and Bianca married—had a big family celebration making Frank the happiest he'd ever been—and then within a year, things went south between them, and he moved out into his own apartment.

"Frank died, but Dax still honors their agreement. He takes care of Bianca financially, paying for her apartment and giving her an allowance like Frank wanted. When there are parties or gatherings within their family or social circles, he plays the part of the loving husband, and she the part of the adoring wife, but everyone knows they're not really together."

The more Lucy spoke, the more Virginia felt her heart sinking. She pictured Lucy on Christmas, celebrating with Virginia, Jack, and Stephanie, while her lover celebrated with his wife. Even if the marriage was a lie and he didn't love Bianca, he couldn't be the partner Lucy deserved if he had obligations to another woman. And Lucy had gone into this knowingly, willingly. Did she not think she deserved better?

"So, yes," Lucy concluded, turning around and leaning

against her hands on the windowsill. "I know about Bianca. Is that all you came here to tell me?"

At this, Virginia dug in her bag for the letter Dax had written and handed it to Lucy. She saw Lucy's eyes constrict. They flicked from side to side as she read. Lucy finally cleared her throat, blinking, and handed the paper back.

"Thank you for the information." Virginia could hear the frayed edge of her voice. She knew then that Lucy hadn't gotten her own letter from Dax.

Lucy spun to face the window once more, then let out a gasp and staggered backward.

"What is it?" Marney stood, and Virginia came out from behind the island to see what was the matter.

Lucy had one hand over her mouth, and the other was pointing, shaking, out the window. Virginia peered out, following the line of Lucy's finger, but didn't see anything out of the ordinary. The window looked out over the apartment complex parking lot. Cars filled just over half the spaces, and small green patches with trees broke up the monotony of the asphalt. At this time of year, they were bare, but in the summer, they'd provide some shade.

"That car," Lucy whispered.

Virginia scanned the lot and her gaze landed on a classic car, a gorgeous tan sedan with a nose that just wouldn't quit. It was a convertible, and Virginia could see the maroon interior from the window.

"That is stunning," she whispered. "Your father would have been drooling."

Lucy turned to her mother, face distorted in surprise. Virginia almost never mentioned Earl to the kids. They'd occasionally complained that they didn't know more about him, but for so long, it was too painful to say his name. The fact that it slipped off her tongue surprised her almost as much as it surprised Lucy.

Lucy shook her head, composing herself, and turned to look at the car again. "I've seen it before. At the gallery."

Virginia's mouth dropped open, and she looked at the car again as if it might reveal some crucial piece of information. Lucy was looking at it as if it were a monster with bared teeth.

"On the day of the...?" Marney trailed off, but they all understood. Lucy nodded.

A pit opened in Virginia's stomach. She unconsciously stepped back from the window, her hand groping for something to steady herself. Marney looked as pale as Virginia felt, and Lucy was frozen in place. While Virginia gaped, Marney pulled out her phone and snapped a picture. They all remained still and silent until a small man in a leather jacket and ball cap approached the convertible, slid inside, and drove away.

CHAPTER 6

Lucy, Marney, and Virginia stood silent in the wake of the classic car's exit. The slam of a neighbor's door eventually jolted them from their trance, and Lucy turned to Marney for guidance.

"Is this something I should tell the police?" she asked. "I didn't think anything of the cars on the street when it happened, and they never asked."

Marney looked from Lucy to Virginia, considering. With her loyalty to Dylan, Marney had always had more faith in the Seaview Police than Virginia did. It had strained their relationship when Virginia insisted on doing her own investigations in the past. Now, though, with her daughter's future on the line, Virginia wanted as many people looking into this case as possible.

"Of course it is!" Virginia yelped. "That car was at the gallery when someone was murdered—someone you were there to meet—and now it's following you around!"

"It's not following me around," Lucy said, though she backed away from the window a bit, looking wary. "Lots of people live here, and plenty of people from this apartment might have been downtown Wednesday. Not everyone on Third Street was there for the gallery."

Virginia turned to Marney. "But it's something the police would probably be interested in, right?" All she could think about was someone showing up at the gallery to take down both Lucy and whoever she was making the briefcase exchange with, but getting scared off before she showed up. And now they were out to finish the job.

Lucy glanced back out the window, still hesitant, like the driver might zip back into the lot at any moment. Then, with a glance down at the dainty gold watch around her wrist, she said, "I'll go by the station and tell them about the car this afternoon. Now, I have an appointment."

Lucy made to shuffle them toward the door, but Virginia remained planted. "On a Saturday?"

Marney, being herded toward the door, turned back and craned her neck for a last look outside. "You said lots of people live here, so you don't think the owner of that car is following you. Have you seen that car here before?"

Lucy stiffened but tossed her hair back and tried to look unfazed. "I haven't paid a lot of attention to the other residents' cars. Now, I really need to get ready for my appointment." At the unrelenting curious glance from her mother, Lucy specified, "Lawyer."

Virginia's palms immediately began to sweat, and acid rose in the back of her throat at the thought of Mr. Murphy, Esquire. She wondered whether he'd assumed Lucy's guilt the same way he'd assumed Virginia's when she sat before him last summer. Was Lucy's freedom hanging on the legal expertise of a man who assumed the worst about her?

Before Virginia could say anything more, Lucy hurried them toward the door. "I promise to answer my phone next time you call if you promise not to break into my apartment again."

"I CAN GO in and give them the tip. You can wait here." Marney's eyes gleamed with sympathy. She knew how much Virginia did not want to set foot in the Seaview Police Station. But Virginia knew she couldn't leave this in the hands of anyone else, even her best friend. In theory, she would trust Marney with her own life, but in practice, Virginia still had a very hard time trusting anyone with anything.

As she pulled open the door—heavy but swinging easily on a well-oiled hinge—and the blast of warm air hit her face, she looked back longingly at the car where she'd told Marney to wait. Marney was twisted in the front seat, watching her.

"I'm here to make a report," Virginia told the woman behind the front desk.

The woman was sipping coffee from a mug so large it could double as a soup pot, and a flash of recognition shot through Virginia as they made eye contact. It was the same front desk clerk who had been working when Virginia had come to retrieve Lucy only a few nights earlier. She was once again working crossword puzzles in pen, although this time the ink was fluorescent orange instead of pink.

The clerk blinked at Virginia. "You need to report a crime?"

Virginia shook her head, then paused, not sure. "I need to report a tip related to an open case."

"One moment." The woman turned away from Virginia, dialed a number into her phone, then wedged the handset between her cheek and her shoulder before picking up her cauldron of coffee with both hands to take another sip. "Yeah, we've got a woman here who says she's got a tip."

The receptionist turned back to Virginia. "What case is this about?"

"Err, it's the..." Virginia realized she didn't know the victim's name. "The murder in the art gallery last week."

The woman pointed to the benches off to the side, spoke a few more words into the receiver, then hung up the phone. "One of the detectives will come get you in a minute."

By *get you*, Virginia assumed she'd be escorted to the detective's office—maybe even Dylan's old office—or a conference room with a cork board full of potential suspects. She wasn't sure if she wanted that; Lucy's picture would be up on that cork board, she knew, and she wasn't sure she could bear to see that. But when the detective stood in front of Virginia, whipped out his notebook, and said, "Alicia tells me you wanted to make a report?" before looking at her expectantly, Virginia felt slighted.

"Aren't we going to go somewhere?" she asked in a

hushed voice. Weren't murder investigations need-to-know business? Shouldn't this discussion be had somewhere more private than a bench in the station lobby? The only other occupant of the benches, a man in a suit scrolling furiously on his phone, cut his eyes to Virginia and then back down to the phone screen.

The detective shook his head. "No need, ma'am. Now, what is it you wanted to report?"

Virginia took a deep breath. "I have a tip related to the murder at the art gallery last week. Someone who may have been there at the time of the crime. My daughter is the one who discovered the body, and she also witnessed a car parked nearby."

The detective dropped his hands, the notebook hanging by his side.

"It's a very distinct car. A classic car. Tan, with a maroon interior. A Mustang. And it—"

"Did your daughter see the car's driver enter or exit the gallery?"

"Err, no, I don't think so, but—"

"Why do you believe a car parked on a busy street downtown has any connection to this crime, then?"

Because my daughter and the murder victim were both participating in some sort of illicit business, and the driver of that car is now following my daughter around. Instead of saying that, Virginia said, "I just think it's worth looking into since it was parked right there. Maybe the driver saw something? Again, it's a vintage Mustang convertible, tan with maroon inside."

The detective didn't write down the description.

"Thank you for coming in," the detective said by way of dismissal, already walking away from her.

Back in the car, Marney was still twisted around when Virginia returned, and she winced and massaged her shoulders while Virginia recounted the interaction.

Frowning, Marney pulled out her phone. "He didn't even write down the description? That's not right. I'm giving Dylan a call."

"No, it's not—"

But before Virginia could object, Dylan's voice was ringing out through Marney's phone's speaker.

"You're on speaker phone," Marney said in greeting. "Virginia's here."

"Hi, Virginia. Hi, Mom. What can I do for you?" Intermittent happy shrieks of a toddler playing pealed in the background, and Virginia could feel Marney glow. Since Dylan had begun seriously dating Officer McNeil and spending more time around his two young children, Marney had reveled in seeing her daughter in this new light.

"We have a lead on the art gallery murder, but the guys at the station didn't take it seriously when Virginia reported it."

Silence hung for a moment, and Virginia waited for Dylan's response. No longer part of the Seaview Police, she shouldn't get involved. And with a personal connection, she really shouldn't get involved. Still, Virginia could feel Dylan considering on the other end of the line.

Finally, Dylan sighed. "What is it? I'll pass it along to Brian—err, Officer McNeil. He'll make sure they look into it."

Virginia breathed a sigh of relief and described the car Lucy had seen at the gallery and then again at her apartment. Just as she finished, the toddler's shrieks of joyous playing turned into a howl of dismay.

"I have to go, but I'll pass this on to Brian, like I said." They heard the rustle of fabric as Dylan pressed the phone receiver to her chest followed by the muffled sounds of her attempting to comfort the child. "I'll have him or one of his officers reach out to you if they need more information. Talk to you later. Love you, Mom!"

The phone beeped three times, signaling that the call had ended, and Virginia told herself that this was good. She'd been successful. The police knew about the convertible, and Dylan was making sure they were on it. But her stomach churned, unconvinced. She began the drive back to Breeze Village distracted.

"I'm going to make you pull over and let me drive," Marney threatened after Virginia ran the second stop sign of the short trip.

"The DMV has records, right?" Virginia asked, paying no mind to Marney's threat. "Of who owns what car?"

Marney grunted an affirmative but didn't take her eyes off the road to look at her friend.

"What if we could get those, somehow?" Virginia pressed. "Then we could figure out who our mystery man is and go question him ourselves."

This time, Marney did look over at Virginia, the expression on her face indicating she thought Virginia had lost her mind. "Last week you accidentally changed the language on your phone to Japanese while you were trying to take a picture. I don't think we're about to successfully hack into government databases."

She turned her attention back to the road. "And besides, that's likely to get us caught and arrested for cyber warfare or something."

"Hmph." Virginia was unsatisfied with Marney's logical and practical response, and she busied herself thinking about how she might find someone who knew more about computers and didn't care too much about silly things like the law.

"The police have access to those records," Marney said. "And you gave them a good description of the car. They'll probably have the guy's name in no time."

Virginia's fingers thrummed on the steering wheel. It was good; it was progress. Still, she knew how the police could be. She'd seen them ignore information before when it didn't fit with their established theory, like when she'd pointed out that Ruth Beaumont couldn't have accidentally overdosed on her own medications based on the timer caps on the bottles. They'd brushed her off then just like they were trying to do now.

Even if they did investigate her tip and determine who the driver was, she didn't expect them to call her and let her know what they found out. She didn't want to be on the outside, waiting and wondering if her daughter was still on the hook for someone else's crime.

Virginia swerved and Marney screamed. One of her hands gripped the handle hanging down from above the door, and the other gripped the seat underneath her hip. A passing car honked its horn, the wail shifting from a piercing tone to a lower pitch as the vehicle sped away, just inches from colliding with Virginia's sedan.

"What the hell was that?" Marney demanded, but Virginia didn't hear her. She had her arm extended, pointing to a billboard as it approached.

"What do you say we check out the classic car show next weekend?"

* * *

AFTER PULLING over to let Marney drive, at her friend's insistence, then circling back around to stare open-mouthed at the billboard she'd spotted, Virginia had put no fewer than three reminders in her phone for the Seaview Antique and Classic Car Show the next weekend. While the weekend felt like a lifetime away, and she hoped the police identified the classic car owner who had been at the gallery before then, it was her own best shot at making forward progress on the case. She knew she couldn't miss it.

It was still fully on her mind two days later when she walked into her ASL class, so much so that she didn't notice when Bill walked in and took the seat next to her.

He tapped her on the shoulder and waved, then made a little gesture like turning a key by his mouth, indicating that he was "turning his voice box off," as their professor reminded them to do at the start of every class.

Surprised and still distracted, Virginia muttered a greeting, then apologized for speaking, then apologized again for the verbal apology. Finally, completely flustered, she sat back in her chair and put her head in her hands. Beside her, Bill shook with laughter.

"It's okay. Class hasn't started yet, so we won't get in trouble. I just thought you might want to practice a bit."

An indescribable confidence and assuredness radiated off him and wrapped Virginia up in it, steadying her. She felt calmed and a bit surer of herself as she replied.

"If he fusses at us, I'm telling him you started it." Her mouth curled up in a wry smile as she spoke, and it occurred to her that she wasn't sure when she last flirted. Had she and Earl flirted? That was a lifetime ago. Was she flirting now? She was pretty sure she was. She meant to, but now that she thought about it, the idea made her panic.

Bill flashed a million-dollar smile at her, and the panic instantly gave way to that comforting feeling of calm again.

"How was your weekend?" Bill asked.

She started to shrug and give the typical, expected response. *Good, and yours?* But his eyes were looking directly into hers, seemingly asking her to be open and vulnerable with him, and she nearly couldn't resist. *My daughter's been arrested—wrongfully!—for murder, and I am tormented waiting for the police to clear it all up.*

She stopped short of that answer, too. The vision of Bill recoiling, not wanting anything to do with the mother of an alleged murderer, flashed before her eyes. The thought that maybe he'd pity her instead, having to wait for the rusty gears of the justice system to slowly turn and free her beloved daughter while she stood helplessly by, was even worse.

"It was fine," she finally said. "How was yours?"

"Brutal. A buddy of mine needed help fixing his fence. I'm paying for it today." He stretched and flexed his arms, wincing.

The professor flicked the lights on and off to get the class's attention, then began to sign. Virginia, eyes still lingering on Bill's arms, didn't see what he'd said. Bill cleared his throat and nudged her with his elbow, and she was startled to find heads turned in her direction, the professor pointing directly at her.

"Me?" she asked, pointing to herself.

The professor lowered his eyebrows in frustration and motioned turning a key by his mouth, a reminder to try to speak only with sign language and not with her voice. She tried to compose her face in a picture of an apology, unable in her embarrassment to recall the sign for *sorry*.

The instructor beckoned her to the front of the room, and Virginia's stomach sank. She shook her head, and her mouth opened automatically to protest, but she stopped herself before vocalizing her distress. He smiled in encouragement, gesturing again for her to come to the front of the room, and Virginia knew she had no choice. She shuffled slowly down the aisle and took one of two chairs beside the projector.

In each lesson, the professor began by introducing the new vocabulary of the lesson before turning the class loose to practice in pairs. He did this introduction by displaying words on the screen, demonstrating the corresponding sign, and having a class member sign alongside him so he could correct any mistakes. It was Virginia's turn to be that lucky member of the class and learn the new vocabulary in front of everyone.

As Virginia settled into the seat, the word *SCHOOL* flashed on the projector, and the professor clapped his hands twice in front of his chest. The curls of his hair bounced slightly as he signed. He made the motion a second time and raised his eyebrows at Virginia, inclining his head slightly in an invitation for her to imitate him.

Virginia copied the gesture, clapping her hands twice, and the professor's face lit up. He made a motion near his chin, then clicked his keyboard so that the projector displayed the word *GOOD*. He repeated the sign, and Virginia realized he was encouraging her. The projector screen changed again, back to *SCHOOL*, and Virginia repeated the sign.

The lesson continued in this way, and when Virginia returned to her seat nearly ten minutes later, her heart was beating hard in her chest, and she could feel the heat in her cheeks. She'd failed to remember almost all the vocabulary from previous lessons, and even though the professor was kind about it, fixing his wide eyes on her encouragingly and demonstrating the signs she forgot, the gaze of the rest of the class felt judgmental. Bill gave her two thumbs up as she approached their row, then offered her a high five as she sat back down.

"You did great up there," he told her when class was dismissed and they could speak aloud again.

"I hope that's the only time I have to do that this semester."

When they both grabbed their belongings and started to leave, Virginia said, "I'll see you Wednesday," at the same time as Bill blurted out, "Do you want to go out sometime this week?"

Virginia's mouth dropped open, and Bill chuckled. He looked earnestly at her, his silver-blue eyes seeming to dance with anticipation, and Virginia felt her head nodding as if of its own volition.

"Oh," she said with a grimace, interrupting his pleased response. "I picked up a few extra shifts at work this week. My evenings are booked."

YOU WORK WHERE?

The casual inclusion of ASL caught Virginia off guard, though they'd just learned the phrase today.

"Where do you work?" he asked out loud.

Virginia looked down at her feet. "I work part-time at Piggly Wiggly."

To her delight, Bill wasn't put off at all by her work as a cashier. Instead, he said, "All right, if your week is booked, how about next weekend? Saturday?"

"I'd like to—really I would—but I've got plans to go to an antique car show on Saturday."

Virginia was ready to suggest Sunday brunch, expecting Bill to think she was putting him off, claiming to be busy, but to her surprise, Bill beamed. "I love cars! I guess that's something we have in common. How about I come with you?" He paused and nervously added, "Unless you're going with someone else."

His anxious addition tugged at her heartstrings, and before she could consider the consequences, Virginia said, "It's a date!"

$\mathcal{A}$ good Southern woman doesn't turn up uninvited, and certainly when she knows she isn't welcome, but there are times in every good Southern woman's life when she must throw that label out the window and do what needs to be done.

As Virginia crossed the lawn toward Jack's and Stephanie's house, she shifted the box of diapers uncomfortably under one arm, the other hand holding a bag heavy with homemade oatmeal cookies. She'd woken up stiff and brought her walking cane with her but had to leave it in the car to carry everything. The going was slow, and she dropped the box of diapers at her feet on the front porch, leaning with the newly freed hand on the side of the house before ringing the doorbell.

"Surprise!" she said when Jack answered the door. Virginia knew that if one must turn up unwanted and uninvited, pretending to be a welcome guest unaware of any ongoing disputes was just as important as bringing gifts.

The screech of an infant rose up from the house behind Jack, and he looked over his shoulder before stepping out onto the porch with Virginia and shutting the door behind him. Even with the door shut, his voice was little more than a whisper when he spoke, as if the house's occupants had superhuman hearing.

"I thought I made my position clear when you came around last week."

Ignoring him, Virginia extended her arm and offered Jack the bag of cookies she'd borrowed Marney's kitchen to make. He just waved the bag away.

"Is everything okay with Lucy?" Jack asked. Worry battled annoyance for dominance in his tone, and dark circles ringed his eyes. "If you're here, I hope that means there's an update."

"She's fine. The police have a lead, and I'm on the case, too—"

She was interrupted by the door opening behind her son and Stephanie poking her head out. Her hair was pulled back in its usual ponytail, but loose strands stuck up in all directions. Her eyes were ringed with the same dark circles as Jack's, and her face lit up as she spotted the bag Virginia held.

"Virginia! Does this mean you're feeling better?" She took the Ziplock from Virginia and pulled it open, inhaling deeply. "These smell divine!"

Feeling better? Virginia looked to Jack, figuring that was the excuse he'd given Stephanie for her not staying after she brought food from Luigi's the previous week.

Leaning against the closed front door, Stephanie handed her husband the baby monitor, freeing her other hand to reach into the bag and stuff a cookie in her mouth. "I'm perpetually starving these days. I'd invite you in, but I just got Emily back down to sleep. I'm glad you're feeling better, though."

"That's all right. I just wanted to bring you those cookies. My mother made them for me when I had both Jack and Lucy. Oh, and I brought some diapers, too. I know we went through more than I could have ever imagined."

Stephanie looked down at the box of diapers and frowned. "We're cloth diapering, actually."

Virginia blinked, wondering what exactly that meant, but Stephanie provided no further explanation and only took another cookie from the bag.

"We appreciate the thought." Jack stooped to pick up the box of diapers and hand it back to Virginia. Her face flushed embarrassment, and she turned away so they wouldn't see.

As she was leaving, a piercing cry from Emily blared from the baby monitor. She turned in time to see Stephanie put her face in her hand, then crumple, sliding her back down the front door until she was crouched on the stoop. Jack knelt beside her and whispered something in her ear and she nodded, both standing before she went inside and he walked with Virginia toward her car.

"Please," Jack begged, his voice lower and more urgent now, "just keep your distance. Especially if you're turning Lucy's case into another amateur detective moment and getting yourself involved in something dangerous. Keep it away from us. Things are hard enough around here without the stress of worrying about you and Lucy involved in a murder case." He took another shuddering breath and said again, "Please. Just… just stay away."

* * *

WHEN VIRGINIA TOLD Marney she would be going to the car show with Bill, she expected Marney to chastise her for upending their plans. Instead, Marney clapped her hands together and brought them up under her chin, peering over them at Virginia with glistening eyes.

"I never thought you'd go on a date again!"

Truthfully, neither did Virginia, and if she'd had her wits about her, she wouldn't have accepted this one. They were supposed to be at the car show to track down a killer, not to explore the possibilities of new love.

"He thinks you like cars?" Marney asked, giggling.

Virginia's stomach, aflutter with the nerves of having a date lined up for the first time in decades, dropped. "I don't know anything about cars." She spiraled, panic welling up. "I mean, I know they've got four wheels, usually. And an engine. They all have engines, right? Gosh, Earl's rolling in his grave hearing this."

Hearing his name rolling off her tongue again, Virginia flinched, expecting a wave of guilt to crash over her—she was dating again, and doing it at a car show, one of Earl's favorite hobbies. But the guilt never came.

Marney, for her part, was gleeful. "I think since you're a woman, you're allowed to just coo over the pretty ones without knowing too much. Besides, you'll probably be too busy getting to know one another to talk much about the cars."

Virginia groaned. "This wasn't supposed to be a date in the first place! We were supposed to find and interrogate a convertible-driving killer so we can bring him to justice."

"I'll handle the interrogation," Marney said. "You enjoy your date."

But the closer the car show drew, the more dread pooled in Virginia's gut. Marney might be willing to take on the task of confronting their main suspect, but Virginia couldn't come to terms with leaving Marney to do it on her own. Images of Marney in danger because of Virginia's past investigations—kidnapped and held at gunpoint—haunted Virginia. It was her family who was in this mess; she had a duty to try to fix it. Not Marney.

But Marney was over the moon that Virginia was interested in a man, the first in the decades since Earl had died, and she insisted that Virginia let her take over the investigation for the day and instead focus on enjoying herself.

She spent the last few evenings before the car show Googling "Top Classic Cars" and variations on the theme, trying to absorb enough information that she could convince Bill she actually had an interest in cars, but everything she read left her brain as quickly as she could take it in. When she pulled up at the large field full of gorgeous cars gleaming in the winter sun, she wasn't sure she'd be able to make a single intelligent remark about them.

"Virginia!"

She turned to see Ronald hustling toward her, each step lurching to the side as he propelled himself along with his cane. Patricia flanked him, and Virginia could see that Jimmy and Gemma were only a few steps further away, though they were too engrossed in one another to notice Virginia's arrival.

"What are you doing here? I didn't know you liked cars," Ronald said. "I'd have invited you to come with us."

"Oh, actually, I—"

"Why, hello there." Bill's smooth voice sounded from behind Virginia, and when she turned to greet him, he took her hand in his and kissed the top of it.

Virginia looked back to Ronald and Patricia. Patricia's face was carefully composed, giving away no reaction, but Ronald was nowhere near as collected. His mouth hung open, revealing toothy disbelief.

Bill looked from Virginia to the others. "I didn't realize your friends were joining us."

Virginia opened her mouth to respond, but Patricia beat her to it.

"We aren't here together. We just spied Virginia and had to say hi. I'm Patricia, and this is Ronald." She stuck out her hand, and Bill shook it firmly. "And we've got to be on our way now. It was lovely to meet you…?" Patricia raised her eyebrows in question.

"Bill."

"Lovely to meet you, Bill," she repeated.

Patricia bodily turned Ronald around and tugged him away from Virginia and Bill, into the field where owners had parked their antique cars and stood beside them, regaling anyone interested with facts and stories about their treasured vehicles. Ronald tried to crane his neck to get another look at Bill, but Patricia gave him a sharp pull, and the two hurried along.

"I didn't mean to tear you away from your friends." As he spoke, however, Bill's body relaxed. He was clearly relieved they'd left and he had Virginia to himself, and a fresh pang of guilt struck Virginia. She was already glancing around for any sign of the man they'd seen get into the convertible at Lucy's apartment; no matter how hard she tried to leave this to Marney, she'd be distracted all afternoon.

"We all live at Breeze Village together," Virginia confided, making eye contact and working hard to focus only on him. "I can see them any time. They don't need to spend time with me while I'm here with you." She watched Bill for any reaction to the mention of Breeze Village. Would he think twice about his interest in her when he found out she lived in an assisted living community? Though she loved it there, she still felt like it was one thing to be retired and another thing entirely to be *old*.

But Bill didn't comment on her living arrangements, instead looping her arm through his and setting off toward the show, keeping a healthy distance behind Ronald and Patricia.

Virginia hung back while Bill spoke to the cars' owners. She knew Marney would be somewhere nearby, searching for the tan convertible, but there was no sign of her. Beside a vintage blue Cadillac with tail fins, Bill got to talking with the owner and discovered they had the same alma mater. "Go tigers!" they said, clapping each other on the back. After a lengthy discussion about which university buildings were present during the years they each spent on campus and which off-campus haunts they'd shared in common, Bill turned to see Virginia on her tiptoes, peering with narrowed eyes at the next row over. She could just make out white wisps of fine hair she thought was Marney's, a sparkling tangerine shawl covering the shoulders beneath the curls as she walked away from Virginia. *There you are.*

"I didn't mean to abandon you," Bill said. "Is there something over there you'd like to see?"

Virginia shook her head and tried to turn her attention back to the nearby vehicles, but a tan glint caught her eye and she gasped. It was the car she and Marney were looking for. And Marney was heading right for it.

"What's that tan car over there?" she asked, pointing. "The convertible?"

Bill put his hand up to shade his eyes, squinting as he tried to make it out.

"It's hard to tell from here, but it looks like a Mustang. Should we go take a closer look?"

Virginia gave an eager nod. She might have agreed to let Marney do the interrogating, but she wanted to get within earshot.

They were still twenty yards away when shouts sounded, and they stood taller, trying to see what was the matter. Suddenly, the crowd ahead of them parted, and Virginia saw the tan convertible's owner sprinting headlong in their direction. Marney was chasing after him but falling farther behind with every step. Her bright shawl had slipped from her shoulders and billowed out behind her.

"Stop that man!" Marney shouted, but the crowd seemed disinclined to follow the orders of a strange elderly woman. Instead, the people simply stepped out of the way, gawking. One or two held up cell phones, recording the chase.

The man was getting closer now, and Bill grabbed Virginia by the waist, pulling her out of the way. At the last second, Virginia stuck out her leg and tripped the man.

"Ow!"

He started to push himself up off the grass, and Virginia stepped toward him, out of Bill's grasp.

"I'm so sorry! Let me help you up." Virginia stuck out her hand, and the man took it, brushing dust and dead grass from his clothes as he stood. He looked behind him in the direction of Marney, who was approaching with an expression equal parts horrified and relieved.

The man turned to resume his run, wrenching his hand free from Virginia's, but Virginia stepped directly into his path before he could take off again.

"I'm terribly sorry for tripping you," she repeated, blocking his escape. "Are you all right? I can't believe I'm so clumsy!"

"I'm fine." The man cast another look over his shoulder to where Marney was now only a few yards away. "If you'll excuse me—"

"Let me buy you a lemonade," Virginia continued, cutting him off once again. The interested crowd had begun to return to other things, and Virginia leaned in close. "I insist."

Unable to shake her off, the man sputtered in place

while Marney approached. She grinned at Virginia, then turned the smile on the man, the grin morphing into something predatory.

"I see you've met my friend," Marney said. The man's face blanched, and he spun frantically, looking for an escape. Marney turned to Virginia. "I simply told this man I had a few questions to ask him regarding his recent presence at the art gallery downtown, and he took off running."

Virginia's nails dug into his forearm as she held him in place. This man was present when the murder took place. A murder Virginia's daughter was being fingered for. Based on the ghost-white shade of his face when Marney mentioned the art gallery, Virginia was sure he knew something.

By then, Bill had stepped closer to see what was the matter, looking in baffled horror at her nails buried in the man's arm. Virginia willed her brain to come up with a convincing lie that would explain her need to talk with this stranger whom she'd just laid out on the grass, but she came up with nothing. Finally, she said, "I can't tell you what's going on, but I need to talk to this man." She saw pain and confusion in his eyes as she continued. "It's important. And it needs to be now. I'm really sorry to do this. I'll see you in class on Monday?"

If they successfully got any information out of their mystery man, she wanted to follow up on it immediately. And if they weren't, she didn't think she'd be a particularly fun date for the rest of the car show. She didn't wait for Bill to respond, instead muttering another apology and turning to Marney and their classic car driver, her back to Bill as he walked away.

Dragging their captive by the arm toward the cart selling drinks and food, Virginia muttered in his ear, "I just chased away the first date I've had in forty years. You'd better make it worth it."

Though he could have snatched himself away from the two octogenarians and made another break for it, the man seemed wary of causing another scene and accepted the lemonade Marney handed to him before settling in at a nearby picnic table. Marney sat beside him, a bony hand on his forearm on the table, reminding him that he wasn't free to go. Virginia sat across from them, wanting a good view of his face as they questioned him.

She remembered hearing Jimmy talking at dinner one night about the cop shows his former neighbor, Ed, had watched too loudly for Jimmy's liking. He'd said it would get quiet for a few minutes and he'd think Ed had turned off the television, but then the noise would start up again.

"It's a tactic," Jimmy had said. "The police sit quietly in the interrogation room, just letting the suspect stew, and then eventually, the suspect can't take the silence and says something to get himself in trouble. I fall for it every time, thinking Ed's done watching, and then when they start shouting again, it's even louder than before! It's unbelievable."

Taking a page out of the fictional police officers' book, Virginia sat quietly, sipping her lemonade and letting their captive stew. It was January, but the sun was out, and in the Southern town of Seaview, iced tea and lemonade were appropriate year-round. Sweat even began to bead on her upper lip as she turned the straw in her hand, swirling the ice inside the Styrofoam cup.

Finally, the man took the bait.

"Did Loretta send you? Who are you, her mom? Auntie? I was at the meeting place, I swear. She didn't show! But I didn't skip out—I was there exactly when she said."

Loretta. A name they didn't have before. It was a start.

"I understand completely, Mister...?" Virginia prompted, even though she didn't. She hoped that by the end of their talk, maybe she would.

The man didn't give his name. He narrowed his eyes at her, and Virginia clenched her jaw and tried to look intimidating. Under the table, her legs were trembling, her body acutely aware that she might be sitting across from a murderer, and even if she wasn't, she was sitting across from a strong, angry man who now had a reason to want to hurt her. But she kept her chin up, doing her best not to show fear.

"Look," she said when he didn't give his name. "My daughter's in trouble because of you. You know all that 'mama bear' stuff they put on cutesy shirts and whatnot? Well, you're dangerously close to seeing the grislier side of this mama bear."

"Loretta's in trouble?" The man's eyes bulged, and his fingers dug into the table. "Oh, God, I knew something was going to go wrong. She just—look, no offense to you, of course—she just wasn't cut out for this kind of stuff, you know? Too trusting. Naive."

The man ran his palms down his pants and looked around again. His tongue flicked from his mouth and wet his lip. The entire picnic table shook as he bounced his knee nervously. "I don't know anything about whatever trouble Loretta's in, I swear. And I don't have the stuff with me, but I can get it for you. I stashed it in my house when Loretta missed our meeting."

Virginia looked at Marney, silently begging for advice on how to proceed, but Marney's face was expressionless. Her hand still rested on the man's arm, the frail threat of a determined elderly woman keeping him firmly in place.

Finally, Virginia sighed. "Loretta isn't my daughter. Whoever she is, I don't know her. I don't know why she missed your meeting or if she's in trouble. But I do know that my daughter is in trouble, arrested for a murder she didn't commit. You were present at the crime scene when it happened. Your car was parked outside, and based on your reaction when Marney asked about the art gallery, you weren't parked there to visit the movie theater up the street. So, if you don't tell me everything you know about whatever happened at that gallery, the Seaview Police are going to swoop in on your house and find whatever 'stuff' you stashed there. How does that sound?"

"Whoa, whoa, whoa!" The man jumped up, nearly tripping backward over the picnic table bench. "I don't know anything about a murder."

Marney was standing beside him quicker than Virginia thought she could move. "That's too bad, because *my* daughter is the Assistant Chief of the Seaview Police." She held up her phone in front of the man's ghost-white face. "Should I call her now?"

"Wait!" The man sat down, his entire body shaking. "I'm serious. I don't know anything about a murder. I was only there to pick up the goods for Loretta. I met her at a bar. We went back to my place, and she… she asked me to take some pictures of us. In the act. I just thought she was a bit of a freak, but then, next thing I know, she's threatening to send them to her husband if I don't help her out with something. She said if she did that—if her husband saw those pictures—he'd kill me, and the way she said it… I don't think she was lying."

The man shuddered, then looked up from where he'd been staring at his hands and made eye contact with Virginia. "All I did was act as a middleman. A delivery guy, really. Well, I don't know if you can call it that if she didn't make the meeting to pick up the package, since I didn't actually deliver the goods."

"What goods?"

"I don't know!"

Marney held up her phone and began to dial Dylan. She put the phone to her ear, and the man held up his hands. "Wait! I was supposed to go to the art gallery to pick something up, pay the guy who gave it to me with the money Loretta gave me, and then bring it to Loretta. It was a duffel bag. I wasn't supposed to look inside, but after Loretta didn't show, I did. It was a bunch of fake driver's licenses and passports."

Marney lowered her phone.

Virginia strained to keep up. "Someone at the art gallery is selling fake IDs?"

"And Loretta wanted you to pick them up for her," Marney added. "But then she stood you up."

The man nodded vigorously. "That's it, I swear. I don't know anything about any murder, nothing like that."

Virginia narrowed her eyes at him. He seemed sincere, and she found herself feeling sorry for the guy, caught up in more than he bargained for. "What were you doing at my daughter's apartment complex?"

"Where?"

"The fancy apartments over by the new high school. Last Saturday. We saw you there."

The man looked skyward, thinking, his lips moving as he counted back the days.

"Oh!" he said. "I was picking up a leather jacket I bought on Facebook Marketplace."

CHAPTER 8

Virginia headed for Marney's cottage as soon as she got back to Breeze Village from the car show. Marney, having sailed through a yellow light and beaten Virginia back, was bent over in the kitchen, spooning a can of cat food into Pancake's bowl. Virginia pulled a glass from the cabinet and started to pour herself some tea, then reconsidered and reached for a bottle of wine.

"It's three o'clock," Marney observed, though she got out a second wine glass to join Virginia, so her judgment was superficial at best.

"What do you make of our guy's story?" Virginia asked.

"I think there's an awful lot of shady stuff going on at that art gallery." Marney shuffled into the bedroom, and Virginia could hear a rustling of papers. When she returned, she laid a page down on the dining table in front of Virginia.

"I couldn't sleep last night, so I started making a list of everything we know about this case."

On the page were stick figures labeled *Dax*, *Lucy*, and *Deceased*. Dax and the murder victim were on opposite sides of the paper, with Lucy positioned in between. Under a dotted line connecting Lucy and Deceased, Marney's crisp handwriting spelled out *EXCHANGE BRIEFCASE*. A third stick figure, labeled *Bianca*, was off to the left, a line connecting her to Dax with the word *WIFE* neatly underneath.

"Now," Marney said, tapping her pen against the wooden tabletop, "Our classic car lover and Loretta are also linked to the gallery, but it's unclear if there's a connection to Dax."

At the bottom of the page, she added three more stick figures in the same configuration as Dax, Lucy, and Deceased. This time, the labels were *Loretta*, *Mr. Mustang*, and *Mystery Supplier*. Then, in the center of the page, she drew a child's rendition of a house, a small rectangle with a triangle on top. This, she labeled *Gallery*.

"What do you think is more likely?" Virginia asked. "That two different people are running some sort of illegal activity out of the art gallery—both our murder victim and the mystery supplier—or that it's the same guy supplying both Loretta and, err, Lucy?"

"You think the murder victim was supp—"

Before Marney could finish her response, a knock sounded at the door, immediately followed by the quiet squeak of the door opening.

"Is Virginia here?"

Ronald stepped inside, pausing to lean his cane against the wall and scoop Pancake into his arms. Then he approached the table, where Virginia was shoving the diagram under a basket of napkins. Patricia lagged behind him, glaring affectionately at his back.

"You can't just barge into people's homes!" she said.

"I knocked! And, speaking of things you can't just *do*, why on Earth did you blow off your date?" Ronald demanded. He turned a censorious look on Virginia, and Pancake seemed to echo the expression, his tiny cat eyes squinting in reproach at her from Ronald's arms.

Patricia said, "We saw him talking to one of the car owners by himself and asked him where you'd gone. He said you had to take care of something. Something about a man tripping and you needing to talk with him?"

Pancake squirmed in Ronald's arms, and he dropped the cat, moving both hands to his hips to give Virginia a disapproving look. "That man is handsome, Virginia. He's got all his teeth—not all of us can say that—*and* all his hair."

"He looks like George Clooney," Patricia added with a nod.

Virginia didn't have to come up with an explanation, for Ronald had turned his attention to where her hands were resting on the napkin basket she'd moved over their diagram.

"What's that?"

"Nothing," Virginia said, too quickly.

Unconvinced, Ronald moved the basket aside and took in the paper with wide eyes.

"'Deceased?'" he read, jabbing a thick finger at Marney's writing. "You're on a new case!" He whirled, looking at Patricia. "Did you know?"

Patricia vehemently shook her head, coming closer to see the page for herself.

"Who's dead?" Ronald demanded. "And why are *you* investigating? Are we in danger again?"

Virginia held up both hands to quiet him, lest Gemma hear from the cottage next door, then assured him and Patricia that the residents of Breeze Village were in no danger.

"As to why I'm looking into things…" Her voice shook, surprising her, and she took in a quavering breath before she could continue. "My daughter is—"

She broke off, unable to say more, and the blood drained from her friends' faces. Realizing their fear, she quickly added, "She's fine. She's okay. She's just… she was arrested for the murder, but she didn't do it. I'm trying to figure out who did. That's why I'm investigating."

None of her friends tried to turn her off from doing her own detective work. They accepted that if there were a case that threatened or concerned someone Virginia knew and loved, she'd be on it.

After a beat of silence in which they took in the situation, Ronald asked, "So, what are we going to do next?"

Virginia could protest, she knew. She could insist that they ought not to get involved, that this was her family's mess and she was going to clean it up herself. There was no *we* to speak of. But she knew enough to know that that wouldn't work.

She let out a sigh. "Do you think you could convince Diana to organize a field trip to the art gallery?"

* * *

THE SEAVIEW SEAGULLS BOWLING TEAM, Lawrence's main social group, hosted family nights at the bowling alley every few months. In the winter, their marketing was essentially, *"It's cold outside. Bring your kids bowling to tire them out so they don't destroy your house."* It seemed to be effective, as the place was packed when Virginia and Marney showed up on the Monday after the car show to watch Lawrence bowl and congratulate him on the event's success. The teammate who usually planned their events had recently injured his leg and had passed on his responsibilities to Lawrence, who had spent the last two weeks worrying about whether he'd ordered enough food from the catering group and trying to track down a machine to blow up the hundreds of balloons he'd bought.

"I just hope we can bring some young blood onto the team," he said, wrapping Marney and Virginia in an embrace. "We're great when no one's out recovering from a hip replacement or down with particularly bad arthritis, but when the average age of the team is seventy-eight, we can't exactly count on that."

Virginia looked around. Bright, colorful lights flashed in the dark space, and music thumped, making Virginia want to nod her head in time. Balloons adorned the ball return machines, and the catering spread at the back of the room was going fast. The room was fuller than she'd ever seen it, and pride at her friend's accomplishment overwhelmed her.

"You are incredible. You know that, right?" She beamed at Lawrence, who gave a self-effacing smile.

"Skip's granddaughter posted on her social media accounts. I'm pretty sure she's to thank for most of this turnout. I didn't even adequately prepare—we're low on food already. I'm going to have to send someone out to get extra."

Virginia put a hand on Lawrence's shoulder. "Hey. This is amazing. Stop worrying for one minute and just be proud." She looked behind him at the table and added, "I'll run by Cancun and get more food. They're no Miss B's, but they're certainly the fastest turnaround in town for large orders."

Marney gave her a piercing glare. "You absolutely will not. You've got class!"

Virginia was supposed to go straight from the bowling alley to her ASL class, but every ounce of her being wanted to go home instead.

"Under no circumstances will you skip your class to help me with this event," Lawrence said. "And if you do get it in your head to try to skip, I'll know."

How would he know? Virginia had no clue, but she knew he would.

"Who's this man you've been on two dates with?" she asked, changing the subject. "Is he here?"

Lawrence's skin deepened, and she could tell he was trying to bite back a giddy smile. "Five dates," he corrected, fully beaming as he thought about them. "He had a prior obligation tonight so I'm afraid you'll have to wait to meet him, but I know you're going to like him."

Marney gave Lawrence an affectionate squeeze on the arm, then checked out the catering table and her watch before shooing Virginia off to her class and heading out to pick up more food.

"I'm not kidding, Virginia," Lawrence called after them. "If you cut class, I'll know!"

Even with the weight of his threat hanging over her, Virginia loitered outside the door to the community college building, unable to will herself to enter until the moment class started. She snuck in and took a seat at the back, though her eyes found Bill sitting in the same row they'd chosen the last few classes. He was sitting alone, and she had an urge to go to him when she saw him look around for a partner to pair up with for the practice exercises, but she averted her eyes, turning her full attention to the woman sitting next to her, a traditional college student who couldn't have been older than twenty.

NAME YOU?

Virginia fingerspelled her name, then asked the young girl the same. Her hands moved rapidly, her fingers nimble in a way Virginia's hadn't been in years, and Virginia had to ask her to repeat herself more slowly.

I V-A-N-E-S-S-A.

By the time they'd exhausted their ability to converse, asking each other if they liked learning sign language, where they were from, how many siblings they had, and where they worked, Virginia's mind had become entirely focused on the task at hand—communicating. It was a challenge, and she felt more than a little embarrassed when she didn't understand Vanessa's quick signing and had to ask her to clarify, but with every question she was able to comprehend and answer, a little piece of her seemed to click into place. A bit of confidence. A reminder that old dogs could learn new tricks. The guilt she felt for blowing off Bill and the anxiety around the inevitable discussion she'd have with him later faded away as her mind became completely engaged in the exercises.

Too soon, the lights flickered off and on, catching the class's attention, and the professor pointed to the projector screen. This week's vocabulary focus would be emotions. For a second, Virginia felt a beat of excitement at growing her ability to communicate her feelings in this new language. Until the professor held up a finger, searching the room, and selected a student to come to the front of the room to demonstrate the vocabulary for the lesson.

Bill stood slowly, leaning on the desk, and any fervency Virginia felt for the lesson evaporated. When he took his seat by the professor, Virginia saw his eyes roving the room until they met hers. They hardly left her for the duration of his time in the hot seat. When he signed ANGRY, SAD, and FRIEND, especially, she felt them boring into her, the unspoken accusation coming across loud and clear.

Bill didn't approach her after class, though. She expected him to come up to her and dress her down or at least to ask her why she'd blown him off. Instead, he hung back, waiting for her to make the first move to apologize. As she tucked her notebook into her bag, she met his gaze, then hurried out the door to her car.

CHAPTER 9

"*I* call shotgun!"

The residents of Breeze Village ambled from the main building of the retirement home toward a small bus waiting in the parking lot to spirit them away to the art gallery. It was the first field trip since the ill-fated trip to the bingo tournament last summer, where the former Breeze Village owner was murdered. While a few residents made quips about hoping no one wound up dead on this excursion, all were eager to get off the premises and explore a bit.

"No fair! I have longer legs. I should get shotgun."

"There's no shotgun. It's a bus," Diana said, taking up her post beside the door to the bus to assist residents stepping up into the vehicle. The Activities Coordinator had loved Ronald's idea for a trip to the art gallery, apparently unaware of the gallery's recent events, and the gallery owner must have been more than happy to charge a discounted group admissions rate and fill the gallery with visitors so soon after it was closed for the removal of a dead body. Virginia was still stunned that they'd managed to get a trip arranged so quickly.

Behind Virginia, a woman grumbled. "Well, I think there ought to be a shotgun. And if there was one, I think I ought to be allowed to sit there."

Diana gripped the woman's forearm as she began to climb the stairs up into the bus. She hid a small smile as she said, "Miss Summers, if there was a shotgun, you'd be allowed to sit there."

The woman took the first seat behind the driver, her arms folded across her chest, and the rest of the group climbed aboard.

"All the cool kids sit in the back," Ronald insisted, leading their small group all the way down the narrow aisle. When they were seated, he leaned in close. "So, what's the plan?"

Patricia's and Marney's heads turned with his to face Virginia, all waiting for direction, and Virginia stammered. She hadn't thought out a plan.

"Well, uh, I suppose we want to find out what we can about the gallery employees." After Marney and Virginia had filled Ronald and Patricia in on what they knew so far, they'd all theorized at length—with more enthusiasm and less intelligence as the night grew later and the drinks flowed—about who at the art gallery might be capable of producing fake IDs and running a business selling them. How that business tied in with the murder was even murkier. "Let's see if we can find out who owns the place and who all works there. Maybe we'll be able to find out who was there when the murder took place or if any of them have connections to Lucy's rat boyfriend Dax."

As it turned out, it was no trouble at all to find out who owned the gallery—they were greeted warmly at the entrance by the owner himself, who gave a quick overview of the gallery's history before encouraging the visitors to wander and enjoy the art.

The Benson-Barnes Art Gallery was Seaview's largest and longest-standing art gallery. The building, a historic home, had been in the Benson family since its construction in 1918. Madeline Benson, a prominent member of Seaview society at the time, was an art enthusiast and collector. She had a number of works by well-known artists on display in her home and regularly invited guests to small parties to appreciate her collection.

Following the death of her husband, she'd remarried Timothy Barnes, an artist himself and a frequent guest at her parties. At Timothy's encouragement, the couple began hosting artists to live with them for residencies and showcasing their work. Then they began selling paintings, both of Timothy's and the resident artists, and hosting curated events where they charged for admission. In 1938, they officially opened as an art gallery, though the couple lived in the home until their deaths years later.

"My grandfather was Madeline's nephew and took over the gallery in the '70s. He was the owner until three years ago when I took it over from him." The owner swept his arms as if showing off a grand space, though the room was quite small and cramped with the group buzzing shoulder-to-shoulder within.

Virginia raised her hand and the owner, who had introduced himself as Hugh Porter, raised his brows in surprise.

"A question already! Of course, what would you like to know?"

Virginia wanted to know who in this art gallery was printing fake IDs and selling them to Loretta. She wanted to know whether they were also involved with the shady business between Lucy and the dead man. And she wanted to know whether the owner—the man in charge—knew what was going on beneath the surface of his gallery. If maybe he had a direct role. But if she was going to find anything out, she first needed to win the owner over, make him think her an unsuspecting old lady just visiting with her retirement home.

"Are you an artist, too? And was your grandfather?"

Mr. Porter gave a guilty smile and shook his head. "Gramps thought of himself as an artist. The Curby Room, that's all the way back and to the left—" he gestured toward a doorway to a hallway leading deeper into the gallery, "was exclusively filled with his original works while he was alive. Never sold a single one!"

Mr. Porter barked a laugh, and the group chuckled along with him.

"Gramps was a better businessman than artist, luckily. Even though he never sold a piece of his own, he grew the gallery's collection and expanded the artist residency program while he lived."

"You still have a residency program? Artists come and live here, even today?" Ronald asked. Excitement in his eyes, he turned to Virginia and gave her a look as if to say *"We've got a fresh batch of suspects!"* She gave him a nod and turned back to Mr. Porter, willing Ronald to maintain his composure, though she was as intrigued as he was to know who might be living at the gallery now. Who, with their artistic abilities, might be running a covert side-gig out of the gallery creating fake IDs?

The owner nodded. "We have three apartments where we host artists, although instead of the residency program of the past—that was more of an internship where artists would learn from Timothy Barnes and other prominent area artists—it's more of a retreat now. We don't have masters here to give intensive instruction, but we provide a space to get away from regular life for anywhere from one week to three months. We cater meals and take care of everything, so all the artist has to do is create."

"Has anyone famous stayed here?" one man asked. "Like Picasso?"

"Well, Picasso never stayed here, no," Mr. Porter chuckled. "The best-known artists who did residencies here back in the day or spent a retreat here more recently would be, let's see... Mary Grant? Jonathan Glickman? Oh, and there were the Charge sisters, Evelyn and Rosie. Jesse Spencer was here just last year."

The man grunted in disappointment, clearly unimpressed by those names, but Mr. Porter shrugged off the dismissal.

"Feel free to wander," he said. "And find me or my assistant, Gerald, with any other questions you have."

As if summoned, a young pimply boy entered the room. He wore a paint-covered apron that made Virginia think of Stephanie, and she wondered if her daughter-in-law had ever had any pieces in this gallery.

The group from Breeze Village disbanded, with Diana

leading the way into the next room. Ronald, Patricia, Marney, and Virginia formed a small circle.

"We should find out if any artists were staying here two weeks ago," Ronald said, bouncing on the balls of his feet in excitement.

"And what the owner's and Gerald's schedules are like," Marney added. "Lucy said the owner was here that day, right?"

"He was leaving when Lucy got here and found the body," Virginia said, nodding.

Patricia had been looking hawkishly around the room and now turned back to her friends. "The owner probably has a calendar of when the visiting artists are here. If I can get a glimpse of it…"

Patricia's photographic memory had helped Virginia on investigations in the past. She'd seen the Breeze Village paperwork for Cece last fall and recognized that she was going by a fake name. Though Cece turned out not to be the killer they were looking for, they'd discovered her crochet shop—how she'd stolen patterns and was undercutting Marney's crochet sales. Before that, Patricia had recalled an address she'd seen on a form when she'd moved into Breeze Village. The address of a dead man, which she'd passed along so Virginia could interrogate his widow.

"We've got to get you into his office." Virginia spun, sneakers squeaking on the wood floor, eyes crazed as she looked for any room that might be an office. Getting Patricia's eyes on Mr. Porter's schedule could be the key.

"I haven't seen anything that looked like an office so far," Patricia said.

"Should we split up?" Marney suggested. Ronald looked at her like she'd just lifted her head off her shoulders and tossed it across the room.

"Are you crazy?" he demanded. "Split up at a *murder scene?* Have you seen a single movie? Are you not the same woman who's been kidnapped and held at gunpoint pursuing Virginia's suspects before?"

Virginia winced at Ronald's casual remark, but Marney didn't react.

"Split up in an *art gallery surrounded by people,*" Marney said. "We can cover more ground."

Ronald opened his mouth to tell Marney what a terrible idea it was, but Patricia held up her hand to stop him. "We'll compromise. I'll go with Virginia. You can go with Marney. We'll cover more ground than if we all stuck together but no one's alone."

Appeased, Marney and Ronald set off toward the back of the art gallery, eyes peeled for an office that might hold the next clue.

Patricia turned to Virginia. "The office is upstairs. I looked up pictures of this place online to get an idea of the layout. The Historical Society did a whole feature two years ago."

"Why—?"

"It's your investigation. Your daughter is the one in the mix. Whatever's in Mr. Porter's office, I wanted you to see it first, without the whole group. You should get to decide what you share with us and what you keep to yourself."

A flash of recognition surged between them, and Virginia's chest swelled. She gave Patricia a tight smile and said, "Lead the way."

The pair wove their way through the crowd of senior citizens pointing at the paintings on the walls and luxuriating in getting out of Breeze Village to pass a few hours in public. Patricia's large form cut through the throng, and she turned back frequently to make sure Virginia was with her. For her part, Virginia walked as quickly as she could manage, effortfully breathing through her nose in an attempt to disguise how hard she was working to keep up.

The second floor of the gallery was all-around tighter than the first, as if the building became narrower as it extended vertically. The staircase had walls on either side, and Virginia could easily touch them both as she climbed the stairs. On the landing, the ceiling hovered only an inch or two above Patricia's head.

A velvet rope blocked the stairs up to the third floor, so the two did a quick tour of the second floor. The uneven wooden floor and crooked walls seemed to close in on them as they wandered the floor. The rooms up here were nearly empty—the upper floors would have to hold some pretty incredible treasures to entice the Breeze Village residents to tackle the stairs, it seemed. But none of them was an office.

At the other end of the building, when they'd peered into all the rooms on the second floor, Virginia and Patricia came to another staircase, a mirror of the one they'd climbed before at the front of the building. A velvet rope like the one in the other stairwell with a sign saying *AUTHORIZED PERSONNEL ONLY* blocked the stairs up on this side, too. Patricia wasted no time in moving it aside, and when she turned to Virginia, her eyes seemed to sparkle.

"It's up here, for sure."

Virginia was surprised at how little reverence her friend displayed for rules, but she wasn't any more inclined to stay put on the lower levels, so she brushed past the rope and huffed and puffed her way up the stairs.

The staircase spat them out at the end of a long hallway with doors all down one side. On the other side was only one doorway, a large double-wide entryway with the doors removed. Light poured from the room into the hallway.

Patricia turned and mouthed something to Virginia.

"What?"

Patricia leaned in so her lips nearly touched Virginia's ears, and repeated, "Do you hear that?"

"Obviously not," Virginia hissed back.

"There's voices coming from that room." Patricia pointed to the open doorway.

Stepping as quietly as they could on the old floorboards, the two crept forward until they reached the first door on the left. Patricia put her ear to the door, then reached out and took the handle in hand. She gave it a gentle turn, and the door swung wide, miraculously silent on its old hinges.

The interior was a small apartment with a single bed, a couch, and a coffee table between the two. A mini fridge served as an end table beside the couch, a small lamp perched on top. The surface of the coffee table was entirely obscured by magazines and books.

"One of the apartments for visiting artists?" Patricia suggested.

They backed out of the room and tried the next door, where they found an almost identical apartment, though in this one, the bed was a mess, covers flung to the floor in a night of fitful sleep.

The remaining doors on the left side of the hall were all past the gaping doorway on the opposite side, and since Patricia had heard voices coming from that room, they were hesitant to walk past and risk being caught.

"What should we do?" Virginia whispered.

"It's your investigation," Patricia said with a shrug, just a hair more nonchalant than Virginia appreciated. "Your call."

Virginia needed to get Patricia inside that office. She needed to find records of the artists who had been present at the gallery when Lucy was wrongfully arrested, and she wanted to hunt down a schedule of the assistant's hours while they were at it. Lucy might be content to let this go to trial and put her fate in the hands of an attorney and twelve jurors, but Virginia couldn't bear to wait around and take that chance.

She took a deep breath in and exhaled. "Let's go."

"Excuse me." A mustachioed man stepped into the hallway, startling Patricia and Virginia, and they spun to face him with their hands over their hearts. "This floor is only for artists and staff."

Virginia began to stutter an apology, but Patricia surprised her by affecting a cartoonishly frail voice and hunching over. "What did he say?"

Virginia stifled a laugh. She followed Patricia's lead

and cupped a hand in front of her ear. "I think he asked us if we want a snack."

Two other artists joined the man, stepping into the hallway with confused expressions. The first was no older than twenty, and the other no younger than sixty. The young man wore an apron covered in clay, like he'd just stood up from a pottery wheel. The older woman was dressed impeccably without an apron or smock, though she clutched a paintbrush in her hands as though she'd stepped away from the easel mid-stroke.

"What's going on?" the clay-covered boy asked.

"I think they're lost," the first man replied. He clearly believed Patricia and Virginia couldn't hear or understand him. In a raised voice, he repeated, "This floor isn't open to visitors. It's only for artists and staff."

Patricia feigned a swoon and cried out, one hand bracing her weight against the wall and the other lying limp across her forehead.

"What do we do?" the youngest artist uttered.

Virginia panicked for a moment, Patricia's acting fooling even her, until Patricia muttered, "Chair."

"Chair!" Virginia exclaimed. "Is there a room—maybe an office—where she could sit down to rest a moment? Those stairs must have been too much for her."

The artists conferred amongst themselves, unaccustomed to fainting elderly women interrupting their work, and Patricia cried out again to speed them along.

"This way." The mustachioed man began to lead them into the large room where the three artists had been working. The space was a large studio with pieces in various stages of completion. Virginia wanted to gawk and look around, but the artist pulled up a stool and Patricia shook her head violently.

"My back's not what it used to be. I need something more ergo—, erno—, erlo-whatsit?"

"Ergonomic?"

"That's it!"

The young potter offered, "Hugh's got a fancy chair in his office."

"We can't just take them to Hugh's office," the mustachioed one hissed.

"Oh!" Patricia let out another wail, theatrically clutching her back, and the female painter said, "Oh, for Christ's sake! She's clearly in pain. Let her use Hugh's chair."

The man led them down the hall, grumbling the whole way, until the second-to-last door on the left. It was unlocked like the doors they'd tried earlier, but instead of a small apartment, this door concealed a plain, unremarkable office. The desk chair was the most remarkable thing about the space, and Patricia let out a sigh of pleasure as she sunk into it that Virginia thought wasn't an act at all.

"Thank you, young man," Patricia said to him. She gave a nod of dismissal, and the man looked surprised. He hadn't wanted to bring them here in the first place, and he certainly didn't want to leave them alone.

"Is there a bathroom up here?" Virginia asked.

The artist threw up his hands. "Follow me," he groaned.

When the beleaguered man escorted Virginia back after accompanying her down the hall to his tiny apartment to use the restroom, they found Patricia standing in the office doorway.

"Feeling much better," she said shortly. "We'd best be on our way. Not a lot of art to see up here. Bit of a disappointment, honestly."

The man's face bloomed bright red. "This floor isn't part of the gallery! It's off-limits!"

"Well, you don't have to be so nasty about it," Patricia said. "They ought to put up signs or something."

As they began down the stairwell, Virginia thought she heard the man exclaim something about the presence of signs. It took everything she had to wait until they were out of earshot to ask Patricia if she'd found what they were after in Mr. Porter's office. Patricia nodded enthusiastically, and Virginia felt the excitement inside ready to bubble over.

"There you are!" Marney and Ronald shuffled toward them, enthusiastic glints in their own eyes.

Ronald held up his hand, something glinting in his grasp. "We found something."

CHAPTER 10

Ronald opened his hand to reveal a sparkling earring in his palm. "It was in the tiny portrait room in the back. Isn't that where you said Lucy found the body?"

"Is it Lucy's?" Marney asked.

Virginia's instinct was that it wasn't. It was larger than anything she'd seen Lucy wear, and more colorful. Lucy's go-to was a pair of simple pearl studs. These dangled with blue, pink, and red enamel shapes, all surrounded by clear stones.

"I don't think so."

"You can ask her later," Ronald said, though Virginia recalled the last time she and Marney had seen Lucy, when she was preparing for an appointment with her attorney. Lucy had already insisted to her mother that the way out of this mess was through a trial, where she believed the jury would take her side. Virginia wasn't sure the news that she was poking around the crime scene for her own investigation would go over well. Especially not the part where she'd brought two more of her friends into the mix.

Still, she pocketed the earring Ronald held out and gave a non-committal *mm-hmm* before turning to Patricia. "What did you find in the office?"

"I found the owner's schedule book. He had the arrivals and departures of visiting artists, plus Gerald's schedule in there. And business meetings with a handful of people whose names I didn't recognize."

"Anyone named Loretta?" Virginia blurted. "Or Dax?"

Patricia shook her head, and Virginia deflated, but Patricia promised she'd write everything down once they returned to Breeze Village.

For the remainder of their field trip, the foursome joined the rest of Breeze Village in looking at the art, though at least for Virginia's part, her mind was elsewhere, and she found it impossible to appreciate the oceanscapes and portraits. She was hardly occupying her body as she floated through the gallery and onto the bus back to Breeze Village, fully in her head instead. In her mind, she saw Patricia writing out the list of names she'd seen in Mr. Porter's schedule. She'd show them to Lucy, who would protest at first that Virginia wouldn't leave the investigating to the professionals, but then she'd pause and say, "Hmm, I know that name… Dax mentioned him." And Virginia would share the information with the police, who would bring down the actual killer, clearing Lucy's name and removing Jack's objection to their visiting, now that there was nothing to keep secret to avoid putting stress on Stephanie. All her problems solved, just like that.

"Earth to Virginia."

When she looked up, the rest of the residents had departed the bus, and her three friends were looking at her with concern. She hurried from her seat and got off the bus, and all four of them moved wordlessly toward Marney's cottage. Marney was the only one with a private space outside the main building, but her space was about to become a lot less private as the group made it their operations headquarters.

"Do you still have that board from last fall?" Patricia asked. "I heard you put together a whole TV-style corkboard with strings and everything when that crazy killer was after Colleen and Virginia. We could use one of those for this investigation."

Marney groaned as she descended to hands and knees beside her bed, then pulled out the board she'd pinned information to when Virginia was investigating threats against Colleen. To Virginia's surprise, it wasn't empty.

"After we talked after the car show, I decided to upgrade from that piece of paper…"

Marney had blown up the diagram she'd drawn and shown Virginia just a few days before. Now, each person had their own index card pinned to the board, and the pins were connected with blue yarn.

"Fantastic!" Ronald exclaimed, leaning in for a closer look.

"And a pen and paper?" Patricia asked. Marney handed her the requested supplies, and Patricia copied down what she'd read in the art gallery owner's schedule. Meanwhile, Marney added two new index cards to the center of the board, next to the rudimentary drawing of a house that represented the gallery. These were for Mr. Porter and Gerald.

Patricia handed Marney the paper, and Virginia and Ronald crowded in to peer over her shoulder. It listed everything in Mr. Porter's schedule for the past eight weeks.

"I didn't have time to look further back," Patricia said.

Mr. Porter's logs included the arrivals of two artists, Mona Hauge and Julien Reed. The group figured the third artist, name unknown, must have been on his artist's retreat at the gallery for longer than the eight weeks, and both Mona and Julien had arrived prior to the murder. That meant three more people who may have been in the gallery when the crime was committed—potential witnesses.

Or suspects.

Marney added their cards to the board: *Mona*, *Julien*, and *Artist #3*.

"So, someone inside the gallery prints fake IDs and passes them off to Loretta through your man at the car show," Ronald said, gesturing to the board. "And, in the same art gallery, Lucy—working on behalf of Dax, cheating scumbag extraordinaire—" he looked to Virginia for approval as he added that characterization, "picks up something in a briefcase from a man who is now dead."

"And gives him something in return from Dax," Patricia added.

"What if it's one person supplying both Loretta and Dax?" Virginia wondered. "It just doesn't seem plausible that two people could be operating out of the gallery like that."

"The person supplying Dax is dead. If we can find out if Loretta is getting another duffel bag full of fake IDs, then we'll know if it was the dead guy supplying her, too."

Marney shook her head. "Loretta's in the wind, according to the man she blackmailed into picking up that duffel bag for her."

"Just like Dax," Virginia whispered. "Get someone else to make the pickup. Disappear the same day the supplier is murdered."

She quaked with anger.

"Lucy never looked in the briefcase to know what was in it," Marney said, "but did the police take it with other evidence from the scene? I wonder if Dylan could get Brian to find out if it was full of fake IDs like Loretta was picking up."

Head spinning, Virginia stood to leave. "I need some supper, a stiff drink, and to lie down."

She'd just opened the door when she froze.

"What a fun surprise!" Gemma, Marney's neighbor, had just emerged from her own cottage, a cake carrier in hand. She waltzed into Marney's cottage without hesitation and plunked the cake carrier down on the dining table while Marney hurried to move the cork board into the bedroom, Ronald doing his best to block her from view. "I tried out Dorothea's coconut cake recipe and was looking for some taste testers." She noticed Ronald's behavior and narrowed her eyes. "What are you all doing in here?"

Ronald blurted, "Cards," at the same time as Patricia said, "Watching TV." Gemma looked from one to the other, then to the turned-off television and the table, which was empty of cards.

"Right," she said, with a quick shake of her head. "Anyway…" Virginia breathed a sigh of relief that Gemma had other priorities on her mind, dismissing them as she removed the cake cover with a flourish and beamed down at her creation.

"It looks… Gemma, it looks amazing." Virginia couldn't hide the surprise in her voice, but Gemma only threw her head back in laughter. The cake stood straight. Gemma had waited until it had cooled to frost it, so the frosting hadn't melted and the layers hadn't slid off one another. She'd piped thick rosettes of frosting around the top of the cake—her first attempt at decoration that Virginia recognized for what they were meant to be, even if they were more like blobs than rosettes—and sprinkled the whole thing with shredded coconut.

"I've come a long way, haven't I?"

Ronald and Patricia eyed the cake suspiciously and failed to mask their surprise when they took their first bites and found it entirely edible—good, even. Ronald cut himself a second slice and mentioned that Jimmy was a lucky man to have someone bake him something like this, and Gemma preened. When she packed up the rest of the cake and started off to find more taste-testers, she turned back.

"Oh, Virginia, I almost forgot—Colleen wanted me to pass along a message from the spirits. She said she's been getting the overwhelming feeling that you shouldn't be driving. Or at least, something about a car and major bad vibes, or whatever it's called when the spirits tell her something bad is going to happen. Do with that what you will!" She waved, then was gone.

* * *

"You really didn't have to do this." Virginia gripped the handle above the door and lowered herself precariously from Jane's enormous SUV. The tiny woman slid down from the driver's seat with impossible ease as Virginia worked to steady herself and straighten her uniform. Virginia had asked Marney to drive her, but she was teaching a crochet class, and Jane had overheard the request and insisted she take Virginia to work.

"Nonsense." Jane waved Virginia off with one hand and pulled the wheeled oxygen tank behind her with the other. "If Colleen says you shouldn't be driving, I'm not letting you get behind the wheel. Besides, I needed groceries anyway. I'm down to my last two bottles of wine, and I don't like to let my stores get lower than that."

In truth, after last year's events, Colleen's warning felt ominous, and Virginia wasn't going to disregard it. She insisted that she'd get a younger coworker to show her how to use Uber at the end of her shift so she could get back to Breeze Village without troubling any of her friends, and then headed for the time clock while Jane made a beeline for the wine aisle.

She'd been behind the register for two hours—half her shift that day—when a familiar black beehive bobbed in her direction, the top of the hairdo peeking over the other registers until its owner turned into her line.

"Virginia Walker!" Jan's raspy voice exclaimed a

greeting joined by the jangling chorus of her bracelets clinking together as she abandoned her cart at the entrance to the aisle and tried to hug Virginia across the register. Her bracelets dug into Virginia's arms, and Virginia grimaced.

Jan babbled as she loaded her groceries onto the belt. "I was hoping you'd be working today! I thought to myself today, 'Jan, you have got to give Virginia Walker a call!' But then I thought maybe I'd see you here, and now here you are! Maybe it's that manifesting that Dorothea's been on about. You think about something and then it happens." She placed a pack of Fiber One brownies on the belt, followed by Activia yogurt and cinnamon-raisin bread. "You know, she called me last week to tell me she is officially on the waitlist to move into Harbor Vale. She's selling her condo. Decided she's ready to make the change."

That didn't surprise Virginia, as much time as Dorothea spent visiting Jan there. And, though she'd resisted it so much herself, she'd found the value of a community in Breeze Village to be far beyond what she'd expected. She couldn't imagine living alone again, not having friends right down the hall or in the dining room to eat with every day.

"She was telling me all about Gemma and that new man of hers, too. It sounds like she's been so busy with him that she hasn't organized a Garden Review Society Meeting in a while. After what happened last time..." Jan raised her drawn-on eyebrows suggestively, and Virginia gave a small smile to suggest that yes, she remembered Gemma losing her cool when Ellen brought two new young members who brought with them plenty of new ideas last fall. "Do you know when the next meeting will be?"

Virginia shook her head and scanned a twelve-pack of Diet Dr. Pepper.

Jan let out an exasperated huff. "My best source of gossip at Harbor Vale just passed—God rest his soul—and I'm having trouble figuring out who's connected these days. My second-best source is trying a new thing where she doesn't talk about other people, and it is really making my life more difficult. I have Dorothea, but I'm her biggest source, not the other way around."

Virginia worked to keep the corners of her mouth from pulling into a smile. "I'll let you know if I hear anything good. I'm not sure the folks at Breeze Village are particularly tied into the happenings around town, but I'll be on the listen-out." Not tied into the happenings around town? That was a bald-faced lie, but Virginia wasn't in the mood to gossip. Especially when the biggest news lately was a murder for which her daughter was the prime suspect.

As Virginia scanned the last of Jan's items, Jan pouted slightly and said, "I heard Breeze Village took a field trip. Now that Mr. Odeh owns both retirement homes, it seems like if one of them gets to go on a field trip, we both should."

"Oh, don't feel too bad. It wasn't anything special."

"Someone said you went to a museum and met famous artists."

Virginia couldn't help the guffaw that escaped her. Whoever had been telling Jan about their field trip had certainly embellished. "Nothing like that. We just went to the art gallery downtown."

As Jan took her receipt, she said, "My physical therapist is just down the street from there. I've driven past it for years but never stopped in. I really should, one of these days."

"No!"

Jan stopped short, staring at Virginia with surprise.

Virginia stammered out, "I just meant that it wasn't all that impressive. Probably not worth wasting your time over."

CHAPTER 11

Virginia stood in the bathroom for at least fifteen minutes after her shift, gathering the strength to ask another one of the cashiers for help installing a rideshare app on her phone. The high-school-aged boy, eating a Hot Pocket and a donut from the bakery on his break, started to walk her through the steps, then finally took her phone and downloaded it for her.

"Here," he said, handing it back. "When you need to go somewhere, you click this, put in the address, and then it gives you these choices. If you share a ride with someone else, it's cheaper. And if you need to get picked up right away, here's the option for that."

Satisfied that he'd done his civic duty by helping the elderly navigate technology, the boy returned to his meal, and Virginia ordered a ride to Lucy's apartment.

"I did it!" she said, and he gave her a kind thumbs-up, only half looking up from his own phone.

Outside the grocery store, Virginia checked the license plate of every car and truck that pulled up, her stomach twisting while her anxiety told her that she'd made a mistake and no driver was coming for her. Though it was barely evening, it was dark, and it began to sprinkle as she waited. At last, a white Jeep pulled up and the driver rolled down his window.

"Virginia?"

She nodded, checked the license plate number, and climbed in the back. A thrill went up her spine. She may not be able to drive herself around right now, but that didn't mean she couldn't be independent.

They pulled up in front of Lucy's apartment. "Thank you for the ride." She held out a five-dollar bill but the wiry man in the driver's seat just looked at it, confused.

"You tip in the app," he said.

"In the app?"

"Where you requested the ride." The driver's face took on a look of concern, like he worried Virginia's confusion might be a sign of a medical crisis, and he quickly said, "Don't worry about a tip. Have a nice day."

He gestured with his head for her to exit the car, and she climbed out. She pulled out her phone before entering Lucy's apartment building, clicking back into the app where her coworker had helped her order the ride. Instead of a map, the screen now asked if she wanted to rate the driver on a five-star scale and if she'd like to give him a tip. Face flushed with embarrassment, she gave him five stars and a tip, then followed someone returning from a dog walk into the locked building.

Virginia had promised not to break into her daughter's apartment if Lucy failed to answer her calls. But she'd never promised not to come over unannounced. She reminded Lucy of this fact when Lucy glowered at her from the doorway.

"I told you, I've got a lawyer. I'm following his advice. You don't need to keep checking in on me. I haven't seen that car again since you and Marney were here."

Virginia worked her way past Lucy and into the apartment. Then, she dug her hand into her purse and brought out the earring Ronald had found at the art gallery. She held it aloft so it caught the light streaming in through Lucy's massive living room windows.

"Is this yours?"

Lucy screwed up her face in distaste and shook her head. "Too much for my taste. I opt for neutrals."

Lucy gestured to the pearls studding her earlobes and the plain silver chain around her neck, and Virginia took in her daughter's appearance. She was styled as always, and the bags beneath her eyes had vanished in the week since Virginia had last seen her.

"You look well," Virginia said with an awkward gesture. "Much better than before. How are you feeling?"

"You mean, how am I coping with the disappearance of my boyfriend, who was also my employer, while preparing to go to trial in a few months for a murder I didn't commit? I'm coping enough to at least put on an outfit and go looking for new ways to pay the bills. But I'm glad I look well, Mom."

Virginia felt like she'd been slapped, and at the same time, felt another pang of pity. She hadn't considered that Lucy's dodgy boyfriend was paying Lucy for her involvement in his ventures, that Lucy was financially dependent on him.

Lucy saw the recognition flash across Virginia's face and snorted. "Yeah, Mom. That's right. I told you I was doing marketing for Dax's stupid furniture restoration business. What I was too embarrassed to tell you was that I left my legitimate job to do it. And now I've got no boyfriend, no job, dwindling savings, and an arrest on my record for potential employers to see while I look for new jobs now."

Her voice rose in pitch as she spoke, and she paused to keep from crying, tucking her knees to herself on the sofa and biting her tongue.

"I can't believe I was so stupid," she spat, her words laced with new anger. "The worst part of all this is that the only reason I was even arrested is that I was there, but I wasn't the only one! The owner is always in and out; his assistant is always there. Multiple artists literally live there."

Lucy pinched the bridge of her nose with two fingers. "Actually, that's not the worst part of it all. The worst part is that I actually loved Dax—I still love him—and when he ran, he wrote Bianca a note and not me."

"We're going to fix this." Virginia sat down beside her daughter and gave her knee a reassuring squeeze.

Lucy lifted her head, shaking it firmly. "No, *we're* not going to do anything. I've got a lawyer, and I'm going to let him do his job." At Virginia's frown, Lucy said more fervently, "You can't go digging around in this one, Mom. You'll only make it worse."

Stung, Virginia snapped back, "You're paying that lawyer with what money?" Lucy flinched, but Virginia kept on. "That lawyer is scum, and he thinks you're guilty.

And the longer we sit around and wait for the police to do their jobs, the better the chance that whoever actually killed that man will get away with it.

"That earring I showed you—it was in the little portrait room at the back of the gallery. That's where you found the body, isn't it?"

Lucy's chin dipped in a tiny, stiff nod.

"It belongs to somebody. Maybe the killer. At any rate, it's something the police didn't find. I'm not going to trust that there's not more out there they haven't found."

Lucy just shook her head, the muscles in her jawline clenching and relaxing. She didn't argue, but she clearly didn't agree.

Standing to leave, Virginia remembered the other clue connected to the art gallery. "Do you know anyone named Loretta?"

Lucy shook her head, still visibly seething and refusing to meet Virginia's eyes.

"Dax never mentioned that name?" Virginia probed further. She had no reason to believe Loretta and Lucy's boyfriend were connected, but they'd both disappeared on the same day after having someone else go to the art gallery on their behalf.

"No, he didn't," Lucy snapped. She finally turned her furious gaze on her mother. "Are you leaving now? I can see you out."

The door shut behind her, and the lock immediately clicked into place. Virginia leaned against the wall of the hallway beside the door for a second, angry and exhausted. She spread her hands in front of her like she was gripping a basketball and shook them furiously back and forth, wishing she could throttle some sense into her daughter. Waiting around for the police to find the culprit was unlikely to do anything but give the people of Seaview time to sully Lucy's name, and trusting that slimeball of an attorney to represent her in a trial made Virginia's stomach turn.

She shoved off the wall. Whether Lucy helped or not, Virginia was not going to let this go.

* * *

"Virginia. What a surprise."

Dylan stood stunned in her doorway.

Virginia waited to be invited inside, but when Dylan continued to stand frozen, she asked, "Do you mind if I come in?"

Dylan led the way inside the small home she'd bought for herself fifteen years earlier. It was a tiny one-bedroom bungalow, and Marney had mourned that Dylan's choosing it meant she was closing the door on the possibility of ever having children. Now, bright plastic toys were scattered through the living room from when Officer McNeil brought his children over, and Marney gushed about seeing her daughter playing with her boyfriend's children.

"I didn't realize you remembered my address." Dylan gathered the toys and tossed them into a wooden toybox on her way across the room.

"You threw Marney a birthday party here once."

Dylan raised her eyebrows and cocked her head to the

side, calculating how long ago that had been, then shook her head. "Why are you here now?"

Virginia leaned against the wall to pull off her sneakers before taking a seat on the deep red loveseat. Following Virginia's lead, Dylan sat in the armchair across from her.

"You know about Lucy's… situation," Virginia began.

Dylan nodded. The corners of her mouth tugged up at Virginia's description, but she didn't say anything.

"I came here because, well, frankly, I came here because I'm feeling desperate. I've been doing some digging and—"

"Of course, you have." Dylan's mouth was straight as the horizon over the ocean, a perfectly flat line of displeasure.

"—and that art gallery is really a hotbed of illegal activity." She took a deep breath. "Yes, Lucy was there when that man was murdered. But she wasn't the only one. The owner is always in and out. His assistant is constantly around. Three different artists literally live there."

Virginia's voice sped as she recited the same spiel Lucy had just given her, and she took another breath to slow herself down. "I need to fix this for her. And I don't understand why she's the one at the center of all this in the first place. Whatever reason she had for being at the gallery that day, she didn't murder that man."

"'Whatever reason she had,'" Dylan repeated. "Do you know what that reason was?"

Virginia considered her move. Dylan wasn't on the

police force any longer, but she had the distinct impression she needed to be careful what she said.

"She didn't murder that man," Virginia repeated, finally.

It was Dylan's turn to consider her words carefully. The silence drew on until Dylan let out a resigned sigh. "Lucy wasn't just arrested because she was there. Lucy was arrested because her belt was the murder weapon."

CHAPTER 12

Virginia sat still for a long time. How did they know it was Lucy's belt? How did someone besides Lucy get her belt to use as a murder weapon? Was it possible…?

No. She shook away the shadow of suspicion and looked back to where Dylan was watching her, lines of sympathy drawn across her face.

"How?" Virginia asked, hoping the single word carried across the full scope of her questions.

"The man Lucy found was named Ian Anderlini. He was strangled to death with a women's braided white leather belt. Lucy identified it as hers when police arrived on the scene."

"But Lucy didn't kill that man," Virginia protested quickly.

Dylan's eyes softened, and Virginia's fists clenched by her sides. If Dylan had said aloud, "Yes, she did," that would have hurt less than seeing Dylan's attempt to soften the blow. Dylan thought Lucy had murdered someone, and she was trying to figure out how to say so while causing Virginia the least pain.

"What do we do from here?" Virginia's voice came out choked, her eyes burning with rapidly welling tears. "How does Lucy's name get cleared?"

"She'll have a trial, and—"

"Before that. Faster. Sooner. Lucy is innocent. Trials are slow. What path forward gets her name cleared? Makes this all go away? If I find the person who really did this—"

"You know how I feel about citizen investigators."

"I know how you feel about *me*."

To Virginia's surprise, Dylan looked hurt. "It's never been about *you*. It's about what your investigations have meant for me and Mom. I've seen my mom in the hospital because of one of your investigations. She was kidnapped, for Christ's sake! And every time you interfere in an investigation, you risk stepping on the actual detectives' case. Blowing their operation, making it harder to actually bring the bad guys to justice."

"Are the police investigating this? Are there detectives on the case?" Virginia wanted to know. "Or did they just arrest my daughter and stop looking any further once they logged the belt into evidence?"

"I'm not on the Force anymore." Dylan swallowed. "And if I were—if I knew anything about the status of a case—I couldn't comment."

So, this was how it was going to be. Dylan was done talking. She'd dropped a bomb and was walking away.

"Dax," Virginia said. "Lucy's boyfriend. Did she already tell the detectives about him? His business, the work she was doing for him? Probably not, right? But he sent her in there and then skipped town."

"Virginia, I can't—"

"And there was another man at the gallery on the day of the murder. He drives a convertible—the one I went to the station to make a report about. He was picking up a bunch of fake IDs from someone at the gallery to pass along to someone named Loretta. I suppose she planned to sell them."

"Loretta?" Dylan held up her hand impatiently, cutting Virginia off.

Virginia nodded skeptically.

"Loretta who?"

"The guy just said 'Loretta.'"

"This guy… Would you be able to tell detectives about him? I think they'd be interested in talking with him."

Virginia started to yell that she'd already tried to tell detectives about this man—that, in fact, she'd already told Dylan about him when they thought he was following Lucy. But she kept her composure and, remembering the man's chase with Marney at the car show, just said, "I'm not sure he'd be equally interested in talking with them."

"Immunity," Dylan said quickly, with a casual flick of her hand. "He'd have full immunity if he shared what he knows about fake IDs being pumped into Seaview. And besides, weren't you just trying to insinuate that he could have killed Ian? Shouldn't you be hammering at the detectives to bring him in and string him up by his toenails?"

Virginia's face went hot with anger. It wasn't the connection to the murder case that piqued Dylan's interest but fake IDs. "I was only trying to impress upon you the fact that Lucy wasn't the only one who could have done it."

"And I already impressed upon you that my understanding of the situation is that Lucy was identified as the potential killer not just by her presence at the time of the murder, but by the murder weapon being her belt."

Virginia wanted to scream, *She didn't do it! She didn't do it!* But the response to that would be, *How do you know? Where's the proof?* And she didn't have an answer.

Instead, fists and jaw clenched too tight, she exhaled and asked, "Is it hard? Being off the Force?"

Dylan nodded without hesitation. "It is."

"But worth it?" Virginia asked, nodding toward a tiny, brightly colored xylophone tipped over on the rug.

Again, Dylan responded without a moment's hesitation. "It is."

"You wouldn't have told me what you did—about the belt, about Loretta—if you were still a cop."

"I shouldn't have told you now. Hell, I shouldn't even know about it." The corner of her mouth tugged up in a half-smile, and Virginia wondered what it was like between her and McNeil. Did he come home like Earl used to, bursting at the seams to tell her all about his day? Or did Dylan ask, a part of her yearning for the life she'd given up?

Dylan stood, smoothed her hands over the front of her slacks, and righted the xylophone. "I don't know what it is to have a daughter, but I'm… I'm starting to get a glimpse of it. If someone hurt Kailey… Well, I wouldn't want to be the police dealing with me if they were moving too slow for my liking."

Dylan looked up, and her eyes—crystal blue, exact clones of her mother's—met Virginia's. "With a charge like murder, prosecutors will blanche at offering immunity, but depending on what kind of information Lucy could share, maybe there are bigger fish the prosecutors want to get to. They could—"

"She didn't do it." Virginia couldn't stop herself this time. She spat the words.

Dylan opened her mouth to respond the way Virginia knew she would—*How do you know? The evidence...* But she stopped herself and shrugged. "You know as much as I do now. Do with it what you will." She smiled wryly. "I guess it's not my problem anymore if the police don't like you messing around in their business."

* * *

Virginia waved Dylan off, not letting her walk her out to her car. The show of independence was easily brushed off as her usual don't-you-dare-try-to-help-me behavior, and Virginia hurried down the block and around the corner before Dylan had the chance to notice that her car wasn't parked anywhere along the street. She pulled her phone from her bag, shivering hands struggling to press the screen with precision to open Uber. When the map stared her back in the face, glowing in the winter dusk, she realized she had no idea where she wanted to go.

Back to Lucy's, to demand answers? *How the hell did your belt wind up wrapped around Ian Anderlini's neck?*

To Breeze Village, to share the new information with her friends? *The earring from the gallery isn't Lucy's, but we've got a new physical clue tying my daughter to the crime scene: the murder weapon.*

That wasn't a conversation she was ready to have, any more than she was ready to look her daughter in the eye and confront her. Woozy at the thought, she staggered to a lamppost and leaned against it, then keyed in a destination and ordered a ride to the only place she knew she'd be able to think.

Virginia smelled the beach before she saw or heard it —a small miracle over the combination of stale cigarette smoke and overpowering air freshener that invaded her sinuses and threatened to make her sick, so much so that she'd had to ask to roll down the window despite the February cold. Though the salt of the ocean overcame the miasma, the crash of the waves stood no chance of being made out over the driver's stereo. She wondered if her first few rides with the app were flukes, or if this one was the fluke.

"This all right?" the driver asked her, pulling into the small beachside parking lot, but Virginia was already climbing out of the car and waving him off, heading for the wooden swing.

The beach was mostly empty, free of all but a few evening walkers. The sun had set. Not many people wanted to shiver on the sand in the cold. This was where she could be alone, but it was also where she could talk to Earl. And the longer this went on, the more she felt like if she *didn't* talk with him, it was some sort of betrayal.

"It's, uh, it's me," she said awkwardly, looking out toward the horizon. "If you're up there looking down on us, I imagine you've got a thing or two you'd like to say to me."

Virginia paused and sat in silence. She waited—for what, she wasn't sure. The crash of the waves didn't swell dramatically. A bird didn't swoop out of nowhere. No divine signs of Earl urging her on from the Great Beyond.

"I'll just come right out with it, then. I'm sorry for maybe raising a murderer."

She wasn't sure until she'd said it that the word would even form on her lips, that her breath would give life to it and voice it, but there it was. The niggling doubt at the back of her mind, the frustration with the way Lucy was handling the situation, and the bomb dropped on her by Dylan that evening were all there. *Maybe a murderer.*

"And, uh, for maybe dating, I guess? If I'm here apologizing to you for things. Although I screwed that up before it could even really happen, so maybe I only owe you a partial apology there." Earl's handsome face, the vision of him assuring her she could never wrong him, came to her mind, and she was filled with affection for him. "You got cancer and abandoned me to raise our children alone—and ruin them, clearly—so I guess waiting over forty years and then maybe seeing about dating again is fitting payback."

Though she was alone, with only the break of the waves, the creak of the rusty chain of the swing, and the whistling breeze for company, she felt a presence beside her as she thought of how her late husband would view their children now, grown, as if they were reminiscing together.

Jack, a father himself now, cradling baby Emily in one

arm while he warmed a plate of food for Stephanie with the other hand. The baby sleeping on Jack's chest while he read on the couch with the television on in the background. Jack taking Emily out for a walk and flashing his wedding ring when women flirted with him, practically baring his teeth. Things she hadn't had the chance to see with her own eyes while she wasn't welcome.

And Lucy, always content on her own, finally in love. Leaving her corporate job to work for her boyfriend. And now this. Prim and proper Lucy, always in control of the situation… How had it all gone so wrong?

Her phone chimed with a message from Marney. She shivered, and her shaking hands pressed the wrong spot on her phone screen, bringing up Facebook instead of the message. She began to close out of it but stopped herself. In the search bar across the top, she typed in L-U-C, then clicked on her daughter's profile when it auto-filled the suggestion. She scrolled for a minute down the curated page. Lucy speaking at a conference in Atlanta for her old job. A family photo from three Christmases ago. Shamefully, she eyed Lucy's outfits in every picture looking in vain for a braided white leather belt, the belt that had supposedly killed this Ian, the murder victim Dylan had given a name.

She closed out of Lucy's profile and tried searching for Dax. No results. It seemed Dax didn't want his life online for anyone to see. She searched for Ian Anderlini with similar empty luck. No Ian Anderlini, but Facebook suggested another profile: Loretta Anderlini.

Virginia held her breath, willing her quavering fingers to cooperate, and when she pulled up Loretta's profile, her eyes went wide. In Loretta's profile picture, the dark-haired beauty had her head thrown back in laughter, and multi-colored enamel earrings glittering with clear stones dangled from her ears. They were, without question, the same as the earring Ronald found in the art gallery, in the same room where Lucy had tearfully described finding Ian's body.

PING! Another message from Marney.

> Just knocked on your door to check on you but you're not there. Let me know you're okay.

> You're worrying me!

> I'm fine. At the beach. Made a new discovery. Come pick me up and I'll tell you in the car?

CHAPTER 13

When Virginia climbed into the passenger seat of Marney's car, exhaling luxuriously in the warmth and thanking her lucky stars for the smell- and noise-free transportation home, Marney narrowed her eyes at her.

"What are you doing out here by yourself? And how did you get here?"

"One of my coworkers helped me install Uber. Given Colleen's suggestion that I do not drive, which I'm really hoping she'll announce with some fanfare is over soon, and with you busy earlier, I needed a ride to work. And I wanted to be able to get around without having to ask a friend every time I needed to go somewhere."

Marney harrumphed, and Virginia sunk down deeper into the heated seat.

"And you used your new powers of transportation to come to the beach at night by yourself? What if your phone died while you were out here alone with no car?"

"I guess I'd freeze to death in the sand," Virginia said

acerbically. She felt her chin jut out like a petulant child as she watched her reflection in the window, refusing to look at Marney while her friend chided her. "Or, more likely, five minutes after your last text, if I still hadn't responded, you'd have gone out looking for me, and the beach would have been one of the first places you checked. You know I love it here."

Marney slid a hand over and brushed Virginia's arm. "You said you're fine, but sitting on the beach in the dark doesn't seem like *I'm fine* behavior."

Virginia swallowed hard once, then again, a painful knot forming in her throat at Marney's astute observation.

"What's the big discovery you said you wanted to share?"

When Virginia had sent that message, she had planned to tell Marney everything. The conversation with Lucy, the visit to Dylan, the bombshell revelation about the murder weapon, and how Dylan's identification of the murder victim had led Virginia to Loretta—and the earring. But now, she couldn't bring her lips to move.

All she could think of was how Marney's face would look when Virginia told her about Lucy's belt. Her eyebrows, wispier and wilder now than when Marney was young, would fly upward, but then she would quickly school her face into neutrality. She'd say it must be some sort of mistake, but there would be doubt and curiosity in her eyes. Marney was a second mother to Lucy, but she wasn't her mother. Virginia was. And Virginia couldn't stand the thought of someone she loved wondering the worst about her daughter.

She cleared her throat, struggling against tears. "The earring. I found out who the earring from the gallery belongs to."

They pulled up to a red light and Virginia passed Marney the phone, Loretta's Facebook profile loaded to show the picture.

Marney gasped immediately in recognition, her eyes flaring, but then, just as quickly, she turned an inscrutable expression on Virginia. "How did you find her?"

Virginia felt her mouth open, and she shut it quickly, fighting to maintain a shred of composure. "What do you mean?"

"Loretta," Marney said, handing the phone back and stepping on the gas as the light turned green. "We've been trying to figure out who the mysterious Loretta is who got mixed up in shady business at the gallery and disappeared just like Dax. Now, all of a sudden, you've found a Loretta who has earrings just like the one Ronald found at the gallery. Patricia and I looked at dozens of Lorettas online over drinks last night after you left. None of the profiles we found had any signs of being the Loretta from this case."

Virginia couldn't say she'd been to Dylan's. She'd risk landing McNeil in trouble for sharing information with his girlfriend if anyone found out Dylan had passed it along, and Marney would be all over Virginia for putting her daughter in that position. Between streetlights it was dark in the car, but she could still feel Marney looking over, waiting for an explanation.

"Rumors are starting to spread about the murder," she said instead. "Jan came to visit me at work today." It was true—if not *the* truth. "As it turns out, the victim in the art gallery was named Ian Anderlini. After work, I went to the beach to talk to Earl." She was embarrassed to admit it even though she suspected Marney already knew she still talked to him. "It helps, when things are stressful. Sitting on that swing, I thought that since I knew the dead man's name, I'd look him up. See if he had any kids he left behind. See if there were any clues of who might have done him in. Unfortunately for us, Ian Anderlini didn't have a Facebook. But luckily for us, Facebook suggested a similar profile. Poof—Loretta."

Virginia couldn't help but peer over to assess Marney's expression. Did she believe it? As they turned toward Breeze Village, Marney said, "I guess I get to put some new names on our board tonight."

The immediate relief Virginia felt at having gotten away without revealing her visit to Dylan gave way almost immediately to guilt. She'd lied to her best friend. Sure, all the information she revealed was true. But she'd kept her source a secret, and she and Marney didn't keep secrets.

She woke the next morning feeling even worse and hurried to Marney's cottage as soon as she'd dressed.

"Marney, I need to tell—"

"Virginia!" Ronald's jolly voice greeted her as Virginia rushed inside, and he raised a coffee mug in a *cheers* gesture.

Virginia recoiled in surprise, then put on a warm smile as quickly as she could. Still, Ronald laughed and muttered something about mornings, and Marney came out of the kitchen with a mug of coffee for Virginia. The smell of biscuits in the oven floated in behind her.

"I was hoping to talk to you," Virginia said softly. She took a sip of the coffee, and as it worked its way down her throat and into her belly, it seemed to chase the guilt away. Patricia came out of the kitchen with her own cup of coffee, and in the presence of three friends instead of just one, Virginia's need to spill the truth shriveled up.

"I didn't tell them about your big discovery," Marney said, eyes twinkling as she watched Ronald light up and Patricia turn her head in curiosity. She'd set Virginia up to deliver the news with maximum impact, just as she knew Virginia would love.

Mentally pushing that shriveled-up guilt aside, Virginia basked for a moment in the feeling of having the scoop everyone wanted. "I found something out yesterday." She pulled the earring Ronald had found from her pocket, dangling it so it caught the morning sunlight and threw sparkling beams on the living room walls. "This earring? It belongs to the mysterious Loretta."

Ronald smacked his hand on the dining table and let out a *whoop!*

"There's more," Virginia smirked, reveling in the rapt looks on her friends' faces. "The mysterious Loretta has also become significantly less mysterious. She has a last name. Anderlini. And someone else in this case has that same name. The man Lucy found murdered in the gallery."

If she'd had a microphone to drop in that moment, Virginia would have dropped it. In her mind, she heard the applause of a packed auditorium. In reality, it was just the simultaneous cries of, "What?" and "How on Earth did you find that out?" from Ronald and Patricia, while Marney looked on with amusement in her eyes.

"That part-time job as a cashier is really a part-time job as a collector of hot gossip," Marney joked.

Virginia faltered a hair, then reinforced her smile. "All the freshest news in Seaview comes through the Piggly Wiggly."

She pulled up Loretta's Facebook profile to show Ronald and Patricia the picture of Loretta wearing the earring, eager to breeze past the subject of how she got her information. To her relief, that line of questioning was immediately forgotten.

"Is she the wife, then?" Marney puzzled. "Or a sister? Cousin? Other relation?"

"Wife, definitely," Patricia said, her finger sliding along the phone screen as she absorbed everything Loretta had ever posted to her Facebook profile. "Two years ago someone named Dot Anderlini posted to Loretta's time-line wishing her and Ian a happy anniversary."

Ronald puffed his chest out and began pacing back and forth, stroking his chin, doing his best imitation of an old-timey detective about to fit the last clue into place and blow the case wide open.

"So, this floozy Loretta cheats on her husband and blackmails Mr. Fancy Car into going into the gallery to pick up a bag of fake IDs for her on the day her husband ends up getting whacked... but then she still goes to the gallery herself, as evidenced by the dropped earring." He frowned.

Virginia screwed up her face in confusion. "Why get

someone else to go to the gallery for her if she was already going to be there?"

"She needed to pick up the fake IDs, but she had other business to attend to at the same time," Patricia suggested. "Like murdering her husband."

Virginia's head spun.

Marney waved a hand in the air. "If we're going to take up the position that being present in the gallery isn't reason enough to suspect someone of murder—our own Lucy being innocent, and all—then we might be jumping the gun leaping straight from the earring being Loretta's to Loretta killing her husband."

The oven timer sounded, and Marney went to pull the biscuits out, leaving the other three to squabble over whether Loretta was their new prime suspect.

In Ronald's eyes, Loretta was definitely guilty. She'd seduced the man from the car show and blackmailed him into trafficking forged documents for her. It was proof that she was a bad person, and a woman who would cheat on her husband was only half a step away from murdering him in cold blood. Maybe she missed the pickup because she'd needed more time than she expected to decompress and come to terms with what she'd done.

In Patricia's eyes, Loretta was probably guilty. She and her husband clearly had a rocky relationship. Maybe she wanted him out of the way. Maybe she and the man with the classic car are in love and killed her husband together, and the story about picking up the fake IDs was all a yarn he spun when Marney and Virginia interrogated him.

But to Virginia, the more they talked, the more she thought about how the evidence didn't point to Loretta's guilt any more than Lucy's. She was involved in bad business, and she'd been present in the gallery—but they didn't even know if she'd dropped the earring on the day of the murder or another time. That sounded a lot like the cops' case against Lucy, minus the murder weapon.

Just as Marney came into the room with the piping hot biscuits, the door to Marney's cottage flew open, and Gemma rushed into the room in hysterics.

"I poisoned him!" Gemma cried. A cotton nightgown was doing its best to cover her but not succeeding. One of the sleeves was hanging loose over her shoulder, and the skirt was pulled up on one side. She was barefoot, and her dark skin was blotched angry and red from the cold.

"What's going on?" Marney headed for the door, leaping into action to assist whoever had been poisoned, while Virginia rushed to Gemma's side. Patricia stood by her chair, ready to follow whoever ended up having the right idea, and Ronald remained seated, chewing on a biscuit.

"It's Jimmy!" Gemma choked out through sobs. "I poisoned Jimmy!"

Marney made a break for Jimmy's room in the main building, not waiting around. Virginia gripped Gemma's forearm and spoke to her sternly. "Gemma, I need you to calm down. You have to talk to me. Where is Jimmy now? What exactly happened?"

"M-m-my cottage!"

Patricia hurried after Marney, calling out for her.

"Now tell me what happened."

"I poisoned him!" Gemma dissolved into wails, but

Virginia gripped both of her upper arms and gave her a shake.

"No, no, we're not doing this," Virginia said sharply. "Not right now." Ronald stood and watched in awe as Virginia tried to extract information from the distraught Gemma. "What did you give him?"

Gemma sucked in a staggered breath and finally cried, "Coconut!"

Ronald and Virginia locked eyes, and Ronald nodded before heading out after the others, armed with the knowledge of what Jimmy had consumed. Now Virginia was alone with Gemma.

"Jimmy can't have coconut," Virginia said. "Is that right?" She spoke softly, like she was talking to a child, and Gemma nodded through her tears.

"I didn't mean to! I didn't know!"

Virginia led Gemma to the couch, and Ronald returned only a moment later, laughing.

"Jimmy's all right," he said. "Just a little itchy. He's allergic to coconut, sure, but not like *kill you* allergic. Just *give you a rash* allergic."

Virginia looked over at Gemma, who didn't seem surprised or comforted by the news. "You didn't kill Jimmy," she repeated.

"But I *poisoned* him," Gemma said, descending back into hysterics.

Virginia wasn't sure what to say to convince Gemma that she hadn't poisoned her boyfriend, but before she had to come up with any further ideas, Jimmy himself was led into the cottage by Marney and Patricia. He unconsciously scratched at his left forearm, then quickly lowered his hand and tucked it away, clearly trying hard to look like he wasn't at all inflamed by the coconut.

"Gemma, baby," he said. "I'm all right. See? You didn't poison me." He looked to Marney as if for approval.

Gemma looked up at him with swollen, tear-filled eyes. "I just can't believe my carelessness might have sent you to an early grave. That was a practice birthday cake for you. I didn't even know you were allergic to coconut!"

"Well, that'll teach me to just waltz into your place and start eating whatever's out on the counter without so much as sniffing it first," Jimmy said with a laugh. "This is why I always stay in my room in the main building. No accidental coconuts over there." The joke set Gemma crying again, and Jimmy wrapped her in a hug and comforted her.

"I just wanted to do something special for you," she said. "And now I've hurt you, and it was all from not even knowing your allergies. What else don't I know about you?"

Jimmy's mouth turned up in a playful smile. "How about we go back to your place and talk about it in private?"

* * *

LATE THAT NIGHT, the bright blue light of the phone screen was the only light in Virginia's room, blaring directly into her eyes as she matched gems to clear the board in level seventy-four of her game. She didn't want to think about Gemma and Jimmy, their radiant joy at finding love and a new chance at happiness in life. When she did that, she thought about Bill, how he had seemed genuinely excited to get to know her, and how she'd hurt him. It was her MO, her modus operandi—she plowed ahead in the pursuit of her goals, hurting the people who cared about her along the way.

She swapped a blue gem with a pink so a stack of five blues glowed bright, then evaporated. More gems filled in the spaces left behind. A green jewel landed between two other greens, and they disappeared. The game chimed, and more gems filled in, cascading into two more matches. Sparkles danced across the screen. Bells reminiscent of a Las Vegas slot machine rang, making it feel like she'd won something real, not worthless points in a meaningless game.

When her head was positively pounding with eye strain from staring at the screen, she finally put the phone down. The darkness felt oppressive, and with the distraction removed, her brain roared to life. Her eyes hadn't even begun to adjust to the darkness before she picked her phone back up to quiet her thoughts once more.

After the incident with Jimmy and the coconut cake, she hadn't looked at Loretta's Facebook profile. She worried that she'd find some key to explain away her presence at the gallery and prove that she couldn't have killed her husband, and then instead of being a prime suspect, Loretta would be ruled out entirely. And where did that leave Lucy?

But she couldn't put it off forever. Virginia needed to find out what there was to know about this woman and her involvement in the goings-on at the gallery. And if Loretta hadn't killed her husband, she probably knew him better than anyone else. If anyone knew who might have had it out for him, who they should be investigating, it was Loretta. If Virginia could only find her…

She pulled up the profile, the picture of Loretta's stunning face turned skyward in laughter now familiar to her.

Loretta wasn't concerned about privacy, it seemed. Every photo, every status update, every thought or picture or memory she'd ever shared online was visible to the public. And somewhere in the haystack, Virginia hoped, would be the needle—some piece of information leading to where Loretta might be found.

She scrolled past a picture of Loretta holding up a croissant, a video of a hand that presumably belonged to Loretta clinking glasses of mimosas with four friends, and a picture of the sunrise over the ocean with the caption *Morning Run* followed by a series of heart-eye and sunrise emojis.

Then, something caught her eye.

*Happy birthday, bitch! :**

The message was posted to Loretta's page by someone named Bianca Carabello. Virginia's heart froze.

She clicked on Bianca's name and was taken to the profile of a woman who was decidedly more concerned about internet privacy than Loretta. The only public information was her profile picture—heavily filtered so Virginia could only tell that Bianca was platinum blond and liked lipstick—and her name.

She returned to Loretta's page and scrolled faster now, looking for any other messages from Bianca.

This was her, she knew. Dax's wife. Virginia could feel it. Lucy had never given her Dax's last name, but how many Biancas could there be? Loretta was friends with Dax's wife. She wondered if Dax's connection to Ian went beyond business, further than briefcase exchanges in the gallery, and thought again of the way he'd disappeared the day Ian was killed.

The only other sign of Bianca that Virginia could find on Loretta's Facebook page was a three-year-old photo of Loretta and Bianca together at the beach. They wore bikinis and pouty smiles, and Loretta had a red solo cup in one hand. The other arm was wrapped around Bianca's waist. *Beach, Bacardi, and Bianca, my three favorite things,* read the caption.

Before calling it a night, Virginia dug out a clean sheet of paper and a pen. On it, she listed all the places Loretta had posted about on her page in the last three months—the coffee shop with the best matcha latte, the boutiques where she'd posted pictures trying on clothes, the sushi restaurant that she'd said was her new favorite, and every place she mentioned running. It wasn't a solid lead, but it was the best she had.

CHAPTER 14

"*I*f I tell you what's been going on in my life, will you promise not to step in and try to help?"

Virginia plopped herself down in the seat next to Bill, out of breath from climbing out of the impossibly low-slung sports car that had been her Uber ride to her ASL class that evening. When she next saw Colleen, she was going to ask whether the spirits had anything to say about the duration of this driving curse. She wasn't sure how much longer she could handle riding around in strangers' cars, not to mention the cost.

Bill looked up in surprise and arched a gorgeous, dark eyebrow. "What makes you think my first instinct would be to try to help you?" he asked coldly, and Virginia recoiled. She'd rehearsed this conversation in her mind during the ride to the community college. In her imagination, Bill had cooled off considerably and was relieved that she was ready to open up to him and tell him the truth about what had been going on. Her next line—*My daughter's been wrongfully arrested for murder and I'm trying to figure out who committed the crime so I can prove she didn't* —felt distinctly wrong in light of his frigid response, but she didn't have anything else queued up.

Her mouth fell open, her brain buffering, working hard to come up with something, while Bill looked on indifferently as if he had been expecting this.

"I'm sorry," she said. She still didn't know what came next, but she knew that was first. The apology didn't soften his eyes, though he nodded in acknowledgement. "I shouldn't have abandoned you at the car show. I've—I haven't—" Virginia sighed.

She wanted to tell him everything, to see his jaw soften and his eyes melt with sympathy, to feel him wrap his strong arms around her and tell her it would be okay. To hear him say he would help her whether she wanted it or not because that's what friends did. Also people who were more than friends, and he still wanted to be more than friends if she'd go on another date and promise not to abandon him to tackle and interrogate anyone this time.

But if she told him and he did that, she'd cry. She would absolutely come apart at the seams and dissolve into him and not stand a chance at making it through class. Already, she was going to have a right time of it trying to coax any amount of recall out of her brain.

And if she told him what was happening and he didn't react that way, if she opened up and he said she'd hurt him too badly, or he didn't know her well enough to want any part in her family problems, or this was a job for the police and she was being reckless and should stop trying to solve the case herself... That would be worse.

So, Virginia said, matter-of-factly, "I'm a widow." Bill's eye's didn't change. No aspect of his hard face did. "At our age, I know it's not uncommon. But that was my first date since my husband passed over forty years ago. I'm a bit out of practice, and I…"

She took a shaky breath, as if the next part was hard to say because of its deep truth instead of how surprisingly untrue it was with Bill by her side. "I underestimated the emotional toll of getting out there again. What that would feel like. Clearly, I had a reaction. But, Bill, I want to try again. With you. If you'd give me another chance, I'd like to go on another date with you."

Bill's expression remained inscrutable. Just before she could open her mouth and take the words back, the professor entered the room, flashing the lights on and off to signal the start of class.

"There's an Italian restaurant I love. Luigi's. Their sauce is fantastic. It's just two store-bought sauces mixed together, but there's just something special—" The words were hurried, desperate, almost whispered, but Virginia didn't care whether the professor chided her for using her voice at the start of class. She needed Bill to agree to this. She needed to be normal.

Butterflies churned in her stomach, and it occurred to Virginia for half a second that it didn't feel any different when she was waiting for the man she admired to agree or decline a date than when she was hiding in a bathroom spying on the son of a recently deceased Breeze Village resident. Either way, it was exhilaration and possibility, an electric hum beneath her skin.

The lights flashed one more time.

"Please."

Bill's face didn't change. She felt sure he was going to decline. Maybe even spit something hurtful about how having a dead husband didn't give her the right to go hurting all her dates, abandoning them without regard. And who in their right mind would want another date with her after that, really?

But then he held up a fist and bent it at the wrist twice as if knocking on a door. YES. He winked it her, then turned forward in his seat as the lesson began, his whole body looser, thawed instead of the block of ice he'd been earlier.

For the rest of class, Virginia bungled nearly every word she tried to sign, but she hardly felt ashamed or upset. She was on cloud nine. She had scored a second date with the hottest guy in class.

THE SENIORS of Seaview had mixed feelings about estate sales. Some, given their own ages, had a hard time going to pick through the belongings of the recently deceased hunting for bargains. But Lawrence knew that with every passing year, production quality on home goods dropped, and there was no better place to find quality wares than estate sales.

"We're lightyears from death," he said, flipping through a box of vinyl records with delicate care. "Ages 'til our own precious and sentimental belongings are laid out on display for the nosy Nellies of town to rifle through."

"Lightyears are a unit of distance," piped up a small

child. The three friends looked down in surprise to see the towheaded boy coming out from between his mother's legs, where she stood examining a shelf of glassware. "Not time. It sounds like it would be time, but it's not. You're just years away from dying. Not lightyears."

Embarrassed, the mother apologized, tucking the boy back in beside her and reminding him not to listen to other people's conversations. "It's not polite," she said.

"But how else are they going to know they're wrong if I don't tell them?"

Marney hurried from the room, smothering a laugh with her hand.

When Virginia felt sure she'd recovered the ability to speak without giggling, she turned to where Lawrence had resumed digging through the record collection.

"Do you think you'll buy the player?"

A wooden record player stood beside the box of records. Virginia thought it looked very nice, but she knew nothing about record players and knew she wouldn't be able to tell if it was of good quality or had been well-maintained. Lawrence gave it an appraising look but shook his head.

"I don't think this is the one," was all he said, but the undertone said more. Virginia surmised that the player, though gorgeous to her untrained eye, was a piece of junk. "I just miss that feeling, you know? Dropping the needle, listening to an entire album from front to back. The special feeling that having a record on in the background gives to an evening."

Marney returned in time to waggle her eyebrows and

nudge Lawrence in the ribs. "What *special feeling* exactly are you trying to set?"

But Virginia knew that Marney remembered as well as she did that Lawrence and his late partner Ben had had a record player before Ben died. Ben was the one into records. His collection was vast. Lawrence still had it, boxed up and hidden away. But now, after decades, it seemed he was finally ready to buy a new player and pull out those old records.

Virginia cleared her throat. "Lawrence, you might not have to take on the pressure of doing all the dating for the three of us anymore." Both Lawrence and Marney looked at her, frozen. "I have a date."

Marney clasped her hands beneath her chin, delighted, and Lawrence practically glowed with joy for her.

"He's totally hot," Marney said to Lawrence, and his glow amplified.

"Does he bowl?" Lawrence asked, and Virginia swatted at him. "What? After our family night event we got two new players, but only one of them has ever actually bowled before, so I'm still on the hunt for new additions to the league. I promise not to steal your hot new boyfriend, but if he does bowl and is looking for a team..."

And even though Bill was so far from being her boyfriend, she felt a flutter of excitement and desire at the idea.

Virginia's phone rang in her purse, quelling any further discussions of her date and his potential as a star for the Seaview Seagulls bowling team. Her son's name across the screen sent her stomach plummeting. For years, his phone calls had meant she was in for a lecture of some sort. *I heard you fell; you should move out of the house. Why don't you let Lucy and I take care of more for you? Are you staying on top of your doctor's appointments? You really should consider moving out of that house.* But then she'd moved into Breeze Village, and for a fleeting moment, it had seemed like the strain on her relationship with her children was lifting. And then everything went into a tailspin.

"Jack, is everything okay?"

Jack sighed before even speaking. "This isn't working. It's got—you've got—" He cut off and sighed again. "Sam came over this morning. Stephanie wants her around, and I can't fault her for that. I know I can't keep her mother away from her forever, and with Emily not sleeping right now... God, it's so hard. But then Sam let some comment about Lucy slip, and right then I swear to God, Mom, it was all about to come down. She was *this close* to letting the whole thing loose."

Virginia nodded toward the door, letting Lawrence and Marney know she was heading outside to take the call, then stood in the lone patch of sunshine in the house's front yard to keep warm.

"You know I think you shouldn't keep things from your wife."

"You don't know what Stephanie needs right now." Jack's response was lightning-fast and razor-sharp. "What she needs—and what I need, in order to take care of my family—is for this to go away. It's gone on too long."

Despite the sun shining on her, a chill shot through Virginia. "What do you mean?"

Jack huffed and said, "I need this to go away. I need it to be over. And I need it be over *now*."

"Are you telling me you want me on this case?"

"Solve the case, see if Dylan has connections that can get Lucy's court date moved up—I don't care about the how. But I can't let Stephanie stress about this while it's still up in the air, and this balancing act can't go on much longer."

"Jackson Earl Walker, from the moment I discovered the body of Ruth Beaumont and thought there might be something more to the story than just the natural death of an old lady, you have been nothing but insistent that I play by the rules. Go by the book. Let the professionals do their jobs.

"Ruth. Genie. Byron—Marney was heartbroken when he was killed, and you'd have had me do nothing! Then Michelle. Russ. And even when Colleen and I were under threat. In every single case, your directive has been to back off. Don't make a mess of it. You've spent a year telling me I shouldn't stick my nose where it didn't belong, and now all of a sudden you want me to insert myself in this case, and do it on your timeline?"

Jack's voice broke. "Please, Mom."

Virginia listened to Jack's ragged breathing on the other end of the line for a full minute. "I'm going to solve this case. Not because you want me to, but because my daughter has been accused of something she didn't do." She sent up a silent prayer to Earl that their daughter hadn't actually done the terrible thing she'd been accused of doing. "And I am going to honor your request to stay away from you and Stephanie while the case is unresolved because you've asked me to. But I will not lie to Stephanie if she asks me anything. I will not help you hide things from your wife. And I will go right back to screening your calls like I was doing a year ago if you're only going to call to tell me I'm a lousy, too-slow murder investigator."

Jack's breathing continued, then stopped as if he'd opened his mouth to say something. Then he let out a sigh, and the line went dead.

* * *

Telling someone she wouldn't adhere to their timeline was one thing. But Virginia couldn't help but feel like she needed to *hurry-hurry-hurry*, and Ronald waiting outside her door the next morning when she emerged for break-fast didn't help.

"Err—good morning?"

Ronald flashed a toothy grin, threaded his arm through hers, and began to pull her toward the elevator. He gave her outfit a once-over as they walked. "Heading out for a shift at the grocery store? I wanted to catch you, since it seems like you've been busy. I haven't been able to stop thinking about finding Loretta. Not all of us have jobs getting us out of the house all the time, giving us something to do, you know."

As the elevator slowly carried them down to the ground floor, quaking slightly underfoot the entire way down, Ronald continued. "I stopped by Colleen's room yesterday to see whether she could help us find Loretta. I showed her the Facebook profile, and Colleen was able to latch onto her soul, or whatever it is she does. Not all the way—I didn't have anything of Loretta's to give Colleen to help with the connection. But partially, she said."

He screwed up his face, concerned, and looked Virginia in the eye. "She said, 'This woman does not want to be found.'"

Virginia's nostrils flared. "I don't really care what she wants."

Ronald beamed back at her. "What do you say we bring Loretta's earring to Colleen and see what she can tell us then?"

Colleen was eating her breakfast and reading the newspaper, and Virginia felt the tug of politeness urging her to get her own breakfast and ask Colleen if it was okay before taking the seat next to her. The tug of exhaustion urged her even more strongly to stop by the coffee dispenser for at least a cup of caffeine, but Ronald felt neither the need for caffeine nor politeness. He tugged her straight to where Colleen was sitting and plopped right down. For her part, Colleen didn't seem surprised by their abrupt appearance.

"The woman you came to me about before," she said, her eyes still peering through her spectacles down at the paper. It was open to an article about a town council meeting where a debate over zoning and the potential for new pickleball courts to replace a dilapidated empty strip mall led to an outbreak of fisticuffs. "You're here to talk to me about her again."

Ronald and Virginia both nodded, and Colleen finally looked up from the article.

"You told me the woman doesn't want to be found," Ronald said.

"I did. That hasn't changed." Colleen didn't volunteer anything further, and Virginia frowned.

She pulled the earring from her bag and put it on the table in front of them. "Ronald said you could only partially, err, latch on to the woman's soul before. We were hoping that with this—"

"I do not 'latch on' to people's souls," Colleen interrupted, hands planted on the table before her, fingers spread wide. "I simply cast my soul into the realm where all spirits abide and seek to have a conversation."

Ronald and Virginia exchanged glances.

"Will that conversation be easier with this earring of hers?" Virginia asked, pointing to the piece of jewelry.

Colleen looked down at the sparkling, multicolored piece and took it in her hand. Her mouth pulled taut, and she frowned with concentration as she looked it over. Then she went still.

Colleen's eyes remained open, but her focus glazed and her eyelids fluttered. Her taut concentration melted into an expression of serene neutrality, and it remained that way for several long minutes during which Colleen grunted occasionally and nodded twice. Her lips began to tug into shapes, and a whisper formed in Colleen's mouth. Virginia leaned in to hear but couldn't make it out when Colleen's lips finally formed words.

The moment those words left her tongue, Colleen's head drooped forward and then ricocheted back, and she jumped as if jolted by a shock. Virginia's stomach plummeted. They'd missed it. Colleen had managed to traverse realms for information, but Virginia had failed to hear it.

Colleen continued to recover, blinking rapidly and

shaking her head. She looked up to see Ronald wearing an expression of intrigued horror and Virginia looking absolutely devastated. She herself looked mildly confused, doing a quick glance around the dining room as if to reorient herself. Turning back to Ronald and Virginia, she said, "2320 Chicory Forest Drive."

Sensations flooded Virginia's body.

First, relief. Colleen could remember what she'd learned in her trance. It hadn't been lost when Virginia couldn't hear.

And then, when Colleen kept speaking—"I'm pretty sure that's over by the new high school, those fancy apartments."—dread.

Loretta was at Lucy's apartment.

Lucy was in danger.

CHAPTER 15

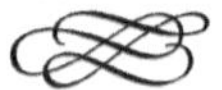

*I*t took everything in Virginia to pretend that the address Colleen psychically recovered meant nothing to her. To thank her and tell Ronald that she really needed to get to work. To insist that he wait for her to finish her shift before he went over to those apartments. To start toward the front door and the parking lot as if everything were normal.

Every cell in her body hummed with an electric need to find and protect her daughter, and she needed to do it herself.

"You can drive again?" Ronald turned to Colleen. "She can drive again? The danger's over?"

Colleen, in her most dramatic fashion, doubled over in her chair and threw her hands up to her temples. "No! You must not drive today! Today is the day. Something terrible will happen." She craned her neck to look up at Virginia. "Promise me you won't."

Virginia switched directions and hustled toward the French doors to the courtyard as quickly as she could.

"Marney will drive me," she called back. "But I've got to go, or I'll be late." If she couldn't go alone, bringing Marney was the next best thing.

Across the courtyard, she pounded furiously on the door to Marney's cottage. *Please be home. Please be home...* With every moment Marney didn't answer the door, dread pulsed through her veins with more vigor.

Lucy was in danger. She needed to get to her daughter.

She banged harder on the door.

"What's the matt—?" Marney's face was cross as she pulled the door back, Pancake tucked beneath her arm, but she cut off mid-word, annoyance falling away immediately when she saw Virginia standing there, desperation all over her expression. She grabbed her purse off the hook by the door and set the cat down in one fluid motion.

"Pancake, be good!" she commanded the cat as she crossed the threshold. She turned to Virginia, the two of them already heading for the car, and asked, "What's happened?"

"Lucy's in danger."

* * *

"Take a right on Hearst." Virginia had already bitten back three urges to tell Marney to drive faster and couldn't keep the direction to take the shorter route to herself.

"We'll get stuck trying to turn left on Oceanfront forever if we go that way," Marney snapped, then softened her voice. "If we go straight here, we get a left turn signal onto Chicory."

In the passenger seat, Virginia clutched her phone to her ear, placing calls to Lucy that rang until they went to voicemail.

"No answer," she muttered. "Again."

"Check her social media," Marney suggested. "Maybe she's posted something."

"If a murderess has her at gunpoint and she can't answer her phone, she'll hardly be posting about it on social media." The memory of Olivia in Virginia's room at Breeze Village assailed her mind. The feeling of her own private space being unsafe had never fully faded since the incident, and now her daughter was facing the same threat. She bit back another request for Marney to speed up.

"I'm trying to help," Marney snapped, then muttered an apology. "There's just nothing else we can do from here, and it's—What's that?"

Marney's head turned to get a better look at a car crumpled against a tree on the other side of the road. It was a gruesome accident, and Marney slowed the car to prolong their glimpse of it, both craning their necks to see.

The front end of the car was completely crushed, and it wasn't until they were even with the accident that Virginia could even tell the car was a shiny white SUV.

Her stomach dropped, and her blood turned cold.

"Lucy!" she screamed, reaching across the console for the wheel. She grabbed it and pushed, sending the car into the beginning of a U-turn in the middle of the road.

Marney shrieked and fought Virginia's turn, the car sawing along a zigzag across multiple lanes. Brakes squealed behind them. Horns sounded.

"Virginia, no!"

"That's Lucy! That accident is Lucy!"

That car was Lucy's. She knew it. How many white SUVs were there in Seaview? Thousands? But somehow, she knew.

Marney's eyes flicked to the rear-view mirror. Virginia's pulse hammered in her ears as they continued down the road, moving away from the accident with every passing second.

"Please," she pleaded, at the same moment that Marney muttered, "Hold on," and yanked the steering wheel hard.

Marney called 9-1-1 while Virginia clambered over to the driver's side window. A country-pop song blared through the broken window, a woman crooning about how no one could love like she could while Lucy lay slumped over the steering wheel, the deflated airbag billowing out beneath her face.

"Lucy!"

Broken glass crunched beneath Virginia's shoes as she crossed the last few steps to the SUV. Lucy didn't stir, and desperation coursed through her.

"Lucy!" she shouted again, then grabbed the handle to the half-crumpled door and yanked with all her might. The door opened only partially, the hinge warped and jammed closed from the accident.

A low groan came from inside the car, so soft that Virginia wasn't sure she heard it, but when she tore her eyes from the stuck door, she saw that her daughter had turned her head. Her eyes fluttered beneath her disheveled hair, and Virginia could see that the broken glass from the windshield had cut her face. Blood trickled down toward Lucy's fluttering eyelid.

She groaned again. "Dax?"

A sob escaped Virginia's mouth, and she braced one hand on the body of the car and the other on her thigh, caving in on herself. Her daughter was bloodied and bruised in front of her, miraculously alive in the pretzeled vehicle, and she was calling out for Dax.

Marney's touch startled Virginia, and she lost her balance, stumbling backward as Marney reached to steady her.

"An ambulance is on the way," she said, reassuring Virginia as she held her upright.

"She's alive," Virginia breathed in answer.

Marney wrapped her arms around Virginia, gripping her so the bones of her forearms pressed into Virginia's back. Virginia's chest heaved, and she let out a wail that was promptly muffled by Marney's shoulder. The sobs quickened until she could hardly breathe, her chest rising and falling against Marney's in a quick, undulating motion.

Paramedics whisked Virginia and Marney to the side, moving quickly in formation. When Virginia tried to ask questions or see what they were doing, she was repeatedly shunted farther and farther back.

"Please tell me what's happening!" she finally cried, and a sympathetic paramedic stepped aside with her.

"Your daughter?" she asked.

Virginia nodded. The lump in her throat precluded any further response.

"We're taking her to the hospital. She's clearly got some cuts and bruises, possibly a concussion. We'll check her over for further injuries in the ambulance. At the hospital, they'll do X-rays. I'd expect the doctors to order a CT scan and MRI as well."

Virginia's head bobbed of its own accord. Her brain grasped onto the words the paramedic spoke, but they floated around in her brain meaninglessly. Lucy was going to the hospital. She understood that much. Scans. Tests. It didn't escape her that the paramedic hadn't said, "Your daughter is going to be okay."

Desperately, she croaked, "Is she...?"

The paramedic's eyes softened, and she looked from Virginia to her peers and back. In a lowered voice, she said, "I can't tell you what will or won't happen. We're specifically not supposed to say that someone is going to be fine." She lowered her voice even further, and Virginia leaned in. Practically whispering, the paramedic said, "But I've seen people make full recoveries from far worse. In my opinion, I'd expect her to be okay."

The rest of the world dissolved away.

"Thank you," she choked out, but the woman was gone. She was back with her peers, working in sync as they loaded Lucy into the ambulance and shut the back door.

Marney steered Virginia back to the car, pulled open the door to the passenger side, and helped her into the seat. She drove them in silence to the hospital. One of her hands rested on Virginia's throughout the drive, giving it a gentle squeeze at each stop light. By the time they arrived, the adrenaline was wearing off, and Virginia was beginning to shake, hardly able to speak. Marney guided her through the double doors of the emergency room entryway and marched up to the reception desk.

"We're here to visit Lucy Walker. She just arrived in an ambulance. She was in a car accident. This is her mother." Marney gestured to Virginia.

The receptionist pursed her lips and frowned, her finger scrolling on the mouse over and over until Virginia wanted to leap over the counter and look up her daughter's room number herself.

The shaking intensified, and Marney led her to a chair and pressed a juice box into her hand.

"Where did you—?"

Marney shushed Virginia, instead taking the tiny straw and poking it through the foil-covered hole at the top of the box. "By the time you finish this, I'll have the room number," she assured Virginia.

And she was right. "She's in 207," Marney said when she returned, trading Virginia's empty juice box for a full one.

They couldn't actually enter Lucy's hospital room for hours while Lucy underwent the tests and scans the paramedic had warned Virginia to expect. However, waiting in the hallway directly outside her door for news felt better than waiting in the lobby. It felt like a child sitting on Virginia's chest, smothering her, instead of an elephant.

When Virginia returned from her fourth trip to the bathroom, owing in equal parts to the apple juice Marney continued to force her to ingest and to her legs begging to be stretched, a doctor emerged from Lucy's room. Instead of padding away down the hall as he had before, he turned to Virginia and Marney.

"Her mother?" he asked.

Both Marney and Virginia nodded eagerly. Virginia was Lucy's mother, but Marney had helped raise her and cared for her just as much.

Unconcerned about the ambiguous response, the doctor addressed them when he read off the results of her scans. As the paramedic had predicted, Lucy was going to be fine.

Dr. Sriharan, as the badge dangling from his coat indicated, elaborated, but Virginia didn't hear the rest of what he said. She didn't care. She knew all she needed to, and she slumped back against the cool vinyl-coated wall while Marney gripped her hand and squeezed.

It was night when a nurse finally told Virginia and Marney they could visit Lucy in the room.

"She's awake. You can go see her if you want, but only for a minute. It's not visiting hours yet."

Virginia steeled herself for the sight of her daughter in a hospital bed, ready to see her usually fiercely independent girl looking pale and vulnerable under the fluorescent lighting with tubes and wires flowing out of her. Still, she gasped at the first sight of Lucy.

The bruising on her face had developed in the hours since the accident, painting her cheeks and chin a grotesque blend of black and purple with sickly green undertones. Stitches held the skin above her eyebrow together, and cuts covered her arms.

"Mom."

Virginia choked at the sound of her daughter's greeting. Her voice was hoarse and gravelly, but underneath the one word, it sounded like an apology, thanks, and relief all in one.

"Lucy," Virginia breathed, her own one-word greeting a prayer, a question, and a reassurance. *You're alive. What happened? Thank God you're alive.*

Neither of them gave sound to whatever else they might want to say to each other. It was late, and they were tired, and Virginia was also terrified to pierce this fragile moment. She pulled up a chair and sat beside Lucy's bed, and they held each other's hands in silence for ten minutes until the nurse came back and told Virginia that Lucy needed to sleep so she would have to come back in the morning. The entire time, Marney stood quietly just inside the doorway, and when she turned to leave, Virginia saw tears in her friend's eyes.

If Virginia had nearly lost a daughter, Marney had nearly lost both something near to a daughter and her best friend in one fell swoop. When Earl had died, Virginia had all but died herself, entirely reliant on Marney and Lawrence to carry her through the days. If she'd lost Lucy now, Virginia would have been lost again to everyone who loved her.

From the hallway, Virginia called Jack to tell him she'd spoken to Lucy. Marney had called him earlier to tell him about the accident, and he had insisted on driving there to wait with them. Marney had put that idea out of his mind by telling him they weren't allowed inside the room, anyway, and that they would keep him updated at every stage. He had his own family to worry about. Virginia could hear him yelling through the phone that Lucy *was* his family—a declaration Virginia thought was rich, given his keeping her away to protect what he called his family, meaning just Stephanie and Emily—but he agreed to stay put at home instead of further clogging the hospital hallway if they promised to text updates every half hour and call when there was news.

Now, on the other end of the phone, his voice cracked. Virginia took a deep breath, feeling her throat quiver and knowing she couldn't keep herself together if he broke down. Neither one big on displays of emotion, they sped through the call and agreed to meet back at the hospital early in the morning.

While Virginia finished her call, Marney texted Lawrence and Ronald updates.

The drive home passed in silence, the deep black sky growing gray as sunrise approached before they reached Breeze Village. Marney opened her mouth and closed it, then again. The third time she did it, Virginia said, "Are you trying to ask if I'm okay to go back to my room and be alone tonight? Because I'm not, but I'm going to do it anyway."

Marney opened her mouth again, but Virginia cut her off. "I know I'm welcome on your couch, and it is as comfortable as my own bed, but I don't have my allergy pills, and Pancake will take that as an invitation to be extra affectionate. And besides, I'm so exhausted, I think I'll only be awake another thirty, forty-five seconds, tops, so I'll hardly have to feel my feelings about all this before I fall asleep. I might just sleep in my clothes."

She looked down at herself and realized for the first time that she was still wearing her work uniform, and that she'd missed her shift entirely, having rushed over to Lucy's instead of to work the moment Colleen had given her Loretta's location. She'd need to call her manager and apologize, and hope she still had a job.

"Are you finished?" Marney asked, and held up a small group of envelopes.

"What's that?"

"It's what I was trying to find a way to tell you. These," Marney said, handing them over to Virginia, "were in the passenger seat of Lucy's car."

CHAPTER 16

The envelopes were addressed to Lucy. No return address. Virginia held them up to the streetlight, trying to place the vaguely familiar handwriting. She opened one, pulling out the letter inside, and as her eyes swept over the sharp points and irregular loops of the lettering, she felt her stomach fall away. She'd seen the handwriting exactly once before, on another letter.

The letter from Dax to his wife, Bianca.

Lucy,

I can't go on without you much longer. I miss you—your voice, the smell of your perfume. I'm so lonely here.

I wish I could tell you where I am, but I know you, Lucy. If you knew where I was, you'd come to be with me, and that wouldn't be safe. I need to know you're safe. That's the only thing keeping me going right now, baby. I'm not anywhere near you, and by keeping it that way, I'm protecting you.

I can't stand knowing you're going to be on trial for something you didn't do. You're so strong. You're incredible. When I can finally come home, I'm casting everything else aside. It's you and me, babe. No one else.

All my love,

Dax.

Virginia's hands were shaking too violently to slip the paper back into its envelope or open the next letter. Marney reached out and took them from her.

"Did you read them?" Virginia asked.

Marney shook her head.

"She's been writing to him."

Marney nodded. She understood who *him* referred to. For a moment, they stood in silence. Virginia knew she should thank Marney for having the wherewithal to take in the accident scene and spot the letters while Virginia could not, but all she could feel right then was hollowness with a low rumbling of rage. She couldn't find it in herself to speak any more, and Marney didn't push. Now wasn't the time.

Eventually, Virginia reached out, Marney gave her back the letters, and then Virginia climbed the stairs to the front door of Breeze Village and slipped up to her room.

* * *

JACK AND STEPHANIE were already in the hospital room with Lucy when Virginia arrived. Her entire body ached with the impact of the previous day and the lack of sleep from staying up half the night reading Dax's letters to Lucy, and she leaned heavily on her cane with every step.

Jack took in her appearance with concern, but

Stephanie rushed over and wrapped her in a hug so tight Virginia's grip loosened, and the cane clattered to the floor.

"Where's Emily?" Virginia asked when she was released and Stephanie pressed the cane back into her hand.

"She's with my mom," Stephanie said.

Virginia forced a smile, or tried, and sent up a silent prayer of gratitude that no one was paying enough attention to her face to notice its insincerity.

"How are you feeling?" She pushed down the black bubble of emotion that the image of Sam babysitting her granddaughter produced and turned to Lucy. The dark bruising had intensified even more since they'd seen her last night, but this time, Virginia was prepared for the sight.

"I'm fine," Lucy said. When Stephanie raised her eyebrows in a challenge to that statement, Lucy said, "They've got me on some great painkillers. I'm going to have to try this car accident thing more often if this is what it gets me."

The joke fell flat. Lucy wasn't usually one for making jokes so it came unexpectedly, and none of the family was in good humor at seven in the morning in a hospital room. Jack's face seemed to turn from ghost-white to fully transparent, and Stephanie's mouth turned down until lines creased her face.

"I'm kidding!" Lucy asserted. "I promise to try my hardest never to repeat yesterday." Her eyes clouded over, and she went quiet.

Virginia shifted her weight from the balls of her feet to

her heels and back impatiently, clutching her purse to her side, the letters Marney had recovered from the accident stuffed inside. She wanted to throw them down onto her daughter's lap and demand Lucy come clean about her communications with Dax. She wanted to teleport to wherever that bastard was hiding and strangle him herself. She wanted to see *him* in a hospital bed, stitched together with skin all shades of purple.

But beneath that anger and indignation that Lucy had been writing to Dax and concealing it, there was still a bottomless pool of love for Lucy and relief that she was okay. The look on Lucy's face looking up from the pillow, desperately trying to joke while still recovering from a harrowing accident, softened the anger and plunged Virginia into that pool. She reached for her daughter's hand and squeezed it tight, relishing in the strong pulse beneath the skin.

Lucy's head had turned to the side, her gaze landing on Jack where he stood, worrying his hands and looking like he was holding back words as much as Virginia was. Stephanie excused herself to go to the restroom, and Virginia followed her out into the hall to give her children a moment alone.

"How are you doing?" Virginia asked, getting her first good look at Stephanie. She marveled at the artsy dishevelment, hairs poking out from under the bandana tied around her head and paint staining her jeans. Adorable. No spit-up stains in sight. She looked like one of the moms she would see while out walking with a stroller and envy, wondering how they did it while she never could quite juggle it all.

But Stephanie's smile slipped a bit, and when she said, "I'm doing great," Virginia heard the false cheer underneath.

Stephanie must have sensed Virginia's knowing assessment, because she immediately let her smile drop, sighed, and said, "It's the hardest thing in the world, having an infant. Some mornings I just want to get in the car and drive and drive and never come back." At the sound of her own words, she straightened and put both hands up. "I never would, of course."

Virginia interrupted her with a soft hand on the shoulder. "I once left Earl with the kids and drove to South Carolina and back. I couldn't leave them, of course, but those few hours where it felt like that's what I was doing, speeding off to freedom… You're not the worst mom in the world for wanting to."

"Oh, thank you for saying that," Stephanie breathed. A nervous laugh escaped her. "I swear I think probably a hundred times a day that I'm the worst mom in the world. I didn't have the best example. But her little face… When she's sleeping, instead of cleaning the house or taking a nap, I just sit there and look at her. And I know I could never, ever leave her."

The hospital door opened, and Jack joined them in the hallway. Before they left, Stephanie turned to Virginia. "If you wanted to come over sometime and see the baby, I'd really like that. Not to babysit—I mean, if you wanted to, I'm not afraid to leave her with you. I just meant, I'm not trying to ask you to babysit. I'm not trying to impose. What I mean is—"

"I understand what you mean," Virginia said with a

soft smile, interrupting Stephanie's flustered offer. Out of the corner of her eye, she caught Jack's hard stare. "I… I truly would love to. To be honest with you, I've been a little afraid of the idea of being around her." She lifted the cane in her hand and waved it in the air. "I'm not as steady as I once was."

Stephanie waved away the concern and reiterated that Virginia should come over any time. Virginia hugged them both goodbye before turning away and rolling her eyes to the ceiling. She bit down on her tongue so hard the tang of blood seeped into her mouth. When she'd recovered enough to reenter Lucy's room, she had new resolve. She couldn't bear to keep putting Stephanie off, having to make excuses to avoid the one thing she most wanted in her life. She took a single step inside the room, shut the door behind her, and held up the envelopes.

"So, Lucy, how's Dax?"

Lucy's eyes went wide, flitting from the letters to her mother and back again. She stammered wordlessly, then slammed her eyes shut and threw her head back against the pillow as if she could will herself back into unconsciousness.

With an icy coldness, Virginia stood her ground and waited. Minutes passed and Lucy opened one eye, saw her mother still standing there, and then let out a moan.

"I don't get a pass while I'm lying in a hospital bed?"

"No," Virginia said harshly.

Lucy considered her a moment. Her eyes flashed coolly, and she finally capitulated, heaving a dramatic sigh like she'd done as a teenager.

"Dax wrote me a few days after I was arrested. I wrote

him back, hoping he'd tell me where he was. He hasn't told me anything useful, and my attorney is aware of our correspondence, so I didn't think I needed to tell you about it. The letters were in my car because I was bringing them to Mr. Murphy in case he thought they'd be useful for my trial."

For her trial? While Virginia could accept that it was wise for Lucy to have an attorney, she still hoped to crack the case wide open sooner than that, and Lucy keeping secrets only made that seem more and more out of reach.

"You should have told me."

"Why?" Lucy demanded. She propped herself up on her elbows in the bed, her face flushing with the effort. "I told you, you digging around can only make things worse for me right now. Mr. Murphy has a law degree and several decades of trial wins that make him the better ally for me in all this."

Virginia's fingers clenched so hard around the head of her cane that her rings bit into the flesh and stung. But try as she might, she couldn't come up with a rebuttal. And if Jack had used his time alone with his sister to try and impress upon her the importance of clearing this case as quickly as possible, he hadn't gotten through to her.

Finally, Virginia shook her head, letting the argument go. "Is that where you were going, when you had the accident? To meet with your lawyer?"

Lucy nodded, her eyes clouding over.

"What happened?" Virginia probed.

Lucy hesitated, her breath suddenly choppy as she recalled the incident. "My brakes just cut out on me. It was like..." She trailed off and shook her head, squeezing her eyes shut against the memory. "I pressed down on the pedal, but it wouldn't go down. It was like it was just stuck, no matter how hard I pressed. I couldn't slow down. I couldn't stop." Her voice was laced with panic and bewilderment.

As she spoke, a leaden ball was forming in Virginia's stomach. She'd been run off the road once in connection with another investigation, and something in her sensed that this wasn't just a freak accident. She swallowed a wave of nausea.

"It felt normal up until the accident?" she asked.

Lucy frowned. "I've never felt anything like that. When I left for my appointment with Mr. Murphy, my window was broken—there was glass all over. Maybe moisture in the car from the broken window could have affected the pedal?" She was grasping for answers, so Virginia nodded in reassurance.

"Maybe. I'll see where they towed your car. There's got to be some sort of forensic automobile investigator or someone who can take a look."

Lucy's eyes widened, and Virginia thought for a moment she was going to protest, but then she nodded and laid back in silence. They remained that way, the sounds of nurses and doctors shuffling around outside the room drifting in through the closed door until there was a knock. The door opened, and both Virginia and Lucy made sounds of surprise when, instead of Lucy's doctor, it was Ronald and Patricia who poked their heads inside.

"We didn't want to disturb you—" Patricia said.

"But we brought gifts," Ronald interrupted and pushed

past her into the room. He placed a plate containing a loaf cake on the table by the window and turned to look over Lucy. "A car accident? Say, Virginia—do you think Colleen got confused and this was the danger she kept warning you about? Why she told you not to drive?"

Patricia hurried in after him with a vase of flowers in one hand and swatted his arm with the other. Lucy's brows were raised in question, but Virginia shook her head and mouthed, "Later."

"Ronald weaseled it out of Marney that you were here," Patricia said to Lucy. "It's not like she's running around telling everyone at Breeze Village you're in the hospital after a car accident. Don't worry, you won't have a whole stream of your mother's retiree friends coming to visit you unannounced."

"How reassuring," Lucy said drily.

Patricia returned her attention to Virginia. "Ronald and I went looking for you this morning, and when we couldn't find you, he pestered her until she told us where you were."

"I still don't think we ought to have to apologize for showing up to wish one of our best friends' daughters a speedy recovery." He walked solemnly to Lucy's hospital bed and added, "I wish you the speediest of recoveries."

Lucy burst out laughing, and the weight in Virginia's stomach lifted a bit.

A doctor interrupted their conversation to let them know that Lucy's test results looked good and that she would be discharged shortly, and the weight shrank further. When Virginia stepped out to bring her car around to the front door in order to drive Lucy home,

Ronald followed her out and grabbed her arm. When she turned, he was looking at her with grave concern.

"I found something." He held out his hand, and Virginia's mouth dropped in disbelief when she saw the colorful glass earring dangling from his fingers. Loretta's earring. But how could he…? She pulled the earring from her purse and looked from one to the other in confusion.

"I went back to the gallery," he said. "This one was in one of the residents' rooms upstairs."

CHAPTER 17

Ronald and Patricia tailed Virginia to Lucy's apartment complex, instructed in a hurried hiss to meet her there and tell her about the earring after she got Lucy home safely. Lucy allowed Virginia to walk her up the stairs and into her apartment without protest, even letting her mother fluff her pillows and pour her a glass of sweet tea.

While Lucy sipped the drink, propped up against the pillows in bed despite her insistence that she felt fine, Virginia rummaged in Lucy's refrigerator.

"How can you live like this?" Virginia cried from the kitchen. "Your fridge is bare!"

"I don't like to cook."

"But you're recovering from an accident. You need your strength!"

"I'll order something," Lucy groaned. "I'm fine. You can go."

Virginia's heart beat faster. "Invite a stranger to come to your door?"

"A stranger bearing food? To come to my door… with the food? Yeah, that's pretty much exactly what I'm planning on doing."

Virginia let out a *harumph* but didn't argue further. She knew it wouldn't get her anywhere with her daughter, and she wasn't planning to leave that door unattended anyway—not when she felt sure that the car crash was no accident and Loretta meant Lucy harm.

With a kiss on Lucy's forehead and an empty promise not to worry, Virginia slipped out of the lush apartment and into the blustery afternoon. She descended the staircase and ran headlong into Ronald, who had been waiting just around the corner out of sight. Patricia came strolling up to them from where she'd been concealed on the other side of the building.

"Well, the gang's all here," Virginia joked.

"Loretta's having an affair with one of the resident artists at the gallery downtown!" Ronald blurted.

Patricia and Virginia hissed in unison for him to lower his voice, and he continued with the closest thing he could manage to a whisper. It still allowed them both to hear without leaning in but was low enough that Virginia thought it unlikely the whole complex would hear him.

"I went back to the gallery yesterday. I was reading the paper and saw that there was an art show in Augusta featuring Major Raymond." Virginia and Patricia just blinked. "The world-famous painter?" Ronald asked. They shook their heads, and he laughed. "I didn't know the name, either, but the article said he's famous—from the pictures of his work that accompanied the article, I can't see why—and looking for his next apprentice. In an interview, he said he likes ambition and confidence, and mentioned how much he would respect it if someone came up to him at one of his shows with their own portfolio to pitch to him. Odd bird, this fellow."

Virginia reeled, struggling to keep up. "You went to the gallery by yourself?"

Ronald plowed ahead. "The article in the newspaper had all these quotes by young artists planning to travel to his shows to try to convince him to take them under his wing. I thought, since the show's only a few hours away, maybe the artists staying at the gallery would take it as their shot."

"And leave the upstairs unattended," Virginia murmured. "Ronald, that's brilliant! You're brilliant."

"It was worth a shot," Ronald said, preening slightly. "And if they weren't gone, I figured I could just do like you two did and pretend to be senile and ill." He let out a barking laugh, but Virginia was shifting on her feet, eager for him to continue. Sensing that he had them hooked, he waited with a twinkle in his eye until they egged him on.

"Tell us, already!"

"I was right! The upstairs was deserted. The whole place was deserted, actually. I'm not sure how much the people of Seaview really patronize the place. And you owe me for climbing those stairs. It was a nightmare! I took that first door after the landing just because I was wheezing so bad I thought I'd have a heart attack."

When Ronald had recovered enough to look around, he'd found nothing of interest in the room but continued his search of the upstairs going room by room.

"I wasn't sure what I was looking for, but I thought I'd

know it if I saw something. For a moment I thought a paint-covered knife might have been bloody, but then I remembered the guy was strangled, not stabbed—isn't that what Gemma heard through the gossip mill?—so that certainly wasn't our murder weapon."

The color drained from Virginia's face. She knew the murder weapon wasn't lying around in the art gallery waiting to be found. It had already been found, and it belonged to Lucy.

Ronald continued, "I was losing steam, but just before I was ready to admit defeat, I found this." He held the earring up again. "I almost missed it! Actually, I stepped on it, and the post got stuck in the sole of my shoe. I'd made it halfway down the stairs on my way out before I thought, 'What's that sound?' My footsteps sounded off, you know? And that's when I looked down and realized what I had."

"Really good thinking," Patricia congratulated him. "I'm only a little hurt I wasn't invited along."

"You think Loretta was sleeping with one of the artists?" Virginia asked, trying to make sense of it all. When she'd left Ronald, she hadn't expected him to take it upon himself to return to the art gallery alone, and certainly hadn't expected him to find anything. Her brain was struggling to process the new information while it was still hung up on Lucy's accident.

"Why else would her earring be in his apartment?"

"I thought she was cheating on her husband with the convertible owner she roped into picking up her illegal goods."

"She could have been sleeping with a lot of people," Patricia suggested.

"Maybe the artist has an even fancier car," Ronald said.

"Unlikely," Patricia countered. "I didn't see any fancy cars parked near the gallery when we visited."

Frustrated, Virginia poked at the ground with her cane and looked around. They were standing under an awning just outside the apartment door. Balconies jutted from the wall above them, and cotton candy-scented smoke drifted toward them on the wind. A young woman with icy blond hair down to the middle of her back put what looked to Virginia like a glowing ink pen to her mouth and inhaled, then breathed out another cloud of the sweet-scented vapor. She was engrossed in her phone, but even so, Virginia lowered her voice, reminded of the presence of the rest of the world.

"Ronald, do you remember yesterday morning, when Colleen gave us the address where Loretta could be found?"

His face turned serious, and his eyes got wide. As if he'd made a grave error, he said apologetically, "I didn't go check it out. You told me to wait until you got off work, but then I saw that article in the morning paper, got side-tracked going to the gallery, and completely forgot."

Virginia put up a hand to stop him apologizing further. "We're there now. Err, here." She spread her arms wide.

Ronald looked from Virginia to the luxury apartment building rising up out of the parking lot behind her, to the sign at the entrance to the parking lot with the address emblazoned on it, then back to Virginia.

"This is where Colleen said Loretta was," Virginia said. "I wasn't actually hurrying off to work. I was running off because I recognized the address. Loretta was here at Lucy's apartment complex and I needed to make sure Lucy was safe."

But she hadn't made sure of it. She'd been too late, and as Virginia crumpled in on herself, Patricia and Ronald moved in to keep her upright and reassure her that it wasn't her fault, that she'd gone as soon as she'd known.

"Was the accident...?" Patricia asked, gently hinting at the ugly question.

Was it an accident at all?

Virginia took a shuddering breath in through her mouth, saliva stringing between her lips. "She said her brakes just stopped working, like the pedal wouldn't depress. She also had a smashed window." She paused, both Ronald and Patricia pulling faces that indicated they clearly thought the accident was a case of sabotage.

Ronald crossed his arms over his chest and backed toward the building, looking out through narrowed eyes at the parking lot. "This building just got itself a new twenty-four-seven security crew. If Loretta returns—if she tries to make a move on Lucy—she won't know what hit her."

* * *

With Lucy's apartment under Ronald's watchful eye, Virginia knew she could leave—her daughter was safe—but every ounce of her rejected the notion of getting in her car and driving away. Her hand shook as she put the car in drive, and she drove unsteadily, her foot shaking atop the pedals. When she passed the tree where Lucy had crashed, she felt her stomach heave and acid sting her throat. The driver behind her honked, then flew past her in the next lane over.

At the salvage lot when Virginia laid eyes on Lucy's mangled SUV for the first time since the accident, she vomited in the dirt. Her brain couldn't wrap itself around the degree of crumpling, how Lucy could have been inside the car when it buckled on itself like that. With folds and crimps and wrinkles, it looked like a fake car made of tin foil, but when she ran her hand over it and pressed as hard as she could, it remained unmoving under the force. She choked and heaved again, thinking of the impact Lucy had experienced.

"Hey!"

Virginia jerked her head around and saw a huge, bearded man in dark, grease-smeared coveralls moving toward her from the trailer that served as an office across the lot.

"What are you doing here?" he demanded.

She didn't have much time. She ignored him and turned her attention immediately back to the car, looking for anything that seemed like a clue. Anything that would point to who sabotaged this vehicle in an attempt on her daughter's life.

There was a smashed window, just like Lucy had said. The trouble was that every single one of them was smashed after the crash. There wasn't a piece of intact glass left on the car. There was no way to verify that any of them had been broken before, and the car was in such bad shape she couldn't tell if anyone had entered the vehicle through one of the windows. Any footprints on the leather seats were obstructed by the sheer amount of glass and debris inside the car.

Virginia moved toward the front of the car to look at the brake pedal. The driver's door hung open where emergency responders had twisted it from its hinges in order to extract Lucy after the accident. Virginia leaned in. She started to put her hands on the seat to brace herself and get further inside but stopped herself just before placing her hands down on top of jagged fragments of broken glass. Instead, she clung to her cane with one hand and braced the other hand on her own thigh, supporting herself as she bent over and leaned in as far as she could, trying to see the pedal.

"Hey!" the man called again, much closer now. He'd covered over half the distance from the office to where Virginia was examining the car, and he was moving fast.

Virginia continued to ignore him. She was so close. If she could just lean in a little bit farther…

Without thought, she shifted the cane from her right hand to her left, the right hand then going to the leather driver's seat and taking her weight. She hissed and cried out as shards of glass cut into her palm, immediately yanking her hand away, but she'd seen it. For a fraction of a second, she'd been close enough to see something gleam underneath the brake pedal.

"I'm talking to you!" the lot manager yelled out, nearly upon her.

She was out of time.

As quickly as she could, without regard for the glass

already embedded in her flesh, Virginia leaned in one more time, crying out as she braced herself on the seat. She dropped her cane, and with the other hand, she swooped toward the brake pedal, reaching for the object that had caught her eye. She was bent over as much as she could be, with her hamstrings refusing to give any more, stretching her fingers for every bit of reach.

Just as her finger brushed against the brake pedal, the enormous hand of the lot manager curled around her arm and yanked her clean off her feet.

"What the hell are you doing?" he demanded.

Virginia reached out with her bleeding, glass-encrusted hand to try and stabilize herself as she swayed unsteadily in his grasp. His eyes widened at the sight.

"You've gone and injured yourself on my lot? Oh, hell!" he cursed, dropping Virginia and swiping his hand down his face while muttering about workplace injuries and fines. "Come on, then," he finally said, when he'd run through every curse word in the book. "I've got a first aid kit in my office."

Virginia stole a glance back at Lucy's wrecked SUV before she began following the hulking man across the lot, unsteady with her cane in her non-dominant left hand. The man naturally pulled ahead, looking back every few steps to ensure she was following. At first, she strained to keep up, but then she dropped the effort and let him move farther and farther ahead of her. Then, the moment after he spun for one of his checks to see how far back she was, Virginia turned and hurried as quickly as she could back in the other direction.

There was something under that pedal, and she was damn sure going to find out what it was.

She'd covered half the distance back to the SUV before the manager turned to check on her again.

"Hey! What the hell?"

Virginia picked up the pace, her legs screaming at her and drowning out the pain in her hand. She had less distance to cover, but the lot manager was faster. She knew she had to hurry. Resisting the temptation to look back and see how close her pursuer was, Virginia pushed on.

She reached the mangled and dangling driver's side door of the SUV. The lot manager's shouts were close, nearly upon her, as she leaned into the car. This time, she reached in with her cane to knock the item free from beneath the brake pedal, tears running down her cheeks as she grasped the cane's handle in her bloody, glass-encrusted hand to maneuver it.

With the rubberized end of her walking cane, she knocked the crushed drink can free just before the lot manager returned. She grabbed it and tucked it into her coat pocket as quickly as she could, dropping her cane as the pain from her hand pushed in on her vision.

"What the hell do you think you're doing?"

Virginia opened her mouth to respond but didn't get a word out before she collapsed.

* * *

"You should have come to my office and asked to go take a look at one of the cars."

194

The edge on the lot manager's voice was softer now than it had been.

Virginia squinted—why was it so dark in here?—and looked around as her vision came into focus. The interior of the mobile office trailer was a wood-paneled space that looked straight out of the '70s and smelled like an ashtray. She'd awakened sitting in an office chair with duct tape covering holes in the brown faux leather upholstery, and the lot manager sat on a low metal stool beside her, picking glass out of her hand and bandaging it.

Virginia flushed and started to pull away, but he tugged her hand back into his lap and finished cleaning it up.

"What were you so intent to find?" he asked when he finally released her hand and stood up. "What was so important it would make you do *that?*" He nodded to her bandaged hand.

Virginia stuck her left hand down into her coat pocket, feeling the crumpled metal can cold against her fingers. After what he'd done for her, she figured she owed the man the truth. She pulled the can out of her pocket and turned it under the desk lamp, its orange-tinted glow the room's primary illumination.

"That car is my daughter's. She said the brake pedal didn't work, and I wanted to get a look at it. This was underneath the pedal. That's what caused her accident."

The lot manager frowned down at the can, then grunted. "Dangerous, leaving trash loose inside her car. Hopefully, she'll be more careful in the future."

The words echoed in her ears long after she left the dim, smoky office. Alone on the same swing at the beach where she'd gone to talk to Earl days earlier, breathing in the salty air, Virginia turned the can over and over in her hand. It was pink. Some sort of energy drink. She couldn't recall seeing Lucy drinking an energy drink before. Was the can Lucy's—a piece of garbage carelessly tossed in the car and accidentally lodged under the brake pedal? Or was this something more sinister?

Her mind looked for a clear next step. Go to the police and let them know she believed—based entirely on the fact that she'd never seen her daughter consume an energy drink—that Lucy's car accident was an attempted murder? She knew how well that would go over.

The muffled sound of her phone pinging with texts came from inside her purse, and she dug it out to see a series of messages coming in from Marney.

> Gemma dropped off more cake at my cottage. Caramel. I didn't wait for you before having a slice.

> I called Dylan, too, by the way. She was beside herself when I told her about Lucy's accident. Patricia filled me in—something about her brakes not working?

> I'm having a second slice of this cake. Hurry back, or there won't be any left.

> My stomach hurts.

She navigated back and saw a missed call and a few other text messages she'd missed while at the salvage yard. The missed call was from Bill, and he'd left a voicemail.

"Virginia, it's Bill. I need to reschedule our date. I'm not trying to cancel on you, I promise. I haven't been able to get the

image of your face lighting up while you talked about that restaurant you love out of my head since Friday. But a friend of mine took a tumble and I need to help him out. I won't be at class tonight, and I can't do our date tomorrow. Give me a call back and we'll reschedule."

Warmth bloomed across Virginia's face at the sound of Bill telling her he'd been thinking about her for days, but guilt came swiftly after that. She'd completely forgotten about Bill and their date in the midst of everything going on. She told herself she'd call him when she got back to Breeze Village, after she'd calmed down a bit from the day she'd had, and moved on to check the rest of the messages she'd missed.

The first text message was from Ronald, letting her know that a few of his buddies had agreed to take shifts watching Lucy's apartment. Her building would be under twenty-four-hour surveillance. He'd shown them Loretta's picture; if she showed up again, they'd take her down.

And the other missed message was from Patricia.

> Mr. Porter has a lunch with all the resident artists this Wednesday. It was in his schedule book when I snuck a look in his office. Didn't think much of it then, but given what Ronald found, it might be worth poking around upstairs again while they're out.

A tear slid down her cheek and landed on her phone screen. She might be in over her head, trying to clear her daughter's name and keep her safe, but she wasn't in it alone.

CHAPTER 18

The crushed energy drink can was still sitting lopsided on Virginia's nightstand two days later when she rose and dressed to visit the art gallery with the others. She considered bringing it to Colleen to see whether the spirits had any helpful information, but every time she picked up the can, her stomach felt leaden with the worry that she'd learn something she didn't want to or nothing at all. Colleen and the spirits might have nothing helpful to say about the can's origins, or they might say the can was Lucy's after all. She wasn't sure which would be worse.

She wanted to share the find with her friends, but she similarly couldn't bear the thought of what reactions they might have. What if they thought the can was Lucy's, that the accident wasn't the work of Loretta but a tragedy her daughter brought upon herself, the same way she'd put herself in the midst of an unsavory group through her involvement with Dax? She could be upset with her daughter, could want to shake her by the shoulders and tell her to stop making foolish choices, but the thought of others judging Lucy raised her hackles.

So, Virginia kept the discovery to herself for two days and avoided seeing anyone who might ask about her bandaged hand, taking advantage of the cold weather and wearing gloves when she left Breeze Village.

When the three friends arrived—without Ronald, since he was standing guard outside Lucy's apartment building—ready to make straight for the stairs and look around in the resident artists' rooms on the third floor for any other signs of Loretta's presence, they were surprised to be greeted by Mr. Porter. Virginia nearly collided with the gallery owner on her way in as he left the building. She looked down at her watch. It was ten minutes past noon. Mr. Porter should have been sitting around the lunch table with all three resident artists, appraising the menu and ordering appetizers for the group. Instead, he was appraising the three senior citizens with suspicion written all over his face. And behind him, at the base of the stairs, was the youngest of the artists in residence, wearing a clay-covered apron and apologizing to Mr. Porter for ruining their lunch plans.

The owner flashed a brilliant smile at the artist. "When inspiration strikes, an artist must seize it. Mona's under the weather today, anyway, and even if Julien isn't enjoying the same inspiration as you are, he's on a deadline and ought to be acting like it. Another time."

Then the young potter was out of view, the sound of his footfall on the stairs growing quiet and then being replaced by the squeak of the floorboards overhead as he made his way back to the studio space. Mr. Porter was assessing the three friends once more, his smile gone.

"The Breeze Village crew, is that right?" he asked. "Did you like what you saw so much during your previous visit you had to come back?"

His tone was light, but Virginia sensed an edge running underneath the words. He was testing them.

"I was really taken with the lighthouse paintings," Marney said, gesturing to one of the rooms off to the side.

Mr. Porter narrowed his eyes. "That collection is that way," he said, pointing in the opposite direction to where Marney had gestured.

"Silly me. My mistake." Marney's face turned red, and she stared down at her feet.

Mr. Porter took a step closer and spoke in a hushed voice. "This gallery has faced quite a hardship recently, as I'm sure you're aware. And you, Mrs. Walker, have received quite a bit of press in Seaview over the last year or so. Yes, I know who you are. I don't know what you three think you're going to find poking around my gallery, but I'd appreciate it if people with ulterior motives would stay away. This place is a sanctuary for artists and those who appreciate art. I will not tolerate any threats to it."

Virginia, thoroughly shamed, was two shades deeper red than Marney, staring at her own shoes with equal intensity. They nodded and turned, prepared to leave with their tails between their legs, but Patricia stepped forward.

"My friends here may not be as well-versed in the local art scene as myself, but they're here because I asked them to accompany me. I wanted to have another look at *Untitled No. 4*, by Julien Reed. I just read online that it sold for over five thousand dollars, and I wanted to come and see it again before it heads to its new home."

Mr. Porter's eyes went wide, but Patricia continued, the edge running beneath her own words razor sharp. "In fact, I saw that four different pieces by Mr. Reed have sold for four and five figures in recent months. So early in his career! It's really a marvel. And he's not the only young artist to have done a residency here and then experienced explosive growth, selling works for many times what their pieces went for just months prior. You truly have a knack for discovering and nurturing rising talent."

The gallery owner's jaw went slack as she spoke, and his eyes darted between them. Marney's blank expression matched Virginia's, the two clueless to what Patricia was talking about.

"I have worked hard over the years to hone my eye." His head bobbed as he collected himself. "If you'll excuse me…"

The front door swung open before Mr. Porter's fingers had closed around the handle, a bitter cold breeze blowing in. He stepped back to allow the new patron entry, and the jingle of bracelets that accompanied the footsteps turned the heads of all three Breeze Village friends. Their brows shot up in unison as Jan flitted into the room, and she gasped dramatically when she saw them.

"Look who it is! Investigator extraordinaire, Virginia Walker!" She wrapped Virginia in an embrace without warning, her heavy earrings pressing into Virginia's cheek. "Are you looking into the murder that happened here? I knew you couldn't stay away from an investigation. When I heard about it, I knew I had to come look around, but you've probably already found anything there is to find."

"Out!" the owner bellowed. He spun around in a flash, bearing down on Jan. "This is a gallery of the arts, not a spectacle for lovers of the macabre. I told your friends, and I'll tell you, too—I will not tolerate people coming into my gallery and spoiling the sanctity of this space."

On the sidewalk, half-shoved out the front door by Mr. Porter while he fumed about society's obsession with true crime and the uncultured masses ruining his business, Jan blinked and pulled her coat around her against the winter wind.

"Can you believe that? What a way to run a business." She turned to Virginia. "Did you find anything good before he kicked us out?"

Virginia froze, then squeaked out, "There was a murder here?"

Jan's eyes widened. Virginia kicked herself. There was no way Jan would believe that Virginia hadn't already heard. But as a smirk spread across Jan's face, Virginia remembered how much Jan loved to be able to break a story, to be the first one with a hot piece of gossip. She was so excited to be the first to the scene that she didn't question it.

"You didn't know?" Jan breathed. She was positively glowing as she stepped closer, pulling the three friends toward her until her breath was hot on their faces. In a whisper, she said, "Someone was killed here—inside the art gallery, of all places—just a few weeks ago. I thought for sure you'd know by now." She frowned, and Virginia's breath caught. "In fact, what are you doing here, if you didn't know about the murder? Virginia, I thought you said this place wasn't anything worth visiting after the Breeze Village field trip."

Patricia and Marney watched as Virginia stuttered out, "I—it—I didn't think—"

"I wanted to come back," Patricia jumped in, repeating the line she'd fed Mr. Porter about wanting to see a particular piece before it left the gallery for its new home. "It seems I'm more easily impressed by art than Virginia."

Jan moved past the explanation, already back to reveling in knowing something big before Virginia. "I just can't believe you didn't hear about something like this. I thought my sources inside Harbor Vale were miserable. I'm miles behind when it comes to knowing what's going on in this town these days. But it seems Breeze Village isn't doing any better. What's becoming of us?"

She peered into one of the gallery's ground-floor windows, muttering that she'd find a way inside once that horrible man was gone. Marney, never overflowing with patience for Jan's antics, put her hand to her head.

"I'm not feeling so well, ladies. Virginia, Patricia, I think I need to head back home."

With kisses to the cheek and exclamations that they'd see each other again soon, the three friends started back toward Patricia's car while Jan slipped back into the gallery, determined to try for a look around. They were passing the alleyway along the side of the building when Virginia saw a teenager leaving the gallery through a side door and heading for a beater of a car parked at the back of the narrow lane.

"Wait up a minute," she said, then turned down the alley. The young assistant had headphones on and didn't hear Virginia's steps as she approached. When he turned to get into his car, he jumped at the sight of her. Virginia held her hands up non-threateningly. "You're Mr. Porter's assistant, right?"

The boy's face went a blotchy red and he nodded, seemingly unused to being recognized. "I'm Gerald." He rubbed his palms down the front of his pants. A streak of black paint rubbed off from one of his hands, and he muttered a curse and tried to wipe it off but only made the black splotch bigger.

"My retirement home came here last week. I recognized you and thought you might be able to help me." Gerald watched, confused, while Virginia tugged off her glove and pulled her phone out of her pocket before pulling up Loretta's Facebook profile. "Have you seen this woman at the gallery?"

Without even looking at the phone, Gerald started to back away, shaking his head insistently. "If this has anything to do with the mur—I mean, with what happened here, I'm not supposed to talk about—"

"It's nothing to do with that," Virginia assured him. He looked uncertain, his gaze drifting from Virginia to the gallery he'd just left. Finally, seeming to decide it would be easier to give her what she wanted so she'd go away than to stand his ground, Gerald leaned in and looked at the profile.

"Yeah, I've seen her before. But I don't know who she is or anything."

Virginia frowned. The gallery assistant turned and climbed into his car, not sticking around to answer any more questions. With the door still open, he leaned out and gestured to where Virginia was blocking his exit. "Do you mind?"

As Virginia tucked her phone back into her purse, she had a thought. "Do you remember if you've ever seen that woman drinking a soda or energy drink? Something in a pink can?"

Gerald immediately shook his head. "No outside food or drink allowed in the gallery. Do you mind?" he repeated, waving her out of the way. "I'm running late."

She stepped back, and Gerald turned the key in the ignition. With a dirty growl, the old car peeled out of the lane, leaving Virginia in its wake.

CHAPTER 19

*L*uigi brought Virginia and Bill to the best table in his restaurant—a window view, out of the way so they weren't bumped into as other patrons were escorted to their tables, but with a good view of the rest of the restaurant so they could people-watch if conversation got difficult. He even had the decency to mostly refrain from winking or making otherwise suggestive remarks as he escorted them to their table and placed menus in front of them.

"This wine is my personal favorite," he said, pointing to the wine list. "An aphrodisiac, if you catch my drift?" He waggled his eyebrows and departed, leaving Virginia beet-red and Bill belly-laughing across from her.

"How's your friend doing after his fall?" she asked, steering the conversation away from the two of them and the fact that they were on a date. "You haven't been to class all week. Are you still helping him out?"

The evening before, Virginia craned her neck to look

for Bill in their Friday ASL class, hoping that he'd be back to his usual routines by then, but he never came.

Bill nodded. "Stanley's a stubborn fellow—won't ask for help and will kill himself trying to get by without it. He won't let me stay overnight, but I've been heading over every day with a hot meal, then staying to help him get cleaned up afterward. Just getting from the kitchen to the living room is tough for him right now, but he won't say so. At least he's got the good sense not to turn me away when I show up, even if he won't ask me to come in the first place."

Bill was to Stanley as Lawrence and Marney were to her. Able to see the need even when she was too damn stubborn—or blind to how bad things were—to ask, and determined to help whether she wanted it or not.

"He's lucky to have you," she said quietly. "Even if he doesn't see it." She knew she hadn't always seen it. In the worst moments, she'd resented the people who showed up because she hadn't wanted to need them. But they'd shown up for her anyway.

Bill smiled back at her. "What do you recommend here?" he asked, picking up his menu.

Virginia pointed out her favorites. "I get the gnocchi alla Sorrentina every time. Extra parmesan on top, if I'm feeling crazy. My daughter-in-law is nuts over the lasagna."

"What's this you mentioned before about the store-bought sauce?"

Her cheeks reddened. "I'm devastated! But I swear, it's fantastic."

Bill's laugh soothed her anxiety. By the time Luigi came back to take their orders, the conversation had picked up, and Virginia hardly noticed when Bill ordered a bottle of the wine Luigi had suggested. The restaurant filled up, boisterous with conversation and laughter as wine flowed. The sunsets were growing later as February pushed on and spring came closer, but it was fully dark outside by the time they refilled their wine glasses and their entrees arrived.

"Tell me about your kids," Bill said later between bites. "You said you have a new granddaughter?"

Virginia nodded, grateful that her own mouth was full. It gave her a moment to decide how much to tell. "Lucy and Jack. Jack's older. He's an accountant. Lucy's in marketing, although I've never really understood what she does. I've never really understood what either of them do, to be honest. Jack is married. His wife is quite a bit younger than he is. I'd pretty much given up on either of my kids becoming parents, so I'm just over the moon."

Bill didn't say anything in response, just stared at her, marveling slightly.

"What?" she asked, looking down at her plate. His eye contact was too much. It felt like he could see inside of her, sense all the things she wasn't saying. *Lucy's mystery marketing job turned out to be illegal, and she's currently suspected of murder. Jack won't let me near his wife and kid until the whole thing is cleared up, lest I reveal to his emotionally fragile post-partum wife that the family is in turmoil. Oh, and Lucy's belt was the murder weapon, so now I'm a monster who can't help but question her own daughter's innocence.*

"You glow when you talk about your family," Bill replied. "You're beautiful all the time, but when you're talking about someone you love—or some*thing* you love, like when you brought up this restaurant—it's really something special to see."

It had been decades since anyone had called her beautiful, and Virginia was stunned into silence. Bill's eyes shined as he watched her wrestle with the compliment, like it gave him great pleasure to create such dishevelment.

In that brief moment, with his adoration gleaming at her from across the table and Luigi bringing them a tiramisu to share, Virginia felt like she could come clean and he might still look at her that way. Like she could tell him her secrets and he would nod and accept her and maybe even still think she was wonderful despite everything.

"It hasn't been easy with the kids," Virginia said, beginning her confession. "I used to screen their calls. Aging can be… Well, you know how it can be. I didn't take it well when they started to bring up moving me into someplace like Breeze Village. They were right. The kids are smarter than we old fogeys give them credit for, sometimes. But I didn't want to hear it, and we didn't have much of a relationship for years. And now…" She trailed off, mustering the courage to share the rest of her story.

Her phone rang, and Virginia quickly silenced it. It was from Ronald. Not thirty seconds later, it rang again.

Smiling easily, Bill said, "You can take that if you need to."

"No, no. It's just my friend, Ronald. He's probably just trying to see if I'm up for a game of poker."

When her phone rang a third time, though, Virginia apologized to Bill and picked it up. Ronald's usual jollity was absent.

"There's been a bit of a situation. My friend Ray and I are in jail and need you to come get us out."

* * *

BILL'S SURPRISED, hurt face haunted Virginia as she rode in Patricia's back seat to the police station. She didn't have the money to pay whatever bond was set for Ronald and his friend, and she didn't want to be alone at the police station again, even if it was to spring her friend from the pen, so she'd stopped by Breeze Village to gather the team before rushing to Ronald's rescue.

"Did he say—?"

"No." Virginia cut Marney off before she could ask yet again what Ronald had said over the phone. "He didn't give an explanation, and I didn't think to ask." She'd been too caught off guard to consider the questions she should have asked.

"It has to be about Loretta, doesn't it?" Marney speculated. "He was watching Lucy's apartment tonight."

Virginia clenched her jaw and looked out the window, letting her vision blur so the streetlights flew by as nothing but orbs of yellow light in the darkness. Ronald had been at her daughter's apartment to ensure Lucy was safe, and now he was in jail. Guilt and shame rose inside her, voices in her mind saying this was all her fault, competing only with the anger working to displace the blame onto Lucy. She had to get involved with a lowlife criminal for a boyfriend, and now Virginia's friends were out here laying their lives on the line to keep her safe.

For the remainder of the drive, she took measured deep breaths, slowly siphoning off the anger and guilt. Still, she sprung from the vehicle the moment they were parked, eager to get the story from Ronald. Maybe this was entirely unrelated. Maybe he'd gotten too rowdy at the American Legion spaghetti dinner and never made it to Lucy's apartment in the first place.

AS IT TURNED OUT, Virginia needn't have worried about paying Ronald's bail. No charges were pressed, and only hours after being arrested, Ronald was released back into the world, along with his grinning friend Ray.

"Finally!" Ray said, climbing into the back of the SUV and laying his head against the headrest like he was right at home instead of in a stranger's car. "I thought I might die in there. Took you long enough. I thought Ronald was lying to me and hadn't called us a ride at all! Can we stop by a Wendy's on the way home? While I was doing hard time, I had a lot of time to think, and one of the things I was thinking about was what my last meal might be. I want a frosty."

"What the hell happened?" Marney demanded, spinning around from the passenger seat to glare at Ronald and wait for the answer they all wanted.

Ray spoke up before Ronald had the chance. He was

missing as many teeth as Ronald was, as if they divided up one full set between them.

"What happened," he barked, "is Ronald was relieving me of my shift—late, so late I was ready to pass out from starvation and in desperate need of the facilities—when the lady we've been watching out for walked by. Ronald saw her first, seeing as I already had my back turned and was heading to my car, and he started shoutin' and making a general fuss, and then I turned around and saw her and my training kicked in."

"What training might that be?" Patricia asked.

Ray described, in great detail, the Taekwondo classes he'd taken as a child, and the whole car stifled giggles.

"I jumped on her, of course. Took her straight down onto the sidewalk. And then Ronald came over and jumped on *me*. So now the lady and I are both gasping for breath, and Ronald's screeching about how he hurt his elbow jumping on us, and the lady's hollerin' about being attacked. I told her I was making a citizen's arrest, but she didn't stop her fussing, and then someone called the police. I was glad when they arrived, thinking they'd haul her away and Ronald and I could go celebrate with a beer, but then they put *me* in handcuffs!"

They pulled into the Wendy's drive-thru, and the moment Ray had his frosty in hand, he fell quiet, giving Ronald the chance to tell his side of the story. It lined up almost exactly with Ray's, including total surprise that they were arrested for assault after leaping on top of Loretta and pinning her to the ground.

"Did you ask her about her husband's murder?"

Virginia wanted to know. "Or about sabotaging Lucy's car? How did she react? Why was she back there?"

Ronald lowered his eyes, looking at his own ice cream. "I did ask her about it, when I could get a word in between all her screaming. It turns out she lives at that apartment complex, and that's why she was there."

CHAPTER 20

The dining room was bustling the next morning, typical for Sunday breakfast. Virginia craned her neck, looking for her friends. Patricia was finishing her plate at one of the round tables next to a group of residents dressed in their church clothes, waiting for their children to pick them up and drive them across town for Sunday service, but Ronald was nowhere to be seen.

After eating, when Virginia and Patricia crossed the courtyard and knocked on Marney's door, he wasn't there, either.

"That's odd," Virginia said, frowning.

Ronald was heroic, but not humble. If he had the opportunity to leap atop a suspected murderer in the name of protecting a friend's child, the entirety of Breeze Village was going to know about it by ten the next morning.

And yet, he was conspicuously absent from the dining room and seemed to have told no one about the prior evening's events.

The threesome marched back across to the main building together and knocked on his door, and Virginia felt her mind spinning out while they waited for an answer. What if Loretta had been lying about living in those apartments? What if she'd come back for revenge? Ronald had made it clear he suspected her of killing her husband and trying to kill Lucy—maybe she needed to take him out before he could expose her.

Her worries were assuaged when Ronald answered the door with bedhead and wearing a stained nightshirt and ushered them quickly inside.

"Are you sick?" Marney asked, hanging back near the door and looking around Ronald's room with a frown.

Ronald didn't answer. He just poured cereal into a bowl and began to spoon it, dry, into his mouth.

"What happened?" Virginia asked.

"I had a visitor." Specks of cereal flew from his mouth as Ronald answered angrily. "Mr. Odeh found out about my arrest and came to talk to me. He's 'nervous' about having someone who's been arrested for assault living in Breeze Village—but they didn't even press charges!" He drew air quotes around the word *nervous*, then took another bite of dry cereal and chewed furiously.

"What does that mean?" Marney asked. "Hashim being 'nervous,' I mean."

Ronald shrugged as he finished his bite. "I'm on thin ice, I guess. Don't cause any more problems, or I'm out."

Virginia fixed her gaze on the beige wall behind Ronald, unable to look at him. This was all her fault.

"Well, since you don't need to surveil Lucy's apartment anymore, that shouldn't be too hard," she said. They'd caught their woman, and she had good reason to be there if she was telling the truth. They didn't have any further idea who might have sabotaged Lucy's car, and they couldn't exactly hang around outside Lucy's building, interrogating everyone who came and went.

"Don't you dare try to cut me out of this investigation now." Ronald pointed his spoon at Virginia and sent more cereal flying.

"It's too risky."

"It's not. I'm the one who found those earrings at the gallery. I'm the whole reason we know the murder victim's wife was in the art gallery at all—plus, she was hanging around upstairs in one of the artists' rooms. Loretta might have a legitimate reason to be at those apartments, but that doesn't mean she didn't kill her husband. It doesn't even mean she couldn't have sabotaged Lucy's car."

"So, what? What do you propose we do now? Go door-to-door around the apartment complex? Knock on every unit until Loretta answers the door, then ask her if she killed her husband?"

Ronald slammed the cereal bowl down on the counter. "I don't know! I don't know what's next, but whatever it is, I want to be included."

All three friends had flinched at the crash of the bowl on the countertop, and Ronald softened at their frightened expressions. "I retired and moved into this place all in one year. Worked 'til I couldn't anymore, and couldn't keep up a house, either. Everything that defined me— gone! Just like that. In one fell swoop.

"I took up playing poker and got good. That became

my thing: poker champion of Breeze Village. It felt good to be good at something again. And now I'm good at being an investigator. I've helped you on your cases before, but this one's the first one where I found a clue on my own. I matter to this investigation, and I'm not going to let go of that."

Marney and Patricia were nodding, but all Virginia could think of was how much Ronald had come to matter not to the investigation but to her. Hashim owned both Breeze Village and Harbor Vale. If Ronald couldn't live there, she didn't know where he'd go. And she couldn't be the reason he had to figure that out.

"You're right," she said, lying. "We'll figure out what's next and see this investigation through together."

In reality, she had a clue sitting in her room that she hadn't shared with the group, and now her mind kicked into gear trying to figure out how she could close the case on her own before Ronald lost his home. Before she missed every milestone of her granddaughter's life. Before a jury heard a prosecutor say Lucy's belt killed Ian Anderlini and had to decide amongst themselves whether to convict her.

CLASS HAD ALREADY STARTED by the time Virginia hurried into the lecture hall at the community college and took a seat at the back of the room. She tried to avoid calling attention to herself, but even with her glasses, it was hard to see from the back. She scanned the seats and found a familiar head of salt-and-pepper hair—more salt than pepper—and snuck down the aisle to take the seat beside Bill. Her heart swelled to be back in his presence, while her stomach knotted anxiously. She'd never reached out to apologize for running out on another date over the weekend.

She cut her eyes over toward Bill, missing the professor's demonstration in order to search for some sign of whether Bill had forgiven her behavior, but his eyes were straight ahead on the professor, and his face gave nothing away. She couldn't stand the uncertainty—she had to do something.

NICE SEE YOU.

Bill raised an eyebrow and turned toward Virginia in response to her greeting. He looked surprised she'd greeted him in ASL—she was surprised her hands remembered how. But he merely tipped his head in a short nod, then turned back toward the front of the room. Virginia swallowed the sting of his rejection.

For the portion of class involving partner work, Bill was all business, focused entirely on practicing the new vocabulary. His usual smile when Virginia flubbed a word or got flustered was gone, replaced with a stony coolness.

"I'm glad to see you're back," Virginia whispered. "Does that mean your friend is doing better?"

Bill put his pointer finger and thumb together and twisted them beside his mouth, like turning a key in a lock. Not in the mood to bend the rules tonight, it seemed. Virginia was thrown, and for the remainder of the class, she struggled more than usual to recall previous vocabulary or absorb anything new. The gray mass inside her head was interested only in how many minutes were left until class ended and she could apologize to Bill and make this right.

When the professor dismissed them, Virginia worried Bill would hurry away since he'd seemed so disinterested in talking with her earlier. She was surprised when he lingered near her as the room emptied.

"I was hoping to talk with you," he said.

Virginia blinked. She'd tried to talk with him, and he'd rejected her. "It sure didn't seem like it." She tried to make her voice sound light, but it came out harsh, her pain laced in every word.

"You ran out on me." The statement was hardly out of his mouth before Virginia had hers open, ready to make excuses and defend her behavior. Bill held up a hand to stop her. "I'm sure it was important. I could tell by the look on your face, and I know you wouldn't just run off without a good reason. I'm sure there was a good reason at the car show, too—you didn't just panic because it was your first date since your husband passed. I know something is going on in your life. The problem is, you're not ready to tell me about whatever that is. And I'm not up for dating someone who runs off every time we have a date. For Christ's sake, you didn't even call me later to let me know you were okay!"

Virginia's throat bobbed, painfully tight around the apology she was trying to push up through it.

"I—I'm so—"

"I know," Bill said, and Virginia thought his eyes looked wet. "But I'm old, Virginia. I'm well past the age of letting myself be yanked around by a woman, no matter how wonderful she is. You look at me, and it's like the sun shines right out of your eyes. I'm warm right through to my core. It's February, but it's summer when you're looking at me over a plate of pasta. But then you run off, and it's the coldest winter on record. Fifty years ago, I'd have weathered it, but I'm eighty. I'm not cut out for this anymore."

Virginia's eyes were wet now, tears stinging, and the taste of blood flooded her mouth as she bit down hard on her tongue, trying to hold them in.

Bill took a shaky breath, then said, "Take care, Virginia," and hurried off, the door to the lecture hall slamming hard behind him.

CHAPTER 21

Virginia snuck out the side door the next morning. She'd brewed her own coffee in the ancient Mr. Coffee pot that was covered in scale and almost never used anymore since she could pop down to the dining room for coffee and company. Then she'd splashed water on her face, swollen with red, puffy eyes from crying after Bill's rejection. He was right; she wasn't treating him well, and he deserved to be with someone who did. The list of people she'd hurt just grew and grew.

So, before dawn the next morning, Virginia downed her burnt coffee to try and revive her sleep-deprived body, then lumbered slowly down the stairs, one hand clutching the top of her cane and the other gripping the railing as she descended. She slipped out the side door at the end of the hallway, staying clear of the lobby and dining room with their sounds of silverware clinking and the smell of breakfast meats and syrup.

The apartment complex felt bigger without a specific, known destination within. Though she knew the idea of going door-to-door looking for Loretta was ludicrous, she didn't have a better one, so now she stood looking up at the four floors of possibilities. She eyed the front door, a large awning extending over the walkway to the sliding glass doors of the front office. She could pretend to be a relative visiting Loretta and ask at the office for her apartment number, but it was still too early for them to be open, and that ran the risk that they'd call up and verify with Loretta that she had a visitor coming. Instead, she made for one of the side doors to the building, gripping the freezing metal handle and tugging hard.

The door was locked.

Virginia let out a frustrated sigh, her breath clouding in the cold of the morning. *Is this how this is going to go?* She tried to force aside her doubts and turned, ready to try another door until she found one unlocked, when a pinch-faced woman with a tiny dog came walking up and tapped a small fob beside the door. With a beep and a click, the door unlocked, and the woman pulled it open. *A-ha!*

Virginia stepped toward her, ready to follow her inside, but the woman frowned and looked Virginia up and down.

"It's dangerous to let people tailgate inside. Just last weekend, a woman was assaulted here."

The assault in question was Ronald and his friend tackling Loretta, Virginia knew. She widened her eyes and let her jaw drop.

"Oh, that's awful! I just keep forgetting to bring my little doo-dad with me." She gestured at the fob in the woman's hand and took another step forward.

The woman's frown deepened, and she slipped all the way inside, pulling the door closed behind her. Just before it clicked shut, Virginia asked, "Is the woman okay? Do you know who it was? I hope it wasn't my neighbor—she's a pretty young woman who lives alone, and I worry about her sometimes."

The woman's frown remained, but she didn't pull the door shut. "It was that pretty woman who drives a Mustang. Lives on the other side of the building." She gestured with her head, not letting go of the interior handle of the door.

Virginia faked a sigh of relief. "Not my neighbor, then." She took another half step forward, daring to reach for the door, but the woman shook her head and pulled the door the last inch, so it closed firmly. Virginia was alone again, cursing in the frigid air, but she had some idea now of where in the building she should be focusing her efforts.

She moved around the building in that direction, trying each entrance as she passed them. Just when she was ready to give up, she came to one where a resident had propped the door open with a rock. She could see the man animatedly talking on his phone while his dog crouched and did its business. The man had his back to the door, and Virginia hurried inside before he might turn around and notice her.

Directly inside, Virginia found herself inside a stairwell. There was another door in front of her, and she pulled it open and stepped into a carpeted hallway, apartment doors lining both sides of the wall. Some had doormats out front, a few had wreaths or other decorations hanging on the door, and many were just plain, black doors rising up from the dull gray-and-beige paisley patterned carpet.

Worried that the man with the dog might come in behind her and realize she didn't belong, Virginia hurried down the hall and around the corner and decided to begin her attempt there. She walked until she heard noise coming from behind one of the doors so she knew the occupants inside were already awake, and then she knocked.

The man who pulled open the door looked confused to see Virginia standing there. In a locked apartment complex, she figured he didn't get strangers knocking on his door very often.

"You're not Loretta!" she said, pretending to be as surprised to see him as he was to see her.

He didn't respond, looking behind him into the apartment where two toddlers were eating breakfast on the sofa while cartoons played on the television, then back to Virginia.

"I thought this was my granddaughter's apartment," she added. "I must have the wrong apartment number."

The man remained standing, not making any move to close the door on her face but not offering any help, either.

Hiding her frustration, Virginia pulled Loretta's photo up on her phone and showed it to the man. "You wouldn't happen to know which unit she's in, would you?" She looked around the hallway, letting her eyes go wide with overwhelm. "I'm so bad remembering numbers these days, and all these doors look the same."

"I'm pretty sure she lives upstairs. I've seen her in the stairwell but don't know which floor. Sorry."

Virginia thanked him, then slowly made her way up one level before repeating the process. The first person on the second floor was no help at all, but the next person she encountered said she was pretty sure Loretta lived upstairs.

More stairs, Virginia lamented internally.

On the third floor, she had three different neighbors direct her down the hall. All were certain Loretta lived close by, but none remembered which door was hers exactly until a frazzled mother with a screaming infant in her arms pointed at the door across the hall.

Standing in front of the plain black door, no welcome mat out front, Virginia swayed with warring emotions, simultaneously in disbelief her tactic had worked and anxious that now she'd have to have the confrontation she'd been waiting for. Her heart beat so hard in her chest that she thought Loretta would be able to hear it when she opened the door. If she opened the door.

She knocked, but there was no answer. After several long moments, she raised her fist and knocked again, harder. She'd not even lowered it all the way when the door swung open. The woman behind it looked disheveled, in pajamas and with her hair falling out of a ponytail, a far cry from the put-together images of her online but plainly recognizable. It was Loretta Anderlini in the flesh, and she looked less than pleased to find Virginia standing on her welcome mat.

"Can I help you?" Loretta looked Virginia up and

down, a hint of disgust shining through the annoyance at being disturbed.

Virginia summoned all the courage she could find. She stood as straight as she could, her grip on her cane firm, tossed her shoulders back, and raised her chin a hair higher. "Yes, I believe you can," she said and strolled forward into Loretta's apartment, bumping the woman's shoulder as she moved past her. Her heart beat faster and her stomach churned, uncomfortable with the deeply uncharacteristic move. One didn't just walk into someone's home uninvited, her body reminded her, tensing more and more as she stepped into the space. But if she'd told Loretta who she was while standing outside, she'd still be standing outside now, with a slammed door firmly between her and the woman she desperately wanted to question.

Virginia turned, looking back to where Loretta stood in the doorway, gaping like a fish. "What are—?" Loretta didn't finish her question. Instead, she softened her expression, a look of pity and understanding replacing her shock. "I'm sorry, I think you have the wrong apartment. Can I help you find the right one?"

Virginia pursed her lips, trying to project an image the opposite of the lost, senile elderly woman Loretta believed her to be. "I'm pretty sure I'm in the right place." She waited a beat for Loretta's confusion to deepen, then said, "Loretta, right?"

A hint of fear edged across Loretta's expression, and Virginia couldn't keep the corners of her mouth from sliding upward in a tight smile. She felt powerful, seeing this woman who just a moment before thought her helpless and disoriented now afraid of her.

Virginia spun in the living room, taking in the space. It was identical to Lucy's apartment, with its gleaming floors and expansive countertops, the enormous windows looking out over a grassy field leading to a small patch of woods instead of the parking lot on this side of the building. But Loretta's style was Barbie-pink glitz and glam, nothing like Lucy's minimalist decor. A baby pink sofa with fuzzy white throw pillows sat along one wall, and the coffee table looked like a disco ball that had been squeezed until its top and bottom flattened out. It was covered in tiny, mirrored tiles, and its curved edges tossed specks of light on the walls.

Holding tight to the feeling of power, she walked around the island separating the kitchen from the living room and took a seat on one of Loretta's barstools, a luxurious pink velvet upholstered stool that swiveled when she sat in it. She wondered if Ian had had any say in the apartment's décor or if he'd given his wife free rein to do as she pleased.

"What's going on?" Loretta stayed frozen in the doorway, the door still open to the hallway. From her perch on the barstool, Virginia could see the door to the unit across the hall where the mother and her infant were ensconced inside, unaware of what was happening just feet away.

"Where were you on January nineteenth?" Virginia cut straight to the point, and Loretta's brows flew up in surprise before she put her hands on her hips and narrowed her eyes.

"I've told the police everything there is to know about

that day. I don't know who you are or who sent you here, but you need to leave. Now." Loretta took a half step to the side, clearing the path for Virginia to go, but Virginia stayed put.

Her hands were trembling where she clenched them together in her lap. She was in the home of someone she suspected of murdering her husband, or at least conspiring to have him killed. Someone who may also have it out for her daughter. She patted her pocket, feeling for her phone—her lifeline, if things went sideways—and fought to keep her voice steady and chin high.

"You spend an awful lot of time at the art gallery downtown. For both business and pleasure, it seems." She nodded toward the open door to the bedroom and asked, "If I looked around in there, what do you think I'd find? Maybe a trove of fake IDs?" She didn't know if Loretta had ever collected the loot from the man in the vintage car, but she needed Loretta to know Virginia wasn't floundering with nothing.

It worked. Loretta went white as a ghost. She stuck her head out into the hallway, looked up and down, then slammed the door shut and advanced on Virginia. "Listen, bitch. I don't know who you are or what you want—"

"I want to know the truth." Loretta was upon her now, taller than Virginia, still seated on the stool. Virginia forced herself to hold Loretta's eyes. "You were at the art gallery. You certainly felt no loyalty to your husband. How convenient for you that he—"

"I did not kill my husband." Spittle flew from Loretta's lips as the words sliced through the air. It landed on Virginia's face, and she flinched.

"You were at the art gallery when he was killed."

Loretta shook her head aggressively. "Not that day."

"Because you knew what was about to happen? You conspired to have your husband killed."

"No."

"Tell me the truth!" Virginia smacked a hand down on the island.

Loretta stepped back, eyeing Virginia over again. "Who are you?"

"My name is Virginia Walker." She paused, debated how much to reveal, and added, "I have a daughter named Lucy."

At the mention of Lucy's name, Loretta's face relaxed. Suspicion and hostility morphed into what might have been pity.

Virginia continued, "Lucy is suspected of killing your husband. She didn't do it, so—"

"So, you're playing detective to prove your daughter's innocence," Loretta finished for her. "Sweet."

She sighed, went to the refrigerator, and pulled out a bottle of champagne. Virginia watched, stunned, as she popped the cork and filled a flute. At Virginia's expression, Loretta shrugged and said, "I'm out of orange juice. And despite what you think, I'm not a cold, heartless husband-killer. I wake up every day surprised not to find him here. Coffee isn't quite cutting it for me these days." Loretta's lip trembled slightly as she spoke.

"Where were you?" Virginia asked again.

Loretta drank her champagne in one go, then refilled her glass before looking across the island at Virginia. "I was here. My friend came over to keep me company since

Ian was out. We did face masks and painted our nails. Happy?"

"And the man in the convertible? The one you enlisted to be your middleman, picking up the fake IDs for you at the gallery. He was there. Or how about the artist you've been sleeping with? You might have plotted with either one to take out the husband you no longer loved. Convince them you'd run away and live happily—"

"Enough!" Loretta barked, slamming her champagne flute down on the island so it broke, shards of glass skittering across the marble. Her breathing was ragged, her composure as fractured as the glass. "Ian wasn't the perfect husband—who is?—and I may have looked for love elsewhere, but I didn't want him to die. And I didn't orchestrate his death. I didn't kill him, and I didn't ask anyone else to."

"Did you tell these other lovers about your troubles with your husband?" Virginia couldn't stop from pressing harder. "Might they have thought they were doing you a favor? The man with the convertible, he was here—"

Loretta's eyes narrowed sharply. "Danny's never been here. I met him at a bar, had a little fun at his place, and then convinced him to help me out." A wicked half-smile pulled at her lips at the memory of her time with the man, how she'd blackmailed him into picking up illegal goods by threatening to sic her husband on him. "That wasn't love. It wasn't even an affair, really. It was just business. And a little pleasure."

"And the artist? Was that love?"

Before she answered, Loretta pulled an intact champagne flute from the cabinet and filled it. The bottle was nearly empty then, and she drank the rest directly from the bottle before picking up her glass and taking a sip. "It might have been, but it's not anything anymore. I ended it."

"When?"

"Two days before Ian was murdered. I thought maybe I could fix things, rekindle what we had. I guess time wasn't on our side."

"How did he react? Was he angry?" Had he killed her husband to keep her from going back to him?

"Not angry. Sad. In disbelief. He told me he'd wait for me to come to my senses and have me back when I accepted that I couldn't fix things with Ian. When I realized that I'd never have the love with Ian that I had with him. He still calls me, trying to get me to come back to him." Loretta's words took on a slightly slurred quality, and Virginia knew she didn't have much longer. She changed directions.

"My daughter was in a car accident. Someone tampered with her brake pedal—stuck something underneath it so the pedal couldn't be depressed all the way." She examined Loretta's reaction, waiting for any hint that she might have known about the accident, but none appeared. "You've heard of my daughter?" *Her boyfriend's wife is your best friend.* She couldn't bring herself to say that out loud. "Do you know whether anyone—Dax, or anyone else—might want Lucy out of the picture for some reason, either in prison for a murder she didn't commit or… or worse?"

Loretta's lips pursed at the mention of Dax, but she only shook her head.

"Do you ever drink energy drinks?" Virginia asked.

Loretta shook her head again. "Those things are gross, and they're awful for you. They'll wreck your skin, and your *breath* after drinking one of those!" She mimed a gag.

Loretta was leaning more and more heavily on the island, and even if she kept her senses about her to answer more questions, Virginia wasn't sure she had much more to offer. She stood and started toward the door, pausing to ask, "And you don't know of anyone else who might have wanted to hurt your husband?"

Loretta drained her glass and rummaged in the refrigerator, coming up empty-handed with a frown. "No. I already told that to the cops, who I will absolutely call if you or any of your cronies come near me again." She crossed the room to her bar cart, gleaming with mirror tiles that matched the coffee table, and opened a bottle of vodka.

CHAPTER 22

The mail room at Breeze Village was less of a room and more of an alcove in one corner of the lobby lined with labeled cubby holes for each resident. Virginia rarely checked her mail, but when she walked in through the front door after an evening shift at Piggly Wiggly to the sounds of an uproarious game of cards in the dining room, her body moved on autopilot to hide.

She didn't want to see Ronald. She'd spent the past week since his arrest and reprimand from Hashim sinking deeper into the spiral of avoiding her friends, feeling guilty for avoiding them, dreading what they'd have to say about her avoidance, and then further avoiding them. And knowing she'd betrayed them by going to find Loretta on her own only made it worse.

Every morning she stayed in bed later and later, and every night she retired earlier, and for the hours she was awake, she tried to be anywhere but in her room where her friends might find her. With each day, the tight knot inside her grew tighter until she could hardly bear it anymore.

She tucked herself into the mail room, hating herself, until she heard the card game finish with grand accusations of cheating. She waited with her breath held for another game to start, retreating farther into the alcove as the sound of footsteps marching from the dining room toward the elevator met her ears. When silence fell, Virginia peeked out to see whether the coast was clear for her to make her way to her room, but her eyes landed on Ronald sitting alone in the dining room. He shuffled his deck of cards, waiting for any more potential opponents to come through, and she ducked back into the mail room to avoid being spotted. On her retreat, she bumped one of the cubbies and sent the mail inside it scattering to the floor.

Virginia bent effortfully to pick it up, then started to replace it when she realized it was her own mail she'd spilled. She leafed through it, finding mostly junk. A local theatre group had put fliers for their upcoming show in everyone's mailboxes. There was something from the local election service, a pamphlet from AAA, and several catalogs and magazines. She breathed in a small gasp when she reached the last item. It was a new issue of the *Garden Review*.

"There you are! I haven't seen you around lately."

Virginia jumped, dropping the mail she'd just picked up. Jane was standing at the door to the mail room, wheeling her oxygen tank behind her. She stooped to collect the mail Virginia had dropped, saying, "I was asking about you at breakfast just yesterday morning. What's been keeping you so busy these days?"

"Oh, just the same old, same old."

Virginia reached out to take the mail from Jane, but to her horror, Jane began to flip through it as if it were her own. "Evelyn is trying to convince Diana to take us on a field trip to this production." She waved the theatre group's flier in the air before continuing through the stack. "This issue of the *Garden Review* is really great. I say—how long has it been since you checked your mail? I swear that came out weeks ago. Oh, now this is lovely handwriting." She held up a letter Virginia had missed, then crinkled her nose. "Smells a bit, though, don't you think?" Jane held the envelope out toward Virginia's face, and her nose crinkled at a familiar odor. She couldn't immediately identify it but she'd smelled it before. The upper left corner was empty, no return address, but it was hand-addressed to Virginia in a broad, looping script. "Who's it from?"

"Probably just an old friend." Virginia hastily took the whole stack of mail from Jane, who emptied her own box and left Virginia alone. She dropped the rest of the mail into her purse, then slid one fingernail under the seal of the mysterious envelope.

She pulled a single slip of paper from the envelope and immediately placed the smell. Gasoline. The page had a large, wrinkled patch like it had been splashed with a liquid and dried. Above the stained splotch, a single line was written in the same looping hand as the address.

Keep your nose out of other people's business, or Breeze Village is in for a scorching surprise.

And in the bottom of the envelope was a single match.

* * *

RONALD'S FACE lit up when he caught sight of Virginia leaving the mail room, but the smile slid away the moment he registered her expression.

"Something's happened," he said. Not a question.

Virginia nodded.

"I'll get Patricia. Meet at Marney's?"

She nodded again.

With the letter sitting out on the dining table, Marney passed out glasses of iced tea, and Ronald rummaged in her cabinets for a bottle of vodka, then followed in Marney's wake spiking their drinks.

"We have to tell the police, of course," Marney said, her face drawn with concern. "And Hashim will want to know immediately."

"We can't! He'll kick Ronald out, if not all of us."

"Someone has threatened to *burn down* Breeze Village. We have to tell him."

"We're clearly getting close to catching the killer," Ronald said, concern conspicuously absent from his voice. If anything, he seemed excited when he read the letter before passing it to Patricia, whose eyes oscillated quickly as she took in the text, instantaneously committing it to memory.

"They wouldn't make threats like that if we weren't on the right track," he continued. "The only reason to send you that letter is that we're too close, and they need us to stop looking before we bring them down."

Patricia picked up the letter again, though she'd already taken it in, her photographic memory imprinting it on her brain. Her face was scrunched up in confusion. "Why now? We hardly stepped foot in the gallery in over a week." She pointed to Ronald. "You tackled Loretta almost a week ago. We *have* been basically off the case, keeping our noses to ourselves. Whoever wrote that—presumably whoever killed Ian… Why are they worried now?"

Guilt tangled in Virginia's stomach. She opened her mouth, ready to force out a confession, when Marney said, "Virginia never checks her mail. She didn't at the house, and I'll bet she never does here at Breeze Village. Before tonight, how long had it been since you got the mail?"

Marney was right—the letter could have arrived days ago, or even weeks.

"Jane said the issue of the *Garden Review* that was in my mailbox along with this letter came out weeks ago."

Eyebrows shooting up with an idea, Patricia reached for the envelope that they'd tossed aside after extracting its contents. She pointed to the postmark in the top right corner. "It's postmarked earlier this week."

"So, the killer waits for us to back off, then writes to us to tell us to back off?"

But Virginia knew with a deep certainty that the letter was connected to her visit to Loretta. She cleared her throat and three pairs of eyes turned on her. "I haven't been totally honest with you." She waited for one of them to make a joke—*You? Hiding things from your friends who only want to help you? Who would have thought!*—to make light of her inability to open up, her need to go it alone, but they all just waited. She drained the spiked tea, feeling the burn in her throat and warmth in her stomach. Then, before she could talk herself out of it, she confessed, "I talked to Loretta."

Where she expected anger, her friends responded first with confusion.

"What do you mean?"

"How did you find her?" Patricia questioned.

Virginia answered while entering the kitchen and pouring another drink to avoid facing their gazes. "I went door-to-door. I pretended to be looking for my grand-daughter, like I'd forgotten her apartment number, and I showed people Loretta's picture until someone knew which apartment was hers."

When she peered through the passthrough above the kitchen sink into the living area, she saw the confusion on Ronald's face slowly turning to understanding. "Exactly the plan you mocked when I told you how it made me feel to be told to let go of this investigation?"

Instead of fury, his voice held only disappointment, and she wished desperately she could go back and undo the hurt she was causing.

"I hoped I could tie things up, end the case just like that." The excuse felt flimsy, yet she kept speaking, hoping her mouth would put together some combination of words that fixed everything. "I wanted to protect you. I—"

"Enough." Marney held up a hand. "Get to the point."

Ronald frowned at her but allowed it.

"I don't think she killed her husband," Virginia said, then recounted her visit to Loretta—her grief, her alibi, her affairs. "And there's one more thing."

Eyebrows went up, and Virginia moved to where her purse hung on the hook by the door. She pulled out the energy drink can, held it up, and then passed it around.

"The day after Lucy's car accident, I went to the salvage yard where her car was towed. Lucy said her brake pedal wouldn't work, and I found this wedged beneath it."

"Loretta?" Marney asked.

Virginia shook her head. "She never drinks energy drinks."

"She's not trustworthy," Ronald said. "Cheating on her husband, sneaking around—why should we believe anything she said?"

"I just got a feeling."

"Oh, yes. A feeling from being in the room with her. A feeling none of us can corroborate since we didn't get that same opportunity."

"I'm sorry—"

Marney cut off Virginia's apology by holding up the can. "Do you think there could still be DNA on this?" When no one responded, she added, "Whoever stuck this under Lucy's brake pedal drank it first. They'd have left DNA on the can. Maybe the police can tell who it was."

"And the envelope," Patricia added. "The killer licked the envelope to mail you that letter." Marney was already nodding furiously along.

Virginia forced her chin up and down but couldn't cover up her lack of enthusiasm.

"What's the matter?"

"What if..." She squeaked the words out, stumbling over them. "What if the drink can is Lucy's? What if no one sabotaged her car? What if the killer is in the wind, not following around Lucy trying to take her out, too, and the smashed window was just bad luck, and she should have been more careful about not leaving trash in her car?"

Lucy never left trash in her car. The little pocket in her car door was devoid of receipts, straw wrappers, and whatever other detritus accumulated in other people's cars. Each time she'd ridden in Lucy's car, it had been as pristine as the day she'd driven it off the lot. And yet, the salvage yard manager's remark stayed with her. *Hopefully she'll be more careful in the future.* Like she'd brought the accident on herself. Like the tiny, angry voice in Virginia's head said Lucy had brought her arrest on herself, too.

Marney stood beside Virginia and squeezed her hand. "Then that will be one piece of this mystery resolved, and we can rest a little easier knowing Lucy is safe in her home."

Virginia nodded, the tension in her throat easing by a fraction.

Marney continued, "Right now, all the police have on Lucy is that she was in the art gallery to meet the victim when he was murdered. Wrong place, wrong time, with a side of getting mixed up with the wrong people. But this" —she picked the letter up, waving it—"could provide a physical link to the real killer. It may not tie them to the gallery, but why else would they threaten us if they weren't the murderer? If the police realize someone is sending death threats to senior citizens to keep them from looking into this investigation, they'll realize they have the wrong suspect and drop the charges against Lucy."

The tension came rushing back.

Lucy wasn't being charged because she was in the wrong place at the wrong time. The police already had what they thought was a physical link to the killer: Lucy's belt, the murder weapon.

Virginia swallowed, forcing herself to nod. "You're right," she squeaked.

THE POLICE DIDN'T SWAB the crumpled drink can or the envelope to test for DNA. The officer taking their report chuckled when Marney suggested it, then said police resources were limited and that wasn't feasible. What they did do, to the dismay of the four retirees, was call Hashim right away. He wasted no time in getting there, his olive skin aflame.

"What is the meaning of this?" Hashim looked from the officer to the four residents sitting across the desk from him, his skin flushing deeper and a vein pulsing in his neck.

"You're the owner of Breeze Village Retirement Community, is that right?" The officer was unfazed by Hashim's bluster.

"Hashim Odeh, that's right. Is someone going to tell me what's going on here? Are these four in trouble? I might own the place, but I'm not responsible for—"

"Nothing like that, Mr. Odeh. We've been notified of a threat made against Breeze Village." The officer passed the letter to Hashim, who read it and sputtered unintelligibly. "It seems to have been splashed with gasoline, and there was a match in the envelope with the letter." He cleared his throat and clarified, "The writer seems to be threatening arson."

Hashim rounded on Virginia, waving his pointer finger wildly between her and Ronald. "*You!* You're nothing but trouble, once again. And you, sir—I already told you that you were on thin ice. You've brought danger to Breeze Village's doorstep, and I won't stand for it."

Virginia shrunk away from the attack.

"Do you have any idea who might bring an attack against your business like this?" the officer asked Mr. Odeh.

He recoiled. "Me? It's them you should be asking."

Virginia took the opportunity to repeat the theory they'd originally presented. "We believe this threat was brought by the same person who killed Ian—err..." She turned to her friends, brows raised in a silent plea for help.

"Anderlini," Patricia supplied.

Virginia continued, "Yes, the person who killed Ian Anderlini. The four of us have been following some leads, and we think whoever is responsible doesn't want us getting—"

The officer held up his hands, motioning for her to stop.

"Our best detectives are on that case. There's no need for the citizens of Seaview to get involved."

Hashim crossed his arms over his chest and gave a smug nod while Virginia felt the sensation of falling into a smooth-sided hole, scrambling in vain for purchase. She searched for the magic words to make them understand, but everyone under seventy in that room had made up their minds already. Virginia and her friends were old. They were forgetful. They were confused and meddlesome and not to be encouraged. And no magic words were going to change their minds.

CHAPTER 23

*H*ashim announced at breakfast the next morning that anyone engaging in activity that might reasonably harm Breeze Village, its residents, or its reputation would be evicted, and the place was immediately abuzz with rumors and theories. Virginia looked for Ronald in the dining room but couldn't find him. She waited, sitting alone at the table long after she finished her meal while the room emptied of breakfasters. Finally, the chime of the elevator caught her attention, and she perked up when Ronald emerged.

"Ronald!" She waved him over, but he kept his gaze fixed on the coffee dispenser and wouldn't meet her eyes.

"Busy," he mumbled as he walked right past her. "No time to talk today."

And then he was gone, his absence churning up a pool of remorse in Virginia.

She went by Marney's cottage, but Marney was preparing for a crochet class she was leading that afternoon, and when she knocked on Patricia's door, her friend held up a book and said she needed to finish it before the next book club meeting so she couldn't chat. She'd spent all that time avoiding her friends, hiding while the guilt of keeping secrets built up inside her, and now, in the aftermath of it all coming out, the loneliness was so potent it felt physically painful. She yearned for their company, but she'd pushed them away yet again.

Unable to stand being alone in her room, she brought her e-reader down to the dining room to enjoy the coming and going of other residents and their visiting family members.

"An investigation?"

Virginia jumped, startled, as Gemma sidled up next to her.

Gemma threw her head back and laughed deeply at Virginia's reaction. "It's not often I catch anyone by surprise!" She gestured down at her large body, clad in a pink-and-orange floral dress with a bright orange sweater.

Virginia collected herself, and Gemma asked again, "Is Virginia Walker, investigator extraordinaire, the reason behind Hashim's announcement this morning? Is there an investigation underfoot?"

Virginia only shrugged. "Not anymore."

"You're going to let the threat of eviction stop you from catching a killer?"

The threat of eviction and also arson, potentially endangering the lives of not just herself but everyone at Breeze Village. People who didn't choose to get involved in hunting down dangerous killers. Innocent bystanders who deserved to be safe and secure in their own home.

Besides that, her partners in the pursuit of justice were rightfully upset with her. Though she repeatedly proved she couldn't ask for or accept help, she knew at her core that she also couldn't solve this case without them.

"We all have our limits, I guess," Virginia said.

Gemma leaned in closer and lowered her voice. "Is this about the murder at the art gallery last month?"

Caught out, Virginia said, "Err, no. I—I've got to go. I forgot about something." She stood in a rush and made for the elevator, Gemma's laughter in her wake.

VIRGINIA WAS IGNORING her growling stomach the next morning when frantic, urgent knocks at her door drew her out of the chair where she'd been watching a cooking competition. Sunday mornings were the busiest time in the dining room at Breeze Village. While she had high hopes of getting her friends together and apologizing again for going behind their backs and visiting Loretta alone so they might all make up, she knew the rest of Breeze Village would be abuzz speculating about what she might have done this time to prompt Hashim's announcement. Better to wait until the dining room emptied out a bit before going down to get her own breakfast and seek out her friends.

She was only halfway across the room when another round of frenzied knocks sounded at the door. The handle jiggled in the frame, locked against whoever was trying to let themselves in.

A heavy wave of panic hit Virginia, stopping the

breath in her throat while her eyes fixed on the door handle.

"Virginia, it's me."

Gemma.

Virginia sagged with relief, then unlocked her door. It swung open immediately, and Gemma shoved her way inside.

"What is it?" Virginia asked as she shut the door. She moved to the tiny kitchenette and pulled open the cabinet of glasses, ready to offer Gemma a drink.

"I guess I'll just come right out and say it." But instead of coming right out and saying anything, Gemma let a pause stretch out while Virginia's curiosity grew. After a moment, she looked around and lowered her voice as if they were in public and not in Virginia's 300-square-foot studio. "People are saying your daughter Lucy committed the murder at the art gallery last month."

Virginia went white.

"Don't worry," Gemma said, shaking her head and putting her palms up in front of her. "I put the fear of God in the uninformed busybody spreading that nonsense around town, and I'll do it again if I hear anyone else spouting off something that ridiculous. I just wanted to let you know I'd heard it. Can you believe what people will come up with? Anyway, I can only guess you've been looking into the case. I don't know if you spooked somebody or annoyed the wrong person with a question or accusation, but it seems someone's started a smear campaign against you. Of all the lies for them to—"

Gemma stopped mid-sentence. Her eyes narrowed,

and she stepped closer to Virginia. "Wait a minute… Something's not right."

Virginia forced a swallow, wrenched her face into a picture of confusion, and asked, "What do you mean?"

Gemma raised an eyebrow and leaned back. "You don't seem shocked."

"No, I—"

"Don't lie to me, Virginia Walker. You've heard the rumor, too."

Virginia knew she'd been caught. She blurted, "Lucy did *not* murder that man. It's a goddamned *misunder-standing.*"

Gemma came up beside Virginia and leaned against the counter, waiting for Virginia to continue. She was a master at getting gossip and information out of anyone, and suddenly Virginia was her target. And Gemma knew all she had to do was leave enough space for Virginia to start talking, and eventually, she would.

Virginia caved. "The police think Lucy murdered that man at the gallery because she was present at the scene. She's the one who found the body." Virginia left out the murder weapon detail.

Even without that piece of information, Gemma looked flabbergasted, dramatically clutching her chest and gasping.

"Lucy was only at the gallery in the first place because of her no-good boyfriend, who conveniently disappeared from town after the murder."

"And no one else was around?"

"That's the thing—the gallery owner was there, plus three artists who live there. One of those artists was having an affair with the victim's wife, so he had good reason to want the husband out of the picture. And he isn't even the only one she was carrying on with. There's a second affair partner, and he was there that day, too."

"Why are people saying she's the one who did it? It seems like the cheating wife or her lover would make a better suspect!"

Virginia squirmed. "Well, since she found the body, she was there when the police got there. They brought her in for questioning, and you know how cops can get about not wanting to be proven wrong. They latch onto a theory, and they don't want to look at the evidence against it."

Especially when there's physical evidence for it.

"But you've been investigating."

Virginia nodded, confirming.

"So, which of these folks did it? The no-good boyfriend who skipped town? The cheating wife? One of the affair partners? Someone else entirely?"

It was a solid list of contenders. "We've been focused on Loretta, the cheating wife, mostly because I was pretty sure she tried to kill Lucy by way of sabotaging her SUV." Gemma gasped, and Virginia recounted the accident, the drink can under the brake pedal, and Loretta's presence at Lucy's apartment building just before the accident, which turned out to be because she lived there.

Gemma whistled. "So, someone gets away with murder thanks to your daughter going down for it. Then you look into the case to try to clear her name, and they try to crash her car and take her out—why? To send you a message?"

Virginia shrugged. She didn't even know for sure that the accident *was* an attempt on Lucy's life, much less the motivation behind it. "That, or she saw something she shouldn't have when she found the dead man in the gallery," she guessed.

"I'll tell you, Virginia, what surprises me the most about this mess isn't that you're tied up in another murder case—you've always had a way of getting mixed up in crazy situations like this. No, it's that you'd let Mr. Odeh's threat of eviction stop you from getting to the bottom of it."

Virginia felt her face flush. Gemma thought she was backing down in the name of self-preservation, too afraid of losing the roof over her head to fight to clear her daughter's name, as if she hadn't faced that challenge before. She pictured the Breeze Village dining room with flames crawling up the walls, the confusion and panic that would spread through the home. The death. Because no matter how well the staff responded, not everyone would get out in time. And it would all be her fault.

"It's not just that Hashim could kick us out. Someone sent me a threatening letter." She paused and studied Gemma's face. Gemma had one thick penciled-on eyebrow half-raised, waiting for the full explanation. "They threatened to burn down Breeze Village if I didn't back off. I'm not just backing off because Hashim says so. I want—I *need*—to figure out what happened in that gallery. I want to clear Lucy's name, of course, but it's more than that. Jack won't let me spend time around Stephanie and the baby until this is all cleared up. Stephanie doesn't know about Lucy's arrest, and Jack doesn't want her to find out because of the stress it'll put on her, worrying."

She leaned heavily on the counter, the weight of what hung in the balance of this case pulling at her body. "Everything in me wants to keep looking. But if I don't let it go, someone has said they'll burn this place to the ground. If I keep digging, I'm putting you and everyone here in danger."

Gemma contemplated this, stony-faced. Eventually, she smacked a hand down on the counter as if to say, *it's settled*. "If you keep investigating, we're all in danger. But if you don't, a murderer is going to go free."

It wasn't the response Virginia expected. She absently fingered the hem of her sweater, confused.

Gemma elaborated, "You said yourself that the police latch on to one theory and go with it. In their minds, they've got their guy, or their gal, as it were. Let's say you back off now. Breeze Village is safe. Lucy goes to trial for a murder she didn't commit. If her lawyer is good at his job, she walks. That's it. The police aren't going to go looking for a new suspect after all that. It's case closed. Whoever killed that poor man gets away with it and gets away with threatening a bunch of octogenarians, too. I don't want that."

"But can you make that decision for all of Breeze Village?"

Gemma pursed her lips.

Virginia's phone rang, and Marney's name lit up in large print across the screen where it sat on the side table, in full view of Gemma. Gemma watched as Virginia answered it, leaning in closer to try to eavesdrop.

"Patricia's here," Marney said. "She's told me to round up the gang."

With a little pump of her fists, Gemma said, victoriously, "I'll make sure Mr. Odeh doesn't find out. You go catch this killer and let him know he can't threaten Breeze Village and get away with it."

* * *

RONALD, Patricia, and Marney were engaged in a heated debate over which restaurant had the best margarita in Seaview when Virginia walked in. The sight of all of them together and happy immediately warmed something in her. A grin spread across her face.

"You're all wrong," she said, hanging her purse on a hook in the entryway and sinking down onto the open spot on Marney's couch. "The best margaritas are at Taco Loco, but the first one or two are always iffy. By the third one, though, they're incredible."

Ronald slapped his knee in exaggerated laughter, and Virginia caught his eye. She tried to communicate with him silently. *I'm so sorry. I was wrong. I am so, so sorry.* Whether he got the telepathic message or not, his return gaze felt like forgiveness.

They were still laughing when Patricia cleared her throat and said, "I've assembled you here today because I figured it out. The threat from Virginia's mailbox."

All eyes were on Patricia, the laughter immediately dissolved into silence. She continued. "My photographic memory—I knew the handwriting looked familiar, like I'd seen it before, but I couldn't place it. This morning, it finally hit me: I've seen that handwriting before in the signatures on Julien Reed's paintings."

After a beat of silence, the room erupted, with Ronald ready to find this man and tackle him—Ronald's preferred form of justice—and Virginia probing for more information. Fending off her friends' interruptions, Patricia shared how she'd been looking more into her theory that the art gallery was artificially inflating the value of its residents' works, and that was where she saw his signature again and placed the handwriting. Marney was silent throughout.

Finally, Virginia asked, "So, what do we do now?" Should they confront the artist at the gallery, or go straight to the police to help them identify the threat to Breeze Village?

Marney looked up from her deep contemplation. "Dylan always talked about needing enough evidence to make a charge stick. She never wanted to bring anyone in if they didn't think there was a good chance they'd get a conviction. We need more than just his signature on a painting if we're going to convince the police to arrest Julien for that threatening letter."

CHAPTER 24

"Remind me again what our story is?" Lawrence asked from behind the wheel of his Lincoln.

"We're from the Seaview Arts Society, and we're doing a piece on up-and-coming artists. We want to feature Julien Reed, and we'd love any early artwork of his so we can highlight his progression and growth as an artist," Virginia recited.

Patricia continued, "And, by the way, what kind of kid was Julien when he was young? Did he always want to be an artist? How'd he do in school? Maybe we could see some old homework assignments? Anything to give more color to our feature would be great. Readers love that kind of thing."

Fields of rye sped past along the highway, the sky a brilliant, sunny blue hinting at the coming spring while the cold hung on just a little while longer. Lawrence, Virginia, and Patricia sped farther from Breeze Village by the minute, Ronald and Marney hanging back. Marney, though she'd been the one to suggest they needed more evidence tying the handwriting in the threatening letter to Julien, squirmed at the idea of lying to his parents to get that evidence. Ronald, though Virginia had encouraged him to come with them, said he wanted to stay back in case Julien made a move while they were away.

"Someone needs to be here to stop him," Ronald had said.

Now, Lawrence asked, "And I'm supposed to be the one asking the questions, why?" When Virginia had first asked him to come on an adventure and help them out, he'd agreed without hesitation, either happy to be included or eager to keep an eye on Virginia in order to keep her safe.

"Because if you ask someone something and flash them that winning smile of yours, they'll bend over backward to give you an answer," Virginia said. "You're way more likely to get information out of our suspect's family than Patricia and I are. I don't think a single person has ever told you to mind your own business."

"You have, plenty of times."

"Besides me," Virginia said.

Patricia had dug up an article on Julien Reed in the *Macon Telegraph* from when he was in high school and won a national award for his art, and from there, had called the school pretending to be a museum curator looking for Mr. Reed's address.

"They really pride themselves in having turned out someone exceptional," Patricia had told the group as she proudly recounted her successful inquiry. "Just a hint that I was someone important in the art world, and she was happy to give me his family's address so I might get in contact with him through them."

It was going on two in the afternoon when the three pulled into town. Julien's family lived just outside of Macon on a corner lot in a quiet neighborhood. Bright white shutters matched the decorative white-painted iron porch columns. Neatly trimmed hedges dotted the outside of the home, and the few tall pine trees rising out of the dry lawn had tidy beds of mulch around their bases. A sparkling clean but decades-old sedan was parked under the carport.

"Someone's home," Patricia said with a nod to the parked car.

"They could have two cars, and both went out in one," Virginia argued, her stomach suddenly turning in knots now that they'd arrived.

Without a word, Lawrence got out of the car, using the handle above his door to pull himself up with an exaggerated groan. He put his hands on his hips and circled them twice. "Got to limber up before my big performance." He winked at Virginia and then strode to the door, Virginia and Patricia exchanging a look before scurrying after him.

By the time the two of them caught up with him, Lawrence had already rung the doorbell and was standing in front of the door exuding a confidence Virginia envied. She was still working to catch her breath and tamp down the voice in her head screaming that it was wrong to lie to these people, even if their son might be a murderer and had almost certainly threatened to burn down their home. The door swung open to reveal a short, thin woman with thinner hair and round cheeks—the only soft part of her amongst sharp angles and bones—and Virginia sorted her face into a smile. Her brain seemed to have completely turned itself off the moment it was go-time, and she grinned vacantly while Lawrence started in on his part.

"Mrs. Reed?" he asked, and the woman nodded. "My name is Lawrence, and my friends and I are from Seaview. We're with the Arts Society there. You're Julien Reed's mother—is that right?"

The woman's cheeks flushed, and she beamed, nodding furiously. She took a step back and pulled the door open wider, revealing a living room that matched the exterior of the home—old and dated but meticulously cleaned and well cared for. "Yes, I'm Lisa Reed, Julien's mom." Her brow wrinkled in concern and she added, "He doesn't live here, though. He's down in Seaview, where you folks live. He's doing a residency at the gallery there."

Lawrence gave a reassuring smile, and Lisa's concern faded from her face before he even started speaking. "His work during his residency at the Benson-Barnes Gallery in Seaview is what brings us here, actually. Do you mind if we come inside?"

Lisa beckoned them in, and Lawrence spun their story of working on an article highlighting rising talent with a connection to Seaview. "We want to interview Julien himself, of course, but to paint the most complete picture —no pun intended—we thought it would help to talk with his parents. Get an idea of how Julien grew up and the path that led him to where he is today."

Mrs. Reed seemed to bask in Lawrence's attention, the acknowledgement that her son was special lighting her up until she practically glowed. "Michael—my husband—is at work, but I'd be happy to tell you whatever it is you want to know. Oh, he'll be so thrilled when I tell him! Michael always encouraged Julien's creativity, see. When he was a toddler drawing on the walls, Michael would say, 'Our boy is going to be something big. Have you ever seen a two-year-old draw like that?' He knew Julien was talented. Meanwhile, I had smoke coming out of my ears while I cleaned the walls for the hundredth time."

"So, Julien was an artist from the very beginning," Patricia mused.

Lisa turned to her and looked almost surprised to find her there; she'd been so wrapped up in Lawrence's presence. "Yes. I discouraged it for a long time. Michael's a computer technician, and I was on Julien to do something more practical, something with more security than trying to sell his art. But he wouldn't have it, and now look where we are! It's a darn good thing he never listened to a word I said."

Lawrence gave a thoughtful look and asked, as if the idea had just popped into his head, "Do you have any of his early artwork that we could see? Anything from his childhood?"

He'd hardly finished the question when Lisa was tugging the cord to the trap door in the ceiling up to the attic and pulling down the ladder with an ear-splitting creak. The three friends shared hopeful glances beneath the clatter in the attic, and Lisa emerged several minutes later with a large plastic storage bin filled to the brim with notebooks and papers.

"This is all his old schoolwork," Mrs. Reed explained, kneeling and opening the bin. "His old artwork should be in here, too." Virginia couldn't help but peer over the woman's shoulder as she leafed through the contents. She flipped through one or two notebooks before exclaiming, "A-ha! I knew it would be in here." She turned and held up a battered notebook, the front cover halfway torn off. "Julien's first sketchbook."

Lawrence took the book gingerly as if it were a precious manuscript that might disintegrate with any amount of handling and flipped through it. He commented on Julien's artistic development while Lisa preened, praising her son. Off to the side, Patricia flipped through one of the notebooks Mrs. Reed had set aside. Virginia caught her eye, shooting her a silent question, and Patricia tilted her chin down in a hint of a nod.

Julien's handwriting matched the letter she'd received.

Virginia's fist clenched, the jolt of triumph obliterating any guilt over lying to Mrs. Reed. *We've got him.*

CHAPTER 25

Lawrence had hardly turned the key in the ignition when Patricia produced a folded piece of paper she'd tucked into her pocket.

"An essay of Julien's," she explained. "He wrote his name at the top. It's a labeled handwriting sample, and I think the police will find it matches the letter you turned in."

"We've got him," Virginia repeated, this time out loud.

"We've got him," Patricia echoed, nodding.

"We couldn't have done it without you," Virginia said, tapping Lawrence on the shoulder over the back of his seat as he pulled away from the Reeds' house. "What did I tell you? The moment she opened the door, Mrs. Reed was ready to tell you anything you asked. Your aura is some sort of truth serum. Your smile has people spilling their guts."

Lawrence breathed a laugh, but there was no mirth behind it. "Only women, it seems. Men have no problem lying to me."

Virginia winced. "The latest one didn't work out?"

Lawrence exhaled sharply again and said, "We made it to seven dates before he stole one of Ben's records and sold it on eBay. I shouldn't have shown him my collection. I should have seen it coming."

Patricia frowned. "Why would you see it coming? You can't date someone if you're expecting the worst of them."

"I can't seem to pick a man who's not a scumbag," Lawrence answered with a shrug. "Maybe I had it right all along. Ben was my person. I should just be happy I had love in my life once and stop inviting pain trying to find someone new."

Virginia wanted to protest. She thought of Gemma and Jimmy, the unlikely pair finding love in their eighties. Their joy proved it was possible.

But then she remembered the look of disappointment on Bill's face when she'd hurt him yet again, and that possibility felt flimsy. It felt like love was the proverbial pot of gold at the end of the rainbow, but the rainbow was just scattered light. There was no end, and there was certainly no pot of gold.

She kept quiet, and Lawrence turned up the radio for the drive home.

* * *

"You can't crouch behind a bush that's smaller than you!" Ronald insisted, directing Patricia to conceal herself behind a parked minivan instead.

"I can't see if I'm behind that thing," Patricia argued, but moved behind the car anyway. She stuck her head out, spoiling the hiding spot as she craned for a better view of the art gallery.

The group was a block down from the gallery across the street, trying desperately to catch a glimpse of the ongoing police raid. Lawrence had driven Virginia and Patricia to the police station before dropping them off at Breeze Village. When they gave the police the handwriting sample to compare to the threat she'd received by mail, the police had insisted they'd take it seriously. This morning, Marney heard from Dylan that McNeil would be at the art gallery for work, and they knew it had to be connected.

The four wasted no time careening across town to make sure they were there in time to watch the cops haul Julien out of the gallery in cuffs. Even if they only brought him in for threatening the lives of the residents of Breeze Village, it seemed like a short leap from that to the murder of Ian Anderlini, and Virginia breathed a prayer that he would confess. That it was all finally coming to an end.

A police cruiser pulled up outside the gallery, and Virginia could hardly contain her excitement.

McNeil and a uniformed officer Virginia didn't recognize entered the gallery together, and as the minutes passed, the gang began to speculate about Julien's reaction when they cuffed him.

"My money's on kicking and screaming for his exit style," Ronald said, grinning from behind a lamppost that concealed him even less than the bush had concealed Patricia.

Marney shook her head. "He'll be—oh!"

The gallery door swung open, and McNeil stepped out, holding it open for his partner. McNeil turned back and waved, and Virginia could see Mr. Porter waving back to him from the doorway as the police stepped onto the sidewalk to leave. Virginia's stomach sank, and as she peered out from her hiding place, her eyes locked with Porter's. The friendly smile he'd worn for the detectives vanished, his mouth a tight line as he stared daggers across the street at Virginia.

"What the hell?" Patricia demanded, abandoning her attempt to hide and standing to her full height. "Why are they leaving?"

Marney's mouth hung open in dismay. "Maybe Julien wasn't there. Maybe they'll have to come back later to find him."

Virginia straightened, her knee shooting pain down her leg. "What's McNeil's number?"

Marney shook her head in refusal.

"I know you have it. Marney, give me the number. We have to find out what's going on, why they just walked out of the gallery without our number one suspect."

"If you want to march into the police station and demand answers, I'll go with you. I want answers, too. But Dylan gave me his number for personal reasons, and I'm not going to give it to you so you can harass him about his work."

Virginia let out a slow breath, then turned to the car. Marney's being right didn't make it any easier to swallow. Something had gone horribly wrong. The police should have been arresting Julien Reed. Instead, they were acting friendly with the owner of the art gallery and leaving empty-handed.

She took the painful steps back to Patricia's SUV, then turned for a final look back at the gallery. The front door was closed tight with Mr. Porter nowhere in sight, but his assistant peered out at them from the window. When his eyes met Virginia's, he dropped the curtain and let it fall, disappearing into the showroom.

* * *

HASHIM WAS WAITING for Virginia and her friends when they pulled into the Breeze Village parking lot. His hands were shoved deep into the pockets of his slacks, but he removed them every so often to rub his facial hair, a deep frown cutting grooves through it from the corners of his mouth down to his chin.

Ronald let out a low whistle when they pulled in. Patricia seemed to cave into herself. Virginia stepped ahead of the others, grabbing the railing where Hashim waited at the base of the steps up to the front door.

"Are you waiting here to thank us for figuring out who mailed me that threat against Breeze Village?" Her body swayed, but her voice came out defiant like she wanted. Out of the corner of her eyes, she saw Marney go rigid. Ronald beamed.

Hashim shoved his hands deeper in his pockets as if to keep himself from doing something he'd regret. "I'm here," he spat, "because I received a call to let me know Breeze Village will no longer be the recipient of a grant from the Seaview Community Promotion Foundation.

The board of the foundation decided we weren't the best fit, and other community organizations would be better recipients of the money."

Virginia blinked at him. A quick glance to the others showed no more comprehension on their faces.

"The president of the board," Hashim continued, "is Hugh Porter."

Virginia gripped the railing harder as her head swam. "That's not fair," she said, but the words were barely more than a whisper.

"It's the reality of upsetting a prominent member of your local society," Hashim countered. "And it is the consequence of you directly defying my orders not to go digging around in something that puts my business at risk."

"It's your business, but it's our home," Ronald said, puffing out his chest.

"Not for much longer." Hashim turned and took the stairs two at a time.

The four amateur sleuths stood shell-shocked. Virginia focused her energy on remaining upright and not vomiting. She'd known that investigating put Breeze Village in danger of the killer's wrath. But by bringing the police to the art gallery and upsetting its owner, she had no idea she was putting it at risk in an entirely different way.

"Does that mean he's evicting us?" Ronald asked, taking the first step forward from where they'd all remained planted.

"Or, without that funding, will Breeze Village close down?" Virginia choked out.

fter a night of fitful sleep and a morning spent refreshing the inmate roster for the Seaview Jail, hoping in vain that the officers had gone back later and that Julien Reed's name would be on it, Virginia swiped lipstick across her mouth, fluffed her hair, and grabbed her cane before heading out. Clouds loomed, spiking her anxiety around driving in the rain, but this was a visit she needed to pay on her own, and she couldn't stand the thought of another rideshare, so she took a few deep breaths before turning her key in the ignition. She gunned it across town, trying to beat the rain, and swiftly followed another resident into Lucy's apartment building without issue.

Lucy answered the door on the first knock, fully dressed with her heels clacking on the laminate flooring.

"Were you on your way out?"

Lucy shrugged out of her blazer and kicked her heels off, moving to hang the jacket up before calling out from the walk-in closet, "On my way in, actually." Reemerging into the kitchen, she poured herself a glass of iced tea and offered one to her mother. "I just got back a minute ago. I'm surprised we didn't cross paths in the parking lot."

"A meeting with your attorney?"

"The bank, actually," Lucy said. "I was opening a new account. For my new business." Each sentence came out quieter than the last, with more hesitation, and her smile at the end was more sheepish than proud.

"A new business endeavor! That's wonderful!" Virginia set her drink down to hug her daughter, wishing it felt normal and easy instead of stiff and awkward. "What sort of business? Marketing stuff?" She hesitated, realizing how little she still understood about her daughter's industry and how silly she sounded.

On cue, Lucy scoffed, but seemed to catch herself. She cut off the harsh laugh and gave her mother a soft smile, sipping her iced tea before answering, "Yep, marketing stuff. All the applications for jobs at other agencies require me to disclose whether I've been convicted of a crime. I haven't, and if Mr. Murphy does his job well, I won't be, but it got me thinking about what it would be like to be employed when this actually goes to trial." Virginia winced, and Lucy continued. "So, I figured I'd start my own thing instead. A few clients here and there is better than nothing. And when this whole thing is over, and my name is cleared—" She waved her hand in the air, as if dismissing the crime and investigation that had turned Virginia's entire family's lives upside down. "— things should pick up again."

The ease with which Lucy jumped over everything happening now and envisioned a future where it was as if none of it had ever happened grated on Virginia. She made herself cross the room and sit down before saying anything.

"I have some news on that front," she finally said. "On bringing this case to a close."

Lucy's mouth dropped open in surprise, and then in a flash, her brow furrowed in consternation. "You're not supposed to be—"

Virginia put her hand up, and Lucy quieted. "After your car accident, I received a letter in my mailbox at Breeze Village. A threatening letter." Virginia's stomach constricted at the memory of the single match resting at the bottom of the envelope, the phantom smell of gasoline stinging her nostrils. "They said that if I didn't back off looking into this case, they'd burn down Breeze Village."

Lucy's hands flew to cover her mouth. "That's horrible!"

"The handwriting matches that of one of the artists living at the gallery. One who happened to be having an affair with the wife of the man you found murdered."

"This sounds like something you should be telling the police, not me."

Virginia's eyes lingered on the floor in front of Lucy's feet. She couldn't meet her daughter's eyes as she said, "That's the problem. We *did* tell the police."

"What's the matter, then?"

"They thanked me for helping them keep Breeze Village and all of Seaview safe, assured me they'd take it from there, and then paid a visit to the art gallery."

"That's gr—"

"Where they shook hands with the owner and arrested

nobody. The artist is still free." She didn't add that the gallery owner was so upset at her for siccing the police on his place of business that he'd pulled strings to get Breeze Village's grant money pulled. There was nothing Lucy could do about it, and Virginia didn't know if she'd be able to say the words out loud.

A crack of thunder startled them, and the room darkened as the sky opened up and began dumping rain. Lucy shivered, whether from the late winter chill or the news, Virginia wasn't sure.

"Well, whether the police end up bringing him in or not, my lawyer will be over the moon to hear about this. He's going to want to see the letter. If the police bag the artist and drop the charges against me, all the better, but if not, just having an alternative suspect to present at my trial will go a long way."

The blood drained from Virginia's face. "I didn't make a copy before I turned the letter over to the police."

The police had the letter, its envelope and any DNA it might contain, Julien's school essay identifying the handwriting, and the crushed energy drink can from Lucy's car with whatever DNA might be left on it. And Virginia had nothing, absolutely no concrete evidence left in her possession.

Virginia's phone beeped loudly at the same time that Lucy's vibrated, and they reached in sync for their devices. Lucy's eyes immediately crinkled as she smiled, the same involuntary response that was spreading across Virginia's face as she brought the screen closer to take in the picture they'd both received. Stephanie had sent a photo to the whole family of baby Emily in the bath, laid back in a pink plastic baby tub. Her cheeks glowed a rosy pink and her mouth was open wide in a smile. The text accompanying the photo said, *Em has started smiling!!!* Tears stung the corners of Virginia's eyes, but when she looked over at Lucy, her smile had vanished.

"She's going to be so pissed." There was no need to clarify who she was talking about. Virginia knew she meant Stephanie when she finally learned what the family had been keeping from her. And she knew Lucy was right.

"Rightfully so."

"Even if they drop the charges before the trial…" Lucy shook her head, trailing off. "It's a miracle there haven't been features in the *Gazette* about me. This town is sleepy enough, I'd have thought reporters would have run with this one. I honestly can't believe she hasn't found out yet."

Virginia squirmed. "I don't know how much longer it'll stay this way." Gemma's shocked face swam in her vision, and she recounted the way the first rumors connecting Lucy's name to the murder had made their way back to Virginia. "If the rumors made it to Breeze Village, it's only a matter of time before they make it to Harbor Vale and then out into the rest of town. Once they've breached containment and left the world of the old folks' homes… The *Gazette* won't be far behind."

* * *

VIRGINIA WAS five minutes late for her shift after driving at a snail's pace while the rain pelted her windshield and skyrocketed her pulse. Her manager watched her clock in, narrowed eyes looking down his enormous nose at her.

She flicked on the light above her lane and waved a customer over, ringing the woman up before the manager could lumber over to chastise her for tardiness.

She could feel his gaze on her as her shift progressed, but the store was busy, and in the moments when she did find herself without a customer in her lane, Virginia made a show of busying herself wiping down the conveyor and cleaning up the area. His shift ended halfway through hers, and Virginia breathed a sigh of relief when she saw him leaving the building. She wouldn't have to withstand a lecture or rhetorical questions about whether she was actually cut out for the job and if he could rely on her. Not today, at least.

When she turned from watching his exit, distracted by her good fortune, she was surprised to find a customer in her lane. "Sorry about that!" she said cheerfully, then jolted as she realized she recognized the man before her. "Bill?"

Bill waved, then moved his hands in a motion that felt familiar, though her brain didn't recognize the motion until she realized she'd unconsciously responded in kind. He'd greeted her in ASL, and her body had recognized the greeting and responded instinctively. She beamed, pleased with herself.

"I can't believe I understood you!" she exclaimed. "At least a little of what Professor Gartner tries to teach us is sinking into this old brain of mine."

Bill smiled back, but it was small and tight and sent Virginia crashing back down. For a moment, she'd seen his eyes sparkling as he greeted her, and she'd forgotten how they'd left things, how she'd ruined what they'd had.

But the memory crept back with the hesitancy in Bill's face, and she felt a wash of shame and regret. She rang up his groceries quickly, the silence thick between them, and then as he tucked the receipt into his pocket and started to push his cart forward she signed, impulsively, SEE YOU TOMORROW?

She waited, desperation tugging at her heart, and then his lips pulled back into a more genuine smile and he signed back, YES.

Her mind was scrambled for the rest of her shift, flicking back and forth from the image of Bill smiling at her to the one of his face two weeks ago when he was telling her he didn't have it in him to be led on by someone who was only going to run away and hide things from him. She was just clocking out, still halfway in a daze and breathing a sigh of relief that she'd made it through, when her phone rang.

Gemma's voice had a forced levity as she said, "Virginia, I just got home from my monthly Bible study, and I have to tell you... I heard two different people mention the murder at the gallery during our luncheon afterward. One of them said she thought she'd heard the wife probably did it, but the other woman mentioned Lucy by name."

Virginia's throat caught. An involuntary groan slipped out, causing a few heads to turn in her direction. She hurried out the door and across the parking lot as Gemma continued.

"I asked her, 'Did you say Lucy Walker?' And when the woman said yes, I told her she was mistaken and also that God hates gossip, so she'd better stop spreading rumors.

On the way out, I talked to the woman who was saying the poor guy's wife did him in, and I told her I'd heard the same thing, and that his wife was cheating on him, so she'll be pushing that story all around town."

Virginia didn't respond. She couldn't—not around the lump forming in her throat. She bit her tongue and looked skyward, counting as she blinked back tears. Finally, Gemma said, "Well, I'm sure you're busy. I've got this covered—I just wanted to let you know what I heard. But hardly anyone pays any attention to Laura anyway. That's the woman who was saying it was Lucy who did it. Plus, with Carolyn now going around town saying the dead guy's wife was cheating on him, that's way more compelling than the Lucy rumor. The wife theory is all anyone will be talking about now."

Virginia could only nod, and then the phone beeped, the call ended, and she was alone. A cheating wife did seem like a more believable killer than an unrelated marketing professional. At least until word got out that Lucy was at the gallery for some illegal business deal with the deceased. Until people heard it was her belt that did him in. Until people learned that Loretta had an alibi and the cheating wife was ruled out as a possibility.

* * *

DESPONDENT, her mind on Lucy and the timer ticking down to when all of Seaview found out she was a suspect in this case and why, Virginia made straight for the elevator to head up to her room when she got home to Breeze Village. She jumped and dropped her cane when she stepped out of the elevator and ran headlong into her three friends.

"We were looking for you," Ronald said.

Tears immediately streamed from Virginia's eyes. The surprise had jolted any semblance of composure, and the dam broke. Panic welled in Ronald's eyes, and he took half a step back, caught off guard by the sudden explosion of emotion. Without asking questions, Marney stepped forward and hugged Virginia, rubbing her hand in circles over Virginia's back and rocking gently. A few moments later, Patricia cleared her throat.

"If you still want to cry after this, that's fine, but if you're crying about the case, I have something you'll want to see." She held up a stack of papers. Virginia took them in her own shaking hand, pulling them closer so she could see what they were.

Immediately, she could tell they were scans of something handwritten, but the handwriting wasn't familiar. "What is this?" She squinted, trying to read the print around the blurs from scanning creased papers.

Patricia shifted her weight in anticipation. "This," she said, taking the letters back and waving them with gusto, "is all the letters Julien Reed received from Hugh Porter before starting his residency here in Seaview."

Patricia was looking at her expectantly, but Virginia wasn't sure why she should be excited over the letters.

"Julien's mom found them when she was going through his things after our visit, and she reached out to Lawrence. She said Julien had applied for a residency at the gallery, and Mr. Porter wrote back handwritten letters in the mail. Julien had loved that—the charm of old-school correspondence. But instead of just sending him an acceptance or a rejection, Hugh had wanted to feel out Julien's goals as an artist or something like that." She waved the pages again, emphasizing the quantity. "Anyway, they wrote back and forth, and eventually, Mr. Porter officially accepted him, as we know from his presence in our fine town. Mrs. Reed thought the Arts Society may want to use quotes from the correspondence in our feature, so she scanned the letters and emailed them to Lawrence."

Virginia looked to Marney and Ronald to see whether they understood the importance of what Patricia was saying. Both had excitement behind their eyes that Virginia still didn't comprehend, so she asked, "And the letters also include a plot to murder Ian, a man Julien hadn't even met yet?"

Patricia laughed. "Not quite. But they do include a promise by Mr. Porter to do for Julien exactly what he did for Jesse Spencer last year and a reference to how mutually beneficial the partnership would be."

Virginia was growing annoyed and began down the hall toward her room. "You can explain why that should mean anything to us while I take off these shoes and pour myself something to drink."

"I don't expect that to mean anything to you because you haven't spent the time I have over the last few weeks looking into all the artists who have completed residencies at the gallery recently and all the art they've sold."

Ronald jumped in, shaking his head. "What Patricia already explained to Marney and me, painstakingly and in more detail than I could ever recall, is that Mr. Porter and the resident artists are running a scheme to make money."

Virginia leaned on the counter of her kitchenette and added another pour of vodka into the tea she'd already spiked, ready to scream. She only enjoyed the drama of an overly drawn-out reveal if she was the one delivering it. "A scheme to make money... by selling art? Isn't making money usually the point of selling stuff?"

"They're inflating the values of their work," Patricia said.

A hint of a memory returned to her, though she still didn't understand. "Is this about what you said to Mr. Porter the last time we tried to visit the gallery together?"

Patricia nodded enthusiastically. "The short version is that Mr. Porter buys the art himself through a fake company, or he gets a friend or associate to buy it. All at crazy high prices—way more than any real buyer on the art market would pay for it. Then the art community goes crazy, with word spreading about how great the artist is because people are paying so much for his art. Then other people—real buyers, this time—buy his art at those sky-high prices because they want to get in early with this up-and-coming new artist. The artist gives Mr. Porter a cut, since otherwise the paintings wouldn't sell for anywhere near as much.

"I confirmed it with Jesse Spencer, a painter who did a residency here last fall. So, when Mr. Porter says he'll do for Julien what he did for Jesse, that's what he's talking about."

It still felt like there was a missing piece. Virginia asked, "And you think Ian found out about the scheme, and that's the motive for murder?" She couldn't see how it all fit together.

"Maybe," Marney said quietly, not sounding convinced. "Regardless, it's something we now have on Mr. Porter. He wants to take away funding for Breeze Village… Well, now we've got something that might be able to convince him otherwise."

CHAPTER 27

Hashim's office door was cracked, the sound of aggressive keystrokes loud enough for Virginia to pick up from the lobby on the other side of the door. He was working late. Virginia raised a fist to knock, looked behind her to where Patricia, Marney, and Ronald stood, urging her on, then lowered her arm and pushed the door open.

"Virginia, what—?"

"How well do you know Hugh Porter?" Virginia demanded, stepping into the office before the Breeze Village owner could order her out.

"What is this about?" Spittle flecked the desk in front of Hashim as he spoke.

Virginia felt her friends' presence as they closed in behind her, and she forced her shoulders back farther, making herself stand just a hair taller. "Hugh Porter," she repeated as steadily as she could. "The owner of the art gallery downtown and the reason Breeze Village is in financial jeopardy. How well do you know him?"

Hashim's swollen fingers dug into the wooden desk as he pushed himself up, leaning against it while he spoke. "I'd argue that *you* are the reason Breeze Village is in financial jeopardy, Ms. Walker, and I don't know why you think it's acceptable to barge into my office this way."

Virginia couldn't stop her eyes from flicking down toward her feet, her shoulders from slumping inward just slightly. Before she could respond, she felt the brush of gauzy fabric beside her as Patricia stepped forward. Hashim's head tilted back so he could look up at her face.

"Hugh Porter, President of the Board of Directors for the Seaview Community Promotion Foundation, is engaging in a scheme with the artists in residency at his gallery to artificially inflate the value of their works and line his own pockets." She produced a sheaf of papers and plunked them theatrically on the desk, keeping her eyes on Hashim the entire time. "What's in those papers should be enough to convince the rest of the board of his…" She cocked her head to the side, probing for the right word, "unsuitability for the position. And with his credibility in tatters, I would expect them to reverse their recent decision to revoke our grant."

The ire in his eyes was replaced with a glimmer of something like admiration as Hashim listened, rapt.

"Hugh Porter didn't give a rat's ass that someone was murdered in his gallery as long as he could keep the gallery's image intact." Virginia's voice shook, and she forced it out louder in an effort to steady the words. "Police had a suspect and weren't poking around anymore, so everything was fine and dandy for Hugh. But he can't have us old folks poking around, can he? We might actually draw attention to the gallery, and then things aren't so easily swept under the rug. And he certainly can't let the police zero in on one of his prized artists as a murder suspect; it would upend his entire scheme!"

If Mr. Porter had the sway to yank the financial floor out from under a retirement community, he had it in him to convince a few police officers that the artist they were looking for couldn't have been involved in anything untoward. He was the reason the police hadn't arrested Julien that day, Virginia knew, and he was going to pay for it now.

Hashim's hand was splayed out on top of the small stack of papers, his fingers spread wide and nearly covering the entire sheet. He took his eyes off Virginia to look down at the pages, sliding the stack closer to himself, then looked back up at the group in front of them.

"Who else have you shown this to?"

Virginia flinched. It wasn't the response she had expected. She'd expected a thanks, an apology, and an immediate move to take the pages to the foundation to get Breeze Village its funding back, followed by the police to bring in Mr. Porter, Julien, and anyone else involved in their scheme. Instead, Hashim seemed worried, almost frantic as he pulled the pages closer still to himself, finally gripping them in both hands and holding them to his front.

"No one," Virginia said softly, confused.

Hashim stepped out from behind the desk, moving toward the door and forcing the four out of his office. "Good, good," he muttered.

"So, are you going to go to—?"

The door slammed shut in their faces.

* * *

"WHAT THE HELL WAS THAT?" Ronald demanded the moment they were in Marney's cottage and out of earshot.

"That was weird, right?" Patricia asked.

Marney's face was grim. She hadn't spoken during the confrontation, and her eyes were unfocused now like she was deep in her own thoughts. Even Pancake's figure eights through her legs didn't earn him the usual scratches behind his ears.

"What are you thinking?" Virginia asked her.

The direct question seemed to bring Marney back to the present. She put on a pleasant smile, then leaned down to pet Pancake. "Oh, nothing. I guess I spaced out for a moment."

Virginia frowned at her. "Don't lie. Fill us in. What's going on beneath those gorgeous curls of yours?"

Marney let out a small sigh and said, "Mr. Odeh is a businessman. Not that he's a bad guy, but he didn't take over Breeze Village because his passion is ensuring the seniors of Seaview have a meaningful and enjoyable life in their final years. He took it over because he saw a business opportunity. A financial opportunity. And now... We presented him with a way to do something good, something right. He can go to the foundation right now, show them Mr. Porter is corrupt, and get Breeze Village our grant money so things can go back to the way they were before. But he might have seen a greater financial opportunity in what we showed him."

Virginia's stomach began sinking the moment Marney started talking, and it didn't stop. "What do you mean?" she asked, already dreading the answer.

Ronald finished for Marney. "He's going to blackmail Mr. Porter."

"Damn it!" Virginia slammed her fist down on the table. Marney flinched, and Virginia immediately regretted the outburst. She muttered an apology, pacing across the room to try and work on the frustration. "Every single time I think we have it—the magical key that will get someone to take us seriously, the final piece of the puzzle that will get my family out of this mess and a murderer off our streets—the universe laughs in my face."

Ronald picked up Pancake and bounced the little cat like a baby. "I once knew someone who spent five years in Los Angeles trying to make it as a stand-up comic. He did an entire thirty-minute set, and not a single person laughed. You've got the cosmic forces of the universe laughing—some might consider that a win."

"This isn't funny! My daughter's entire future is on the line here."

"Hashim's blackmailing Mr. Porter instead of taking things through the proper channels. That doesn't mean *we* can't take things through the proper channels," Patricia suggested. "We have all those scans in Lawrence's email. We can print more copies."

"That takes away all Hashim's leverage over Mr. Porter, spoiling his lucrative new side gig as a blackmailer," Virginia grumbled. "He'll evict us then, for sure. Even if Breeze Village gets all the funding it needs, he'll throw us out as a punishment."

"Not if everyone knows it was us who got Breeze Village its funding back," Marney said. "You did those interviews for the *Seaview Gazette* when you brought down Matt and Christine after Ruth's murder last year. People love celebrating when we old folks do something good. If the *Gazette* publishes an article saying a bunch of retirees brought down a crooked gallery owner and got him removed from his position on the board of a charitable foundation making decisions about where grant money goes, we'll be celebrated. Hashim couldn't kick us out. It would look terrible for him."

Ronald perked up at the idea, unconsciously smoothing his hair as if the newspaper interview were going to happen at any minute. But Patricia was still frowning.

"The way I see it," she said, "we've got two problems with Mr. Porter. Number one: he's threatening our home by getting our funding taken away. Hashim may or may not have that one figured out, through... duplicitous means, we'll say. But number two: he's protecting the prime suspect in our murder case, which puts Lucy at risk if we can't prove she didn't do it."

Virginia considered whether they could take a page out of Hashim's book. "What if we blackmail Mr. Porter, too? We'll tell him we'll expose him if he doesn't turn Julien over to the police. If Julien only goes down for the murder but not the fraudulent art sales, Hugh can sucker some other young artist into it to replace Julien. He can keep his reputation intact and his little scheme."

Ronald countered, "The second Julien's in custody, he'll tell the police anything he's got on Mr. Porter and that art gallery. Even if we didn't expose him, if he sends Julien to the jailhouse, Julien certainly will."

And Hugh's scheme with the artists was far from the only illicit activity going on behind those gallery doors. Did Mr. Porter know about the fake IDs and Lucy's brief-case exchanges with the now-dead Ian? Did Julien? If he was happy to engage with fake buyers to pump up the price of his art, what else was he willing to do? Could he be the one producing the fake IDs? How many shady side-businesses could Mr. Porter be running out of his gallery?

Motives and possibilities swirled in Virginia's mind, along with Dylan's comment when Virginia told her about Loretta and the fake IDs. She'd said how interested the police would be in whatever the man in the classic car could tell them about the operation. Virginia wondered if the police were digging further into that after what she'd told Dylan. Maybe it wasn't just Mr. Porter's influence keeping them at bay. Maybe they were holding off on doing anything to disrupt a bust, and that's why they hadn't brought Julien in.

"Whether or not he'd capitulate to our demands, we are not blackmailing Mr. Porter. It goes against our morals. We're good guys," Marney asserted.

Ronald frowned as if uncertain he wanted to be one of the good guys.

Virginia nodded. She wasn't proud of it, but she could use the reminder to pull her back. She was an investiga-tor, determined to dig until she found the truth, but she didn't need to lose sight of who she was at her core while she did it.

"We've given the police evidence," she said. "Julien's old essay and the threatening letter. The drink can from inside Lucy's car. But the way they see it, they've already got the killer. Lucy. Why do any more work trying to connect the dots and find a killer when they've already got a suspect awaiting trial?

"If we want the police to do anything more on this case, we've got to give them something they can't ignore. Not handwriting samples they have to analyze and compare. Not DNA samples they have to pay to send out to a lab for testing."

Patricia's mouth turned up at what was coming, but Marney finished the thought. "A confession," she said.

Virginia nodded. "Let's go see what Julien Reed has to say for himself."

CHAPTER 28

$\mathcal{I}$t took three days to formulate a plan and gather the necessary supplies before confronting Julien, and in that time, Mr. Odeh made no move to evict the foursome. The morning they planned to act, the four friends all gathered in Marney's cottage. Virginia glanced over to the corkboard of suspects and connections in the case and fiddled her hands in front of her. Pancake paced, the little cat seemingly attuned to the nervous energy in the room. When Ronald arrived, last, he laid eyes on Virginia and cried, "You're green!"

"I'm nervous," she muttered.

Marney stepped beside her and grabbed Virginia's hand. "It'll be okay." The words were soft but confident. "It's a good plan. And if it goes belly-up, we'll make a new one. In case you haven't noticed, it's kind of our thing now." She winked, and Virginia straightened slightly, feeling a trace less nauseated.

"It'll be okay," Virginia repeated, trying to make herself believe it.

Patricia, who had been standing off to the side and looking mildly uncomfortable, stepped forward with conviction. "It's time," she said, then patted Pancake on the head, waved to her friends, and slipped out of the cottage to initiate the first stage of their plan.

And that was it. No more waffling. They were on a clock.

Virginia turned to look at Ronald and saw his eyes sparkling with excitement. He grinned widely, his missing teeth on full display. Marney wrapped Virginia in a tight hug and held on as the seconds passed, then finally let go and stepped back, still holding onto Virginia's arms. She took a long look at her friend, then shoved Virginia and Ronald out into the chill morning.

Speeding downtown toward the art gallery, Virginia found herself looking from her watch to the car's clock to the road and back on a circuit until Ronald remarked that her incessantly checking the time was going to get them killed before they even had a chance to enact their plan and told her to keep her eyes on the road. For the rest of the drive, she ignored the almost physical pull of the clock against her eyes, and she breathed a sigh of relief when they neared the gallery right on schedule. She dropped Ronald off and circled the block until he called her phone.

"Mr. Porter's outta here!" he said in what might have been the world's loudest whisper. "Took off like a rocket with his phone pressed to his ear."

Virginia closed her eyes for a moment in appreciation. Marney and Patricia had done their part. Hugh Porter was out of the gallery. Now, it was up to her and Ronald to get Julien alone and get the truth out of him. And to get it on tape.

On Monday morning, the gallery was devoid of customers, and Mr. Porter's assistant was nowhere to be seen as the pair entered the gallery and made their way toward the front staircase. Breathing heavily, Ronald lagging behind as he lugged the heavy leather bag by his side, they climbed to the second floor, checked again for Gerald, the assistant, and then proceeded slowly up the final flight.

The top floor of the gallery was silent. The doors along the right side of the hallway to the artists' rooms and Mr. Porter's office were all shut. Sunlight spilled into the hallway through the open portal to the studio space on the left, and it felt warm and stuffy in the cramped upstairs even in February. With no sound coming from any of the rooms, Virginia couldn't tell whether Julien and his colleagues were in the studio or in their own rooms. She crept forward slowly, agonizingly slowly, and winced as the floor creaked beneath her weight.

"Which one is Julien's?" she hissed, looking back at Ronald and gesturing to the series of closed doors.

Ronald pointed to the second-to-last door, past the wide-open doorway to the studio. "That's where I found the earring."

Virginia winced at his attempt at a whisper. She whipped her head around and held her breath, expecting someone to pop out at any moment and discover them, dashing their plan, but no one did. She was nearly blue in the face from holding her breath before she let it out and took another step forward.

Ronald unzipped the leather bag he'd hauled to the top of the landing. From it, he pulled a green and gray swirled bowling ball, the lightest one Lawrence had. Virginia slipped down a few stairs and waited behind him out of sight, while Ronald lined the ball up and then gave it a shove, pushing it so that it rolled down the hallway and then down the back staircase, clattering wildly down the wooden stairs.

At the uproar, all three resident artists came rushing into the hallway just as Ronald and Virginia had hoped. The female painter, Mona, hurried out of the studio through the open doorway while Julien and the young potter burst out of their rooms.

"What the hell was that?" Julien demanded.

"I didn't see anything."

The three of them followed the sound, and the moment they reached the back stairwell with their backs to Ronald and Virginia, the two hurried down the hall and into Julien's room. They could hear the artists descending the stairwell, investigating the noise. Ronald tucked himself behind the door to lie in wait. Virginia sat on the tiny couch in front of the pristine coffee table, its tidiness a stark contrast to the bed in the corner of the room where the covers lay tangled and thrown halfway off the mattress.

Voices drifted up from downstairs.

"We have no idea!"

"It must have come from upstairs." Gerald sounded angry as he argued with the three residents.

"Yeah, instead of making art, we're up there tossing bowling balls down the stairs," they scoffed.

Footsteps indicated the artists were heading back upstairs. Ronald made himself as small as possible behind the open door. Virginia pulled out her phone and started recording, then set it beside her on the couch and placed her purse on top of it, concealing most of the phone while leaving the microphone exposed. She prayed Julien wouldn't spot it.

In the seconds remaining, she focused on calming her breathing, adopting the coolest exterior she could for the interrogation, though her hands shook in her lap. They didn't have to wait long before Julien returned to his room, muttering under his breath, then stopped dead at the sight of Virginia on his couch.

"Who the fuck are you?" Julien demanded, terror and surprise turning to anger as he registered Virginia's presence before him. He stepped inside quickly, moving toward Virginia until he towered over where she sat. "What are you doing in my room?"

Ronald stepped out from behind the door, shutting it behind Julien and closing them all inside. Julien whirled around at the reveal, looking from Ronald to the sealed door behind him.

"We're here to talk about Ian Anderlini," Virginia said, "and why you murdered him."

Julien spun back to Virginia, throwing his hands up in the air with his palms out in surrender. He started to back away but bumped into Ronald. When he turned around once more, Ronald wore a grin more threatening than Virginia guessed he could produce with so few teeth. Julien positioned himself sideways, his neck swiveling back and forth between the two of them, his complexion a ghastly white.

"We're not going to hurt you," she said, guilt building within her as the fear built in Julien before them.

"Much," Ronald amended. "Provided you tell us what we want to know."

"I'm not afraid of you." The tremor in Julien's voice suggested otherwise, and Ronald raised an eyebrow, challenging his assertion. Julien mustered a bit more force and said, "You can't be here."

"Tell us why you murdered Ian, and we'll be out of your hair," Ronald said.

"I didn't! I swear I didn't!"

Virginia's mouth was a tight line as she watched Julien, looking for some kind of tell but finding none.

"We know about your scheme with Mr. Porter," she said. Julien's eyes swelled immediately, and his mouth dropped open. "We have the letter where he promised to do for you what he did for Jesse Spencer. And we have a confession by Mr. Spencer outlining exactly what that entailed."

"Oh, and we have your letter in response where you profess how eager you were to get in on the action," Ronald added.

A look of shock came over Virginia before she could stop it. They had no such thing; promises by Mr. Porter, sure, but they only had the letters Julien had received, not his responses. They had no actual proof Julien had engaged in the scheme beyond Patricia's analysis of his sales history.

"That doesn't—that doesn't prove anything," Julien

stammered. His head was shaking back and forth as if on a swivel, and he'd backed himself up so that he was nearly pressed against the wall, still with Ronald on one side between him and the door and Virginia on the other.

Virginia forced herself to shrug and maintain an unbothered look as she said, "Maybe not. Whether the police buy into the theory that you killed Ian because you were having an affair with his wife—that's impossible to tell. But whether the art community thinks your work deserves a place on their walls, whether it's worth anything at all…"

"Whoa!" Julien's head shook faster, panic rising in him. "That's not—"

"If the art community finds out what you've done here, your career is over," Ronald said coolly. "And we'll make sure that's exactly what happens if you don't tell us the truth."

Julien looked from him back to Virginia and pleaded, "I didn't kill anyone. I don't know what to tell you." He dove for a chair covered in clothes, then rifled through the pockets of a coat from the pile. "Look! I wasn't even here when that guy was murdered." He held up a tiny slip of paper, and Ronald snatched it from his fingers.

Ronald frowned, then handed the paper to Virginia. It was a ticket stub from a movie theater.

"I went to the movies, and when I got back, the whole place was covered in yellow tape and cops were all over. I wasn't even here when he was killed! I couldn't have done it," Julien repeated.

Virginia's shoulders sagged, the weight suddenly too much as another lead slipped from her grasp. Ronald lifted an eyebrow and said, "Well, that doesn't help us much, does it? See, we're trying to figure out who laid out Mr. Anderlini downstairs. We were pretty sure it was you —you've got a strong motive, what with screwing the dead guy's wife, and threatening to burn down a retirement home over the investigation certainly didn't make you look better."

At the mention of the threat against Breeze Village, Julien's jaw swung wide.

"Yeah, we know about that," Ronald said. An icy chill ran underneath his words, and Virginia had never seen him look so vicious.

Julien staggered back, hands up in surrender. He stammered, "Look, I—I—I showed you the ticket stub. I wasn't here!"

Ronald cleared his throat and repeated, "Like I said, that doesn't help us very much. Why should we keep your secrets if you can't tell us what we need?" He raised his eyes in challenge, and Julien seemed to crumple.

"Don't expose me, please. This thing with the fake buyers, it's not supposed to be forever. Just a few pieces— to get my name out there in the art world, make people take me seriously. My art *is* good!" He stamped his foot, a flush of color creeping up his neck. "But people don't take new artists seriously if someone doesn't set the precedent. 'What a little rising star,' they all croon, but then balk at actually shelling out good money for that rising star's painting." Julien's face contorted in a sneer, and he met Ronald's eyes as he went on. "Then one well-regarded curator says the painting's worth featuring at his gallery in New York. One collector says he'll buy it for five figures. And the art world is clamoring to buy up that rising star's work at ten times what they wanted to pay earlier."

Ronald maintained a cool, unimpressed visage throughout Julien's tirade. "Just because these art buyers have more money than sense, you're happy to defraud them. We get it. And if you don't have anything else to give us regarding the dead guy downstairs, the whole art world will get it, too."

Julien turned his eyes to Virginia, looking for forgiveness or mercy on her face. She schooled it into a hard expression matching Ronald's as best she could, then waited.

Finally, Julien cracked.

"I really wasn't here that afternoon. But..." As he trailed off, Julien's eyes went to his feet. He paused, then took a deep breath, threw his shoulders back, and lifted his head to say, "I know who did it." Virginia found herself holding her breath, waiting for him to go on. "It's why I sent you that letter—to keep her safe, because I'm in love with her."

No.

"It was his wife, Loretta. Loretta killed her husband," Julien whispered, the statement tinged with sorrow and disbelief.

CHAPTER 29

Virginia sank deeper into the small couch, dizzy.

"She didn't," she insisted, head shaking as she gripped the upholstery beneath her. "I already talked to her."

Julien, seeming to relax after his reveal, more secure that Ronald and Virginia wouldn't air his secrets now that he'd given them something big, grabbed the wooden desk chair and tossed the clothes draped over the back onto the floor. He spun it around and took a seat facing Virginia, one ankle crossed over the opposite knee, and leaned back. "I know you did."

While Virginia reeled, mind swimming with confusion, Ronald stepped forward and grabbed Julian's shoulders, spinning the chair with him in it. With his hands still on Julien's shoulders, Ronald leaned in until his face was inches from Julien's. The young artist leaned back, trying in vain to put some space between himself and the toothless octogenarian staring him down.

"Explain," Ronald commanded.

Julien's throat bobbed as he swallowed, then finally nodded.

"I was dating Loretta, but I would have *never*..." He trailed off without saying it. Instead, he shook his head as if to push the thoughts of killing Ian out. "Loretta came by at the beginning of that week and told me—she told me she couldn't see me anymore." Julien's voice broke and he swallowed again. "She said it was over. I protested because what we have is real, and she knows it! She told me she didn't want to end it, but she couldn't come to the gallery anymore. At first, I accepted it, but then when that man was killed... I didn't realize the connection until I heard his name, and I realized she'd only broken it off with me because she was going to..."

A green sheen crept over Julien's face as he worked to get the words out. He turned and fixed his gaze on the wall instead of Virginia or Lawrence, his eyes unfocused as he spoke. "I knew her husband came around the gallery for business. It's how she and I met. She followed him when he wouldn't tell her about his business dealings, found herself at the gallery, and the moment we saw each other, we just knew. It was true love. Once-in-a-lifetime, lightning strike, can't-explain-it true love."

"She clearly didn't feel the same way, if she ended the affair."

Julien narrowed his eyes, a viper-like expression on his face as he turned on Ronald. "I told you, she only broke up with me because of what she was about to do."

Ronald removed his hands from Julien's shoulders but stepped back only an inch. "Have you spoken to her since the murder?"

"No. Well, just the one time. I started calling her after her husband's death. I wanted to check in on her and let her know I still loved her and always would. I left messages. She never answered. But then once, a couple of weeks ago, she answered and just started screaming at me. She told me about an old lady who came around accusing her of murder—that would be you—and that she was under a lot of stress so I needed to give her space while she dealt with it. I thought I could help her by getting you off her back."

"You thought that since your girlfriend killed her husband, why don't you double down on that and burn down an entire retirement community?" Virginia spat.

The venom was gone from Julien's voice, replaced with a childlike nescience. "I wouldn't have actually burned the place down. I just needed you to think I would so you'd back off."

"So your girlfriend wouldn't go to jail for murder?" Ronald grilled.

"So she could have time to heal without being harassed!"

"I'm sorry," Virginia said, pushing herself up from the sofa, "but if Loretta's *healing* comes at the expense of my daughter's freedom, she can go to hell. Or jail. I don't really care."

Genuine confusion twisted Julien's face. "What does your daughter have to do with this?"

Ronald backed away as Virginia closed in on Julien. "My daughter," she snarled, "is the police's prime suspect in this murder case." Julien's eyes went round, and his mouth dropped open, but Virginia continued. "And someone—presumably the same someone who killed Ian —tried to kill her by sabotaging her car."

Julien shook his head, the motion growing more fervent with each cycle. "I don't know anything about that." The words came quickly, tumbling out of his mouth while he continued to shake his head and lean farther back in the chair, moving away from Virginia pressing in.

Before she could say anything more, Ronald cut in. "You seem pretty sure your girlfriend killed her husband, but, as you know, Virginia already paid Loretta a visit. And Loretta had an alibi."

He locked eyes with Virginia, bringing her mind back to the present. She nodded, then turned back to Julien and relayed the story Loretta had given. "She was at home with a friend. They had a spa day and painted each other's nails." As she spoke, Julien's brows furrowed.

"Loretta's never once done her nails at home. She goes to Nail Envy every third Thursday. She's not really an 'at home spa day' kind of woman. She goes to the actual spa."

Virginia turned back to Ronald, searching his face for some clue as to what to do now. She'd completely dropped Loretta as a suspect, taking her at her word when she'd spun her story. How much time had they lost?

"I don't know anything about your daughter, though," Julien said. "Loretta's never mentioned anything."

Ronald extended a hand toward the man, and Julien looked at it like it might burn him if he gripped it. "You've been a help to us today," Ronald said. "We can't stay much longer, but I have a proposition for you. You answer any other questions we might have. You help us bring Loretta down and keep Virginia's daughter out of prison for this crime she didn't commit. And in return, we burn any evidence we have of your little scheme with Mr. Porter. We keep your name clean and your career as an artist intact."

Julien still didn't take Ronald's hand. Instead, he gulped, looking up at Ronald with pleading eyes. Finally, he choked out, "But I love her."

Just then, the walls of the gallery building shook as the front door slammed, and a roar sounded from downstairs. Hugh Porter was back, and he wasn't happy.

Ronald scoffed at Julien. "That's our cue to sneak out the back."

Leaving Julien white-faced in his chair, unable to choose between saving his career and saving a killer he'd fallen in love with, Ronald and Virginia slipped out of the small room. They hurried down the back staircase and out the side door into the alley.

* * *

WHEN VIRGINIA and Ronald burst into Marney's cottage, they found Patricia's arms wrapped in bandages and Marney's eyes glued to an unfamiliar phone buzzing incessantly on the dining table.

"What the hell happened to you?" Ronald demanded, charging toward Patricia, who smelled vaguely of maple syrup.

She waved him off. "I had to really make a show to make sure Hashim left his office."

"She body-slammed the breakfast buffet," Marney clarified, a smirk breaking out across her face even as her eyes remained on the phone. "You could have had a career in professional wrestling, you know."

Patricia's answering smile danced. She recounted the way she'd pretended to get dizzy, gripped the table where the food was laid out, and then, in her words, "sealed the deal by passing out."

Marney shook her head. "I've never seen someone leap into a loss of consciousness like that. She got six inches of air, hollering that she felt lightheaded, then crashed down and took the table out with her. I just wish I could have seen the aftermath. As soon as Hashim came rushing out of his office to see what was the matter, I slipped in and grabbed *that*." She pointed to the phone, which buzzed again as if in response.

"Nurse Kim tried to call an ambulance to rush me to the emergency room," Patricia said. "I recovered my faculties awfully quick after that, but I had a few burns from where I landed in the scrambled eggs."

Virginia was focused on Marney, who pointed to the strange phone and said, "Hashim made a call five minutes after we confronted him with the letters from Mr. Porter to Julien. I figured that call was probably to Mr. Porter, so I texted that number and asked to meet immediately."

"It worked," Ronald said. "When we got to the gallery, he was racing out of there like a bat out of hell."

"He wasn't happy when he got back, either," Virginia added.

Marney nodded, unsurprised. "He's been calling back nonstop, presumably trying to figure out why Hashim demanded they meet across town, then stood him up."

Patricia looked from Virginia to Ronald. "Was it worth

it? Did you get anything good out of Julien? Did you remember to record?"

Virginia pulled her own phone from her purse and set it on the table next to Hashim's. "I recorded. Let's hope it turned out." She pressed play and waited. There was some unintelligible background noise followed by a very clear, "Who the fuck are you?"

Marney's eyebrows shot up, surprised, and Virginia stopped playing the recording.

"It sounds like he wasn't thrilled to see you two," Patricia said.

"But he was happy enough to talk, once we gave him the right incentive." Ronald's lips curled into the same threatening smile Virginia had seen him wield on Julien.

"And?" Patricia prodded, practically vibrating with impatience.

"And he's pretty sure Loretta killed her husband," Virginia said.

She played the rest of the recording.

When it ended, cutting off in the middle of Ronald giggling as they ran out the side door, Virginia muttered, "I feel like a fool. I just took her at her word."

Ronald curled a hand into a fist and shook it in the air. "The moment I see this lying woman, I'm body-slamming her like Patricia did to those eggs." The others laughed, but their response only seemed to bolden Ronald. "What are we waiting for? We know where she lives."

Three pairs of eyes turned on Virginia, waiting for her signal. She only stuttered. Her stomach was grumbling, and her muscles ached. They'd already confronted one suspect today, and she was tired. The thought of putting on a cool, threatening demeanor to try to get another confession out of someone sounded like more than she had in her to give.

"Should we call the police?" she asked. "Give them this recording?"

The eyes all turned to Marney, since she'd historically been the one steering them toward the police and away from their own independent investigation. Instead, Marney shrugged.

"We can give them a recording of someone saying they're pretty sure this woman killed her husband. Or we can go ambush her and see if we can get the confession we thought we were getting from Julien. That seems a lot more likely to get us what we want."

Lucy's name cleared. Virginia's family reunited. That was what they wanted.

Virginia's stomach grumbled again, and her eyes went involuntarily to the couch. Her legs were begging for her to sit down, but she knew that if she did, she wasn't getting up again any time soon.

Marney was right. All they had right now was a third party saying he believed Loretta was a killer. Julien might have obliterated Loretta's alibi, but he hadn't given them any evidence. All Virginia and her friends had on Loretta were theories. Suspicions. Evidence that she was a crummy and disloyal wife, sure. But no evidence that she was a murderer.

Not like the police had on Lucy.

Virginia knew she had to trust. Trust that her daughter had been telling the truth that she didn't murder that man. Trust that if they followed the leads, they'd get the proof they needed to convince the police of the same.

Ignoring the protests of her body, Virginia turned toward the door. "Let's go."

* * *

PATRICIA DROVE, the other three clinging to their seats for dear life. She'd peeled out of the parking lot while Virginia was still fumbling for her seatbelt. In the mirror, she could see Marney in the seat behind her, gripping the handle above the door with white knuckles.

"Don't kill us before I can body-slam that murderous Jezebel!" Ronald cried. The proclamation, combined with the adrenaline, sent Virginia into frenzied laughter.

The foursome sped across town toward Loretta's—and Lucy's—apartment complex. Patricia wound through the streets like a maniac, with Marney whispering expletives and Ronald whooping every time she took a particularly tight corner. They reached the complex in record time, pulling into the parking lot on literal screeching tires.

"Did you have a secret career as a stunt driver?" Marney asked, her face faintly green.

"There she is!" Ronald cried before Patricia could respond.

Sure enough, Loretta was plainly visible across the parking lot, staring at them as she craned her neck to see the ruckus. Virginia's breath froze in her throat as she waited for Loretta to recognize them, but the dark-haired beauty looked away, seemingly unconcerned, and climbed into a beautiful silver-blue sports car. She pulled out of the spot, and Virginia rushed Patricia to *move, move, move!* before Loretta got close enough to make out their identities.

Obediently, Patricia slammed on the gas once more. She headed for the opposite end of the lot from Loretta, saying, "What do I do? What do I do?" Ronald and Virginia swiveled their heads, tracking Loretta's car, and Marney looked increasingly like she might vomit.

"Follow her!" Ronald ordered, and Patricia did.

Forced to hang back and drive at a reasonable speed, Patricia tailed Loretta as they moved farther outside of town. The color had fully returned to Marney's face by the time Loretta pulled into a nearly empty parking lot behind a bar called Rusty's Tavern in a neighborhood Virginia had never visited despite living in Seaview her entire life.

"Now what?" Patricia whispered. She'd kept driving past the lot instead of pulling in, trying to keep from being spotted, and was now inching forward while the others turned in their seats and watched Loretta climb out of her car and enter the bar.

"Now I body-slam her!" Ronald said. "Park and let me out!"

"If I recall correctly, you've already body-slammed Loretta. I had to cut a date short and pick you up from jail because of it."

Ronald shook his head. "That time doesn't count. Ray's the one who actually body-slammed her. I only body-slammed him. It was a dog-pile situation. She was already on the ground when I jumped on 'em."

"If you walk in there and body-slam someone, the

bartender is going to throw you out, and us along with you. There goes our chance at getting a recorded confession," Marney said. "We have to play it cool."

Patricia circled the block and pulled up in front of the bar. They agreed she'd wait outside and keep the car running, ready to make a getaway like something out of a movie. As the other three approached the bar, Marney and Virginia kept a hand on Ronald, gripping the flesh of his arms to keep him from running at Loretta the second they saw her.

But it wasn't Ronald they needed to worry about.

As soon as she spotted Loretta, Virginia dropped her hand and ran toward her, lifting her cane like a bat. Because Loretta was sitting at the bar, a glass of dark liquor in front of her, but she wasn't sitting alone.

Perched on the stool next to her, sipping from his own glass, was a man Virginia had only seen in a photograph but who she recognized immediately.

Seated next to Loretta was Dax.

CHAPTER 30

They didn't get hurled out of the bar for the beating Virginia gave Dax with her cane. Mostly because she only got one good blow in before he tossed her, Marney, and Ronald on their asses himself, and the bartender nodded at them all, considering the matter settled.

"You cheating scumbag!" Virginia cried, trying to push herself up from the floor. She had to roll over onto her stomach and then get on all fours before she could pull herself up to standing, and it was only the anger flowing through her that kept her from feeling embarrassed when she saw Dax's smirk. She raised her cane to hit him again, but his arm shot out faster than she could have anticipated, yanking it from her hand and throwing her off balance. She swayed and fell forward, landing against the bar next to Loretta. The impact rang through her forearms, and she cried out again. Loretta turned and looked at her with a raised eyebrow.

"This isn't the kind of place I'd expect to run into you,"

she said, eyeing up Virginia and her friends. She might still be drinking in the daytime, but she didn't seem one bit the mess she'd been when Virginia had gone to her apartment. Instead, she seemed cool and collected, confident and powerful, and absolutely unafraid of Virginia and her friends.

Ronald ground his jaw but held himself back, evidently not in the mood to be thrown to the ground again.

"You know these geezers?" Dax demanded, whirling toward Loretta.

She downed the remainder of her drink, slid the glass across the bar along with a few dollar bills, and turned to face them. "I do." She pointed to Ronald. "That one and his friend have already been arrested for assaulting me once. That one" — she pointed to Virginia — "is Lucy's mother." The dim lighting made it hard to tell, but Virginia swore Dax's smirk faded, his expression turning somber. Loretta pointed to Marney last. "That one's new."

Marney held out a hand. "Marney Richards. Pleasure to meet you."

While Ronald beamed at Marney, Virginia turned on Dax, practically snarling. "You dragged my daughter into this mess. You sent her into that art gallery with briefcases full of who-knows-what. And then *she*" — Virginia spun and jabbed a finger at Loretta —"murdered her husband, and my Lucy is going down for it because she was there. Because you sent her there."

With exaggerated amusement, Dax turned to Loretta and lifted an eyebrow. "You got so sick of Ian's slovenly habits and inedible cooking you finally took him out?"

Loretta didn't smile at the joke. She kept her gaze on Virginia and said coldly, "No. I didn't."

"Well, that settles that," Dax said with a shrug at the same moment Ronald shouted, "That's not true!"

Ronald surged forward a half step before Dax puffed his chest, and Ronald backed down. Feebly, he said, "She was cheating on her husband with one of the artists at the gallery."

Loretta's stony face crumbled just a fraction, and her eyes cut over to Dax. He frowned, his too-cool-for-everything demeanor slipping. Something akin to hurt flashed in his eyes, and he nodded slightly. "Ian suspected you were cheating," he said softly.

"I know," Loretta said. Sincere remorse flowed beneath the admission. Although she'd told Virginia that what she'd had with Julien was real love, that it wasn't just a fling like she'd had with the classic car enthusiast she'd blackmailed into helping her, the regret at the pain she'd caused her husband was tangible.

"So, she killed him before he could confront her," Ronald accused, unmoved by her sadness. "Now that he's dead, you don't have to split everything in a messy divorce! You can run off with the artist and keep it all for yourself."

Loretta scoffed, and Dax said, "Clearly, we have a few things to sort out. I propose we do so over another drink, preferably in a booth and with less yelling. The bartender here is a friend, but he won't be for much longer if we drive off all his customers." He nodded across the room toward a large booth in a corner, far away from where the other mid-afternoon drinkers occupied stools at the bar mere feet from where they now stood. The others were all blatantly watching the argument unfold, not hiding their interest.

Marney smiled. "Oh, please. We're the best entertainment this joint has ever seen. But I won't say no to sitting down. Or to a whiskey." She started to lead the group across the room, then turned back to add, "Neat."

Virginia and Ronald made eye contact while they scurried after their friend across the room. Loretta followed reluctantly, looking like she'd rather walk barefoot across hot coals, while Dax flagged down the bartender to order their drinks.

"I've told you," Loretta said, sliding into the booth, "I didn't kill my husband."

"We don't believe you." Ronald grunted as he maneuvered himself sideways across the torn plastic upholstered bench.

"Neither does Julien," Virginia said. "In fact, he's pretty certain you did it. He blew a hole right through the *at-home manicure and spa day* alibi you gave us."

A cold laugh erupted from Loretta. She held up a hand and wiggled her fingers, bright red claws extending from each digit. "You caught me. I wasn't doing my own nails with my friend when Ian was killed."

The three friends all stared at Loretta, waiting. Virginia realized she'd never started recording the conversation after they'd walked in, and she reached into her bag, searching for her phone.

Loretta's eyes almost sparkled as she continued. "If you want a better alibi—an actual alibi someone could corroborate..." She looked over Virginia's shoulder back toward the bar, chuckled, and continued, "I was here when Ian was killed."

Virginia frowned. "Why?"

"Does it matter?" Loretta challenged.

"Why should we believe you?" Ronald demanded.

"Ask the bartender. He'll tell you I was here."

"For all we know, you paid him to say that."

Loretta shrugged. "I can't make you believe me. But that guy" — she fingered a man in a torn wool cap who had fully spun around on his barstool to watch the group — "was here, too, so there's another witness. And so was Dax."

Virginia's brows shot up, and Loretta laughed, satisfied with the reaction she provoked.

"That's right," Loretta said. "I was here with Dax. I guess that rules him out, too, before you try to head down that rabbit hole."

Virginia only gaped. Ronald spun back toward the bar, demanding they talk to Dax.

"Too bad he snuck out after sending us over here," Loretta said.

Ronald was hoisting himself out of the booth, not believing that Dax had vanished. Virginia turned and took one look toward the bar and saw that he was gone, knowing immediately that Loretta was telling the truth. Dax wasn't someone who stuck around to answer questions, it seemed.

"Where did he go?" Marney asked.

"Back underground, I'd guess." At the others' confusion, Loretta said, "He didn't kill my husband. Besides the fact that he was here with me when it happened, Dax is terrified that he's next."

"Tell us what you know," Marney demanded. She was in her element, entirely authoritative, and Virginia wished she'd brought Marney to any of her prior interrogations.

After a moment's consideration, Loretta nodded in agreement. "First, turn off that recording." She gestured to Virginia's lap, where she'd been fumbling with her phone. Virginia's face flushed, and she laid the device on the table, face up.

"Dax's theory is that whoever killed Ian is coming for him next. He got a voicemail from Lucy after she found Ian dead at the gallery, and then, from what he's told me, I don't even know if he stopped back at his apartment before running. He said he had a cousin get his things for him and sort things out here. He's convinced their boss is the one who took out Ian, and that he's cleaning house."

Cousin Charlie. The man Marney had intercepted when she'd followed Lucy to Dax's apartment.

"Cleaning house?" Virginia asked.

"Why'd he come back now?" Marney wanted to know.

Loretta turned to Marney first. "He came back to town to try and convince Lucy to go with him into hiding."

All the blood left Virginia's face. Her ears began ringing, and she gripped the table's edge to keep her hands from shaking. Lucy had seen Dax, and she hadn't called Virginia.

Loretta met her eyes and said, "Lucy turned him down. He's distraught."

Distraught? He certainly didn't seem it, all swaggering and cool on the surface.

"You know about the briefcases," Loretta went on. "But that's not all orchestrated by Dax and Ian. They're part of a larger…"

"Gang?"

"Group of people with creative ideas for making money," Loretta countered. "Look, I might have been married to Ian, but he kept a lot of stuff close to his chest. Didn't want me involved. Didn't want me knowing too much about what he was involved in. For my own safety, or his ego because it felt good to have secrets, I don't know. Regardless of the motive behind his secrecy, I don't know the specifics. I didn't even know his work had him at the art gallery until I followed him one day."

"That's how you met Julien," Virginia prompted.

A faraway look clouded Loretta's eyes, and she wiped at the corner as she nodded. "Ian slipped away into some room where I couldn't see him. But then Julien was just standing there. We got to talking, and things… Well, that's not the point. Ian came out, I hid, and then he left with a bag he hadn't gone in with. Instead of following him out, I marched into the room he'd come out of and found myself face-to-face with some teenager."

"Gerald?"

Loretta shrugged. "Could be. I didn't care much about his name—only about the business he was doing with Ian. See, I was tired of being paraded around at parties with their—what should we call them?—business associates, but not being privy to any of the information, and depending on Ian for an allowance. I saw the scared look on that kid's face, and I knew I had an opportunity. I told him I knew what he was up to and that I wanted in."

"But you just said you didn't know what they were doing."

"How far do you think admitting that was going to get me? Thinking he was caught out, the kid led me down to where he had a secret setup in the basement, shoved in between a bunch of pipes and old crates for transporting paintings. He was printing money down there."

Virginia had a thousand questions she wanted answered, but Ronald only had one. "There's a basement? How'd they keep that thing from flooding this close to the ocean?"

Loretta laughed and tossed off a remark about how loaded the family who'd originally built the house had been, but Ronald's brow stayed creased as he considered the feat of engineering.

"So, Ian was collecting the counterfeit money the gallery assistant was printing downstairs?" Marney asked.

Loretta's head dipped in a nod and looked back toward the bar with a scowl. "The least that bastard could do before slipping out would be to actually buy us the drinks he promised." She twisted her fingers together in front of her and said, "Whoever owns Ian and Dax also owns that poor kid. Probably got him installed at the gallery so he could print for the group. Then Ian goes and gets the money from the gallery and distributes it to the washers. Dax is one of the people working for Ian. Ian passes Dax his cut, then Dax launders it and brings back clean cash the next week.

"I didn't want any part in that, though. So, I convinced the kid to go into the business of printing fake IDs for me instead." Loretta smirked, and Virginia pictured Gerald, the young boy on the wrong path now in Loretta's clutches. "Everything was great until I got sloppy. After making one of my pickups, I stayed at the gallery too late with Julien, and Ian spotted me. Instead of grabbing the fake bills and getting out, he started lingering at the gallery. Switched to giving Dax his cut there so he could hand around longer. Anything he could do to try and catch me out. He figured I was having an affair but didn't know there was anything else afoot. He'd be mad if he caught me cheating, but he'd be livid if he knew I was encroaching on his line of work. So, I went out, picked up a man, and got the leverage on him I needed to get him to make the pickups for me."

"The man from the car show," Marney whispered. Virginia nodded.

"I had my own money then, so things got easier at home. Ian and I weren't arguing so much. I didn't care as much about what he was doing, going off for work and keeping me in the dark, since I had my own thing going."

"You thought you could fix things with your husband?" Virginia recalled the way Loretta had told her about ending her affair with Julien, the timing tragic.

Loretta nodded. "I broke things off with Jules. But then Ian died."

"While you were here with Dax."

Loretta nodded. "I was here trying to get Dax to partner with me, actually. He'd been trying to get their bosses to trust him more. He was always at a lower level than Ian, stuck laundering money through some carpentry business that was destroying his body instead of using his brain. I wanted to expand, and I had more to offer Dax than he was getting with Bianca's late dad's crew."

Bianca. Virginia remembered Lucy telling her how Dax had worked with her father.

"You're friends with Bianca," she said slowly. The picture of Loretta and Bianca at the beach flashed in her mind.

"Dax and Ian got close, working together. Dax was like Ian, keeping his work to himself. B and I bonded over it. We became friends through our husbands."

Out of the corner of her eye, Virginia saw that Marney had pulled out a small notebook and was taking notes, but Loretta didn't seem to care.

"So, when your husband was killed, you were here with Dax, trying to get him to leave his current gangster employer and work for you instead. Then what?" Marney prodded.

Loretta chuckled at the description. "Dax turned me down. We left the bar, went our separate ways, and then the next thing I knew, Dax was calling me, frantic, telling me Ian was dead and not to go near the gallery. Then he was gone. I hadn't heard from him until an unknown number texted me today telling me to come here."

"Why is he afraid?" Ronald asked, rejoining the conversation. "Why would their boss want Ian and Dax dead?"

Loretta shrugged. "Specifically? I have no idea. But from the tales I've overheard at the parties Ian dragged me to… Look, the people Ian and Dax are working for are not good people. It doesn't take much for them to feel threatened or offended, and they don't tolerate people who threaten or offend them."

Marney was following a different train of thought and asked, "Who else knows about Gerald and the money laundering? The gallery owner?"

"No. Gerald says he's too preoccupied with his own shady business to look twice at what his assistant is doing, as long as Gerald keeps his nose down." Loretta put her hands on the table, pushing herself up. "Now, I think I've told you enough to get you to leave me alone from here on out."

Virginia forced her head to bob in agreement, though she hardly registered what Loretta was saying. Her mind was still trying to fit the pieces together, but one piece just didn't fit.

The belt.

"Wait," she said abruptly. Loretta turned back, looking impatient. It was a long shot, but Loretta had already given them so much. Maybe she could give them this final piece. "Ian was strangled with a belt," Virginia said.

Instantly, Loretta was seated again, leaning across the table. "The police didn't tell me," she whispered. "Strangled, was all they said. They didn't give me any details."

With shaking, sweaty hands, Virginia pulled out her phone and brought up a picture from the previous Easter. Lucy and Jack posed in front of an azalea bush, smiling politely for the camera. The picture had been taken just before the family lunch that had gone horribly wrong when Jack brought up moving Virginia into an assisted living facility and Virginia caused a scene. Lucy was wearing a pale pink dress with a thin, braided white leather belt wrapped around her waist. She placed the phone on the table and spun it to face Loretta. She pointed at Lucy. "A belt like that."

Though she didn't look away from Loretta's face, she could feel Marney's and Ronald's faces turning toward her, could imagine the shock across those faces. The betrayal as Virginia revealed yet another secret she'd been keeping from them. Her gut twisted with the guilt, but she kept her focus on Loretta's face, which lit up in recognition.

"A belt like that?" Loretta asked. "Or that belt?"

"Are any of the shady criminals Ian and Dax work for women? Maybe one of them has a belt like that."

Loretta stared at Virginia, refusing to say anything while Virginia squirmed under her gaze. Unable to take it, Virginia blurted, "The police think my Lucy killed your husband because she said the belt was hers at the scene. But if it's not hers, if it belongs to someone else and she just thought—"

"It's hers," Loretta whispered.

Virginia shook her head in defiance, her eyes burning with tears.

"It was her belt, but I didn't know." Loretta's voice was still low, as if she were working the situation out in her head as she spoke. "I thought... I took that belt out of Dax's car. I figured it was Bianca's—his wife's. But it must have been Lucy's."

Loretta's forehead was creased with concern. Virginia leaned in, practically laying on top of the table as she willed Loretta to continue, to explain, to make it make sense.

"I wore it out for a date with Ian. It sat in my apartment for a while after that. I haven't seen it in weeks. Not since…" Loretta's normally beautiful complexion turned chalky, and she looked up at Virginia, the concern on her face now horror. "I think Bianca took it from my apartment when she stayed over after a New Year's Eve party."

Virginia's voice was hoarse as she rasped, "Where is Bianca?"

CHAPTER 31

*L*oretta hadn't spoken to Bianca in nearly a week. They'd fought over something petty—whether Bianca looked ugly in one of the photos Loretta posted to her social media in tribute to Ian—and Bianca was icing her out since Loretta wouldn't take the post down. As Loretta explained the fight to Virginia, it was all Virginia could do not to scream. She finally had an explanation. Some way Lucy's belt could have been the murder weapon without Lucy being the murderer. And now, when every cell making up her body itched to chase Bianca down and throttle her with that very belt, the one person who should be able to lead them there—Bianca's best friend—was instead prattling on about social media filters.

When she couldn't take it anymore, Virginia slammed her hands on the table and demanded, "But where *is* she?" Loretta jumped. Virginia pressed harder. "It doesn't matter if you're fighting. You're her best friend. You know where she lives. Take us there, now!"

Loretta dragged herself back up out of the booth and swayed on the spot, muttering, "But she couldn't have… She wouldn't…"

And then she bolted.

Loretta took off at a sprint, straight out of the bar. The three friends weren't even all out of the booth and on their feet when they heard the rev of her silver-blue sports car flying by.

"What happened?" Patricia asked when they climbed back into her car.

"Go after her!" Ronald shouted at the same time as Virginia said, "Can you take us home?"

The other three all looked at Virginia, perplexed. As if in answer, her stomach rumbled loudly.

"I'm hungry," she said. "I've done two interrogations today, one of which got me thrown to the ground by my daughter's boyfriend—"

"Dax was there?" Patricia, now pulling away from the curb, cursed herself for missing all the action inside Rusty's Tavern.

"I don't have it in me to go after her today," Virginia continued. She hardly had it in her to keep her eyes open on the drive.

"If she gets to Bianca first, what's to stop Bianca from running?" Ronald asked.

"You think she'll let her best friend get away with killing her husband?" Marney asked.

Patricia turned her head to look back at Ronald and Marney, eyes popping out of her head. "How much did I miss?"

They filled her in on the drive back to Breeze Village,

interrupted only by a stop at a fast-food drive-thru for sustenance. Though her stomach was no longer growling when they made it home, Virginia felt shattered. She leaned heavily on her cane with every step, her feet shuffling forward only inches at a time. "I'm going upstairs for a nap," she muttered.

Marney grabbed Virginia's hand before she crossed the courtyard to her cottage. "We'll find her. We found Loretta. Hell, we even found Dax."

"Not on purpose. And then he got away."

"We'll find her," Marney repeated, and then the elevator arrived, and Marney turned away.

Virginia awoke in near darkness nearly four hours later to her phone alarm reminding her to leave for ASL class. She turned off the alarm and rolled over, but she couldn't fall back asleep. Her mind had kicked on, and all it could think about was how to find Bianca. The minutes ticked on. As six o'clock approached, footsteps grew more prominent in the hallway as the residents of Breeze Village made their way down to the dining room for dinner. Virginia pulled a pillow over her head to stifle the noise, but it didn't stifle her thoughts. Finally, she gave up.

The dining room was packed, but none of her friends were inside. Awkwardly looking around from the doorway, Virginia spotted Colleen. She hesitated, trying to decide whether to go talk to her or not. Colleen had found people for Virginia before—maybe she could find Bianca now.

But she waited too long to approach her, and then Colleen was gone in a swish of billowing robes.

Suddenly, the noise from the dining room felt like too

much. Virginia's pulse was rising in her ears, and without realizing what was happening, she found herself hurrying across the lobby and out into the evening air. Apart from the birds and some road noise, it was quiet. Virginia felt herself beginning to relax again.

Her phone beeped.

BILL LEVAL

Coming to class tonight?

Can't. Busy day. Not feeling up to it. She erased the last sentence, cringing, then erased the whole thing. *Not tonight, but I'll see you Wednesday?* She stared down at the message for a long time, trying to decide whether to send it. The tiny kernel of hope inside her that maybe she could repair things with Bill urged her to go. Yes, he'd ended whatever it was they'd been starting. But he was reaching out to her again. Maybe it didn't have to be over.

She deleted the second message with a glance at the time. She could still make it, just barely, if she left right away. *Running late but yes!* She hit send before she could talk herself out of it.

VIRGINIA SLIPPED through the doors in the back of the lecture hall moments after class began. Bill's silver-streaked hair caught her eye immediately, about halfway down the room and one seat in from the aisle. It would have been easy enough to move quietly down the aisle and slide into the open seat on the end without disturbing anyone, and part of her yearned to do that, but the uncertainty was too much amid everything else going on.

Instead, she took a seat in the back. She had to slide past one person to get to an open seat and nearly fell over doing so. She let out a tiny yelp as she grabbed onto the table, saving herself from falling. To her horror, everyone in class except the Deaf professor turned to see the source of the commotion, and then the professor looked up to see what had captured the entire class's attention.

Amid all those eyes, one ice-blue pair caught her own, and her face turned beet red not under the gazes of all her other classmates, but under Bill's.

For the first half of class, Virginia stumbled through the exercises with her partner, the student she'd nearly fallen on top of. He wasn't any more proficient in ASL than she was, but where she chalked her struggles up to her aging mind, his could be more accurately attributed to a lack of effort. Virginia fought in every class to remember the signs she needed and tried her best to keep from speaking when she couldn't recall a sign, but her partner had no qualms with ignoring the professor's *voice box off* request.

"Damn," he muttered, flopping his hands down into his lap in frustration. "Garage. I can't remember the sign for garage." She racked her brain in an effort to come up with the sign and show him, but he continued verbally. "Does your house have a garage?"

"Uh…" She signed NO and was considering whether she knew any other vocabulary she could use to describe where she lived when her phone lit up and grabbed her attention. Turning away from her partner, she looked down at the screen to see a message from Lucy.

> Found Dax. With him at his apartment now. You need to come.

She'd hardly finished reading the message before she grabbed up her bag and left without so much as saying goodbye to her partner, only muttering, "Excuse me," as she pushed past him and into the aisle, hurrying for the door. As she did, another message came through from Lucy with an address.

Virginia dialed Marney before she'd even made it through the vestibule leading out to the parking lot.

"Lucy's with Dax at his apartment," she said the moment Marney answered. "I'm heading over there now." If anyone could lead them to Bianca, it was Dax. Loretta had described him as distraught that Lucy wouldn't go with him. Whatever hard exterior he projected, and however much harm he'd caused, Virginia believed Dax did love her daughter. And if they told him what they'd learned about Bianca, he would lead them to her to keep Lucy safe.

There was a pause on the other end while Marney processed the unexpected information. "Didn't Loretta say Lucy already saw Dax and turned him down? Why is she with him again now?"

"I guess I'll find out soon."

"I don't like this. Why don't you come here first, and we can all go together?"

"I can't waste that kind of time," Virginia countered. "What if Dax runs again?"

Marney huffed, frustrated. "Then we'll pay Loretta another visit. We'll come up with another plan. Virginia, what if it's—"

"I've got to get over there. Nothing bad is going to happen. I'll be safe, I promise." Virginia pressed her hand into the push bar, swung the door outward, and then charged into the evening.

Dax's apartment building was older than Lucy's. One of the lights on the side of the building meant to be lighting up the sidewalk and stairway flickered. Virginia double-checked the unit number in the message and stepped into the blinking light. One hand retained a tight grip on her phone while the other gripped the handrail of the stairs. She was out of breath when she reached the landing, but she didn't pause before knocking hard on the door to Dax's apartment.

The door swung open from the blow, and her stomach dropped immediately. "Lucy?" She stepped inside, just barely. When she didn't get a response, she added, "The door was open."

A step forward put her in a mostly darkened living room, orange-hued light from the kitchen illuminating only a fraction of the space. As she stepped farther inside, she made out her daughter and Dax sitting on the couch and exhaled a sigh of relief, cut short by the sound of the door slamming shut behind her.

Virginia whirled and found herself staring down the barrel of a gun, the woman holding the weapon recognizable from a picture Virginia had seen on Loretta's social media.

It was the woman she'd been looking for.

Bianca.

"Wha—?" Virginia's fingers loosened, and her phone fell from her hand, clattering to the floor. Bianca cackled, then stepped forward and stomped once—hard—on the phone.

"Sit," she directed, waving the gun to point Virginia toward the sofa where Lucy and Dax sat. When Virginia braved another look in their direction, taking her eyes off Bianca and that steel monstrosity in her hands, she understood why neither of them had cried out or come to her aid.

Lucy and Dax were slumped, heads lolling together and jaws hanging slack.

"What have you done?" Virginia hurried to the couch and gripped her daughter's face in her hands, then grabbed her wrist to feel for a pulse.

"They're fine," Bianca said. "For now, at least." When Virginia turned her head, Bianca was smiling down at them wickedly. She waved the gun and repeated her command. "Sit."

Virginia's pulse thundered. She tried to calm it, tried to reconcile what she'd expected with what she'd found, her entire world turned on its side. She sat but didn't take her hands off Lucy until she found what she was looking for, the tiny thrum of a heart still pumping blood.

Satisfied that Lucy wasn't dead, she looked around for the first time. Her only mission now was to get her daughter out of there. From where Virginia sat on the ratty sofa, she couldn't see anyone else in the apartment. Just Dax and Lucy, out cold, and Bianca, triumph rolling off her in waves as she stood above them, angling that gun toward them.

"How about a cup of tea?" Bianca asked, then turned toward the kitchen. There was a menacing air of amusement in the words, and Virginia watched closely as Bianca traipsed into the kitchen and began filling the kettle. Metal clanged on metal as she set it back onto the stove and then flicked on the burner. The burner on the other side of the stove from where she's set the kettle began to turn red. She turned, meeting Virginia's eyes, and then pulled a plastic cutting board from one of the cabinets and set it on the now-glowing burner.

"Oops," she said with a giggle. "Looks like I turned on the wrong burner by mistake. At least, that's what the fire department will say when they look for the source of the fire that tragically killed three people tonight."

Virginia shoved herself up from the couch, but Bianca was on her in a second, the barrel of the gun pointed directly at her forehead. She started to ease herself back down when the door burst open.

"Argh!" Ronald rushed into the room, arms up and hands stiff in a karate stance. Patricia and Marney hurried in behind him.

"Virginia? Are you—?" Marney's concern cut off abruptly as the three of them took in Bianca, then her gun.

Bianca blinked, equally surprised at the intrusion, but then a feline grin spread across her face. "Ah. The gang's all here."

Ronald roared again, lunging for Bianca. A crash split the air, and Ronald fell and landed at Bianca's feet, his cry the echo of the gunshot.

"No!" Virginia, Marney, and Patricia all moved toward him without hesitation, but Bianca fired a second time, this time into the ceiling, a warning to put an end to the chaos. The three immediately paused, and Ronald let out a groan from where he lay, blood beginning to seep from his leg onto the carpet.

Never dropping her weapon, Bianca moved to the kitchen, where the smell of melting plastic was beginning to fill the air. With one hand, she grabbed a glass from the cabinet and filled it with water. There was some light commotion, and then Bianca emerged with the glass.

"Sit," she barked, and the three women did, leaving Ronald on the floor, moaning. Bianca frowned down at him, her serene, controlled demeanor slipping slightly, her breath hitching. Shooting someone hadn't been part of her plan. Incinerated bodies from an accidental kitchen fire was simple; case closed. But a gunshot wound in one of the bodies might raise concern.

The smell coming from the kitchen was stronger now. Both Marney and Patricia noticed it at the same time, their heads swiveling in that direction where smoke was rising from the burning cutting board. Any color left in their faces vanished as they understood Bianca's plan.

Bianca handed the glass of water to Virginia first, ordering her to drink. Her eyes slid from Virginia to Dax and Lucy, and Virginia knew that whatever she'd given them was in this drink.

"Why are you doing this?" Virginia asked.

"Drink," Bianca repeated.

"Why did you kill Ian?" Desperation filled every word, but Bianca was unmoved.

"I'd stick around for the monologue, but I'm afraid we don't have time." She nodded to the kitchen. "Now, drink."

Virginia raised the glass to her mouth and took a sip. Bianca took the glass and passed it to Marney next, then Patricia. She cast another look at Ronald, then said darkly, "I don't think he's going anywhere," and dumped the remainder of the drink down the sink.

The smell of smoke intensified, but Bianca still remained, pointing the gun at them and waiting. Virginia's heart thundered, and a whisper of panic swelled in her when Patricia's eyes blinked closed. Then Marney's. Then her own eyes fluttered shut, and Bianca let out a satisfied grunt.

"Good riddance," she said, then strutted to the door as the first lick of flame rose up from the melted cutting board.

CHAPTER 32

The second the door shut behind them, Virginia and Marney opened their mouths in unison, the drug-filled water spilling from their lips. Relief flooded Virginia's veins when she realized Marney had hatched the same plan she had, and when she realized it had worked. They were still conscious, at least for the moment.

"The fire," Marney said, rushing for the kitchen while Virginia crouched down beside Ronald. Her extremities tingled—she'd ingested some of whatever Bianca had given them—but she still had control of her limbs.

"Ronald?" she asked, searching his ashen face. He blinked up at her, and she let out a sob. "I thought you were—"

"Be relieved later," he rasped before launching into a violent fit of coughing. "After you save us."

Marney clattered in the kitchen, searching for a fire extinguisher or something to douse the flames. Virginia stood, pulling herself up on a chair and trying not to think about how heavy her legs felt, and moved to Patricia next. They needed to get out.

"Patricia," she said, her voice cracking as she fought tears. "Wake up. I need you to be awake." She slapped Patricia's cheeks, praying the drugs hadn't fully set in, that maybe her friend would open her eyes. Patricia's head only lolled where Virginia moved it.

"Marney," she called. "I need your help. We've got to move them."

Marney flew into the room from the kitchen, distraught. "I can't put it out. It's growing so fast."

Virginia could see fire spreading across the countertop and up the kitchen wall. It was only going to grow faster and faster. They had minutes, if that. "Help me move them!"

Marney reached her side, and Virginia lunged for Lucy first, shouting an apology at Ronald's groaning form as she looped an arm under one of Lucy's shoulders. Marney followed suit, and the two staggered with Lucy between them to the door. They dropped her on the landing outside and yelled for help, but no one came. No neighbors emerged from their apartments. They were on their own, and they were running out of time.

When they raced back into the apartment, the flames had engulfed more of the kitchen and were creeping along the wall toward the living room. Virginia reached down for Ronald's hand, and she and Marney yanked him into a sitting position. As he tried to stand, Ronald let out a scream of agony and fell back down, Virginia and

Marney unable to hold him upright. Heat beat on their backs as the fire began to swallow up the room.

"I'm so sorry," Virginia wept. "I'm so, so sorry."

Virginia's eyes met Marney's, the pair coughing and choking and waiting until the last possible moment to leave their friends. She didn't realize it would be this loud, a fire. As the flames consumed all the air in the room and roared mightily with it, her own cries were drowned out. The roar only grew louder as the fire grew stronger, and she considered throwing herself down next to Ronald and going out with the friends she couldn't save, the friends she unwittingly lured to their dooms. As the roar of the fire turned into a rhythmic pounding, only the look in Marney's eyes kept Virginia upright and had her moving for the doorway instead of lying down. The look that mirrored her own guilt and despair, the weight of which she might never get over.

The smoke stung her eyes, and she blinked through tears. The tug from Marney's hand kept her aiming for the door. Four figures appeared in the doorway, their movements distorted. Their faces moved like they were shouting, but she couldn't hear over the sounds of the fire and her own heartbeat.

"Alive!" someone yelled loud enough for Virginia to make out the words, then reached out and yanked her bodily through the doorway and onto the landing. "Get her down the stairs," they said—to whom, Virginia wasn't sure—and then they were gone.

"Lucy...?" Virginia scanned the landing for her daughter, but she wasn't where Virginia and Marney had left her. Marney's shaking hand found hers again, and before Virginia could ask anything, a police officer in uniform took her other hand and led them down the stairs toward the parking lot where three police cars were parked along the curb.

"My friends—" Virginia protested at the top of the stairs, trying to point back toward the door to the apartment, but the officer cut her off.

"My guys won't leave them," he said. "Now, let's go."

At the bottom of the stairwell, Virginia could see Lucy laid out on the strip of grass between the sidewalk and the asphalt. Her knees gave out at the sight, and the officer lowered her to sit on the stairs. The blare of sirens was upon them with little warning, and two fire engines careened into the parking lot, launching into action immediately. An ambulance followed right behind. Then, the officer who had escorted them down the stairs was gone, and more emergency responders were streaming up the stairs past Virginia.

"Why don't you come with me?" a new voice asked. Virginia's vision was still blurred, but she made out the forest green uniform of the woman who'd spoken. "Let's get you out of the way and check you out." Too exhausted to object, Virginia let the woman take the bulk of Virginia's weight with an arm under her shoulder and walked with her over to the ambulance.

While the paramedics tended to Virginia and Marney, Virginia craned her neck toward the burning apartment. She needed to know that the responders had gotten everyone out in time, but she couldn't make herself ask.

"Kitchen fire?" the woman asked. Virginia's eyes swam as she turned them back to the paramedic. She thought about how to respond, then settled on just nodding. She didn't have it in her to explain. The woman clicked her tongue, disapproving of what she imagined to be carelessness leading to this tragedy.

A second ambulance pulled up beside the first. More paramedics leaped out and immediately began unloading stretchers. Virginia's eyes dipped closed, her head spinning, and when she opened them again, Ronald, Patricia, Dax, and Lucy were all on stretchers, multiple green-clad paramedics tending to Ronald's leg and shouting to each other. A glance behind her found Marney talking to a police officer. They were standing beside a third ambulance, which must have arrived while she'd dozed.

Virginia lifted a hand and tried to point to her other friends. "How—?" she tried to ask, but the word came out as a croak and sent her into a coughing fit that shook her weary body.

Footsteps alerted her to people coming toward her, and she looked up, expecting to be taken to the hospital and vowing that she'd get answers as soon as she could speak enough to ask the questions, that she'd alert the authorities to who was behind all this. Instead of paramedics approaching to load her onto an ambulance, Dylan came walking toward her with the person she least expected to see.

"Bill," she breathed. And then she lost consciousness.

* * *

Virginia was vaguely aware of being laid out on a stretcher and hoisted into an ambulance. She came to again as two nurses were transferring her to a bed in a starkly lit hospital room, recognizable in Virginia's swimming field of vision primarily by the beeping of the monitoring equipment. Across the room, she could see Marney but no one else.

Panicking, she lifted her head, and pain radiated from behind her eyes. "The others?" she tried to ask. It came out scratchy and inaudible.

"What's that?" one of the nurses asked, and Virginia repeated her question, using all her energy to force the sound out. "Oh, they're here, too. You can see them in the morning."

They were okay, then, or they would be. Right? Virginia told herself that the nurse wouldn't have said that if any of them wasn't going to be okay, and then, feeling slightly better, let herself drift out of consciousness again.

"Ma'am, you can't—" Virginia woke to Dylan charging into the room, a flustered nurse right on her heels, trying to dissuade her. "They're not ready for visitors."

Dylan paid the nurse no attention, marching to Marney's bedside and crouching, holding Marney's hand in her own. Her thumb brushed over the tubes protruding from Marney's wrinkled skin, and her voice was thick when she said, "Hi, Mom."

Deciding Marney could handle the visit and wanting no further argument with Dylan, the nurse left.

Virginia tried to sit up. Here was someone who might have actual answers; she didn't want to let her exhaustion stop her from getting them. Her head swam the moment she lifted it from the pillow, and she lay back, choking out the question that had been on her lips from before the ambulance had whisked them away. "How?"

"It's thanks to Mom," Dylan said. She wiped a tear from her eye and gestured to Marney. "She called me to let me know you were barreling head-first into something that didn't feel right. She begged me to get McNeil and a few officers over there since the police station's closer to those apartments than Breeze Village is. It seems Breeze Village residents drive like F1 racers, though. She and the others beat the officers from the station, who beat me since I was coming from home."

Virginia tried to imagine the police getting a report that one elderly woman believed—without any evidence —that her friend was in danger in an apartment across town and responding that quickly. As if seeing the doubt written across her face, Dylan laughed and said, "McNeil told them that if it turned out to be nothing, he'd bring donuts to the station every day—even his days off—for a month."

"That's what I call motivation," Virginia chuckled. The laughter felt wrong in her body, and the jolt of it shook something loose in her mind. She sat up suddenly, ignoring the pain that shot through her at the motion. "Bianca!" She tried to toss the blanket off her, to swing her legs over the side of the bed as if she could run out and chase down Bianca herself, but she fell to the side and then Dylan was beside her, helping her back into a lying position.

"Shh, it's okay," Dylan said softly, but the reassurance

did nothing to calm Virginia until she added, "She's at the station. In a cell." When Virginia's face remained bewildered, Dylan clarified, "We got her. She's under arrest. For the attempted murder of you six, plus Ian's murder, and the attempted murder of Lucy by way of sabotaging her car."

All Virginia could do was repeat her question. "How?" she demanded again.

"That beau of yours," Dylan said.

So, she hadn't imagined it. Bill really had been there at the apartment.

She looked around, expecting him to come through the door.

"He's still at the station," Dylan said. "He's giving a formal statement. He'll be here as soon as he can." Seeing the way Virginia's face fell, Dylan added, "I saw the look on his face when he saw you outside that apartment. That man loves you, Virginia. He'll be here."

Bill did come, and just as Dylan had done for Marney, he rushed to Virginia's bedside and fell to his knees, taking her hand in both of his own. "You're okay," he breathed, running his hand over hers again as if to reassure himself.

"And the woman who put us here is behind bars thanks to you, we hear," Marney said from across the room. Bill noticed her presence for the first time and smiled at her.

"The police officers deserve all the credit," he said, and Marney laughed.

"I deserve some of it," she said. "I got them there. How'd you end up there, anyway?"

Bill looked back to Virginia and said softly, "I followed Virginia out of class and heard her on the phone. It sounded like she was having a little argument, and then she promised to be safe. While I don't know this woman as well as I hope to in the future, I get the sense that Virginia doesn't say she'll be safe when she actually intends do the safe and responsible thing. So, I figured she was about to do something dangerous, possibly related to the other times she's run out on me, and I followed her."

Marney's brows were raised in appreciation. Virginia was just listening, rapt, taking in the actions of this man who had possibly saved their lives.

Bill turned to Virginia. "I saw you go into that apartment and not come out. I dialed 9-1-1 but couldn't press *call*. I didn't want to waste the police officers' time if it was nothing. So, I just waited." His voice wavered, and he shook his head, upset with himself. "Then your friends went in after you, and I kept watching. And then, finally, I saw a woman exit the apartment with a gun in her hand. I thought I saw smoke coming out the door, too, but I couldn't be sure." He took a deep breath. "And then I did the hardest thing I've ever done. I followed her, leaving you in that apartment when I didn't know if you were dead or alive or what had happened in there. I called the police the moment I saw her walk out with that gun, but I knew I couldn't let her get away. I followed her instead of trying to save you."

Virginia's throat pinched too tight for her to respond. He sounded so regretful, but Dylan had just told them it had worked. Bianca was behind bars, and it was all thanks to Bill.

"She talked," Bill said. "That woman, Bianca. She drove to one of those new-construction neighborhoods on the south side and went into one of the houses there. I stayed a few blocks away on the phone with the police, and when they pulled up, I pointed out the house. She heard the sirens and came shooting out of the garage in her car, *Grand Theft Auto* style. She took out the garage door and everything! She tried to speed off, but she hit a trash can and spun out. She was railing at the police—'I'm innocent! I demand a lawyer! This is an illegal arrest!'—but then she saw me. I guess since I'm old and half the people she'd just tried to incinerate are old, she figured I was with you. She pointed at me and said I'd regret this. Told me I'd burn just like my friends, and that she knew people who could get to me even if she was behind bars.

"The police just let her talk, and it's like the more she said, the less she could keep it inside. She said that none of this was ever supposed to happen, but then, in the same breath, she said she had to kill you because you just wouldn't let it go. That you deserved what happened to you in that apartment."

It was a weird sensation, hearing that someone had confessed to killing her while looking down at her very-much-still-alive body. She reached over and rubbed one hand across the opposite forearm, feeling the tickle and confirming that she was, in fact, alive.

"Why?" Virginia still wanted to know. "Why do any of it? I wouldn't stop investigating, sure, but before that— why kill Ian in the first place?"

Bill swallowed and looked to Dylan before saying anything, looking for the approval of someone who wasn't currently laid up in a hospital bed before he dropped any more information on them. Dylan nodded, so he answered.

"She kept saying, 'It was supposed to be Loretta. It was supposed to be easy.' It sounded like she tried to frame someone named Loretta for the murder, but it didn't work. Then she said…" He swallowed again, working up the courage to say, "She said that if it had to go sideways, at least it was Lucy getting pinned for it, but that prison wasn't enough for people like her. She deserved to die. Bianca said that if she was going down, at least she could go knowing she gave Lucy what she deserved first."

Virginia closed her eyes and breathed deeply through her nose, fighting off the wave of nausea that was sweeping over her.

"Lucy is your daughter," Bill said, and Virginia nodded confirmation. "Oh, Virginia." Bill's body shook as he began to cry.

There were two quick knocks on the door and then it swung open to reveal the nurse. "Someone else wants to see you two," she said. She saw Dylan and Bill and looked like she wanted to tell them to leave but didn't want to fight if they protested.

Without waiting to be told, Bill stood. "I'll be back tomorrow," he said, brushing Virginia's hair back in a way that sent goosebumps up her arms. "Get some rest."

He walked out, and Lawrence walked in, his usually calm face absolutely furious. "If I have to visit you two in a hospital one more time!" But his face softened the moment he saw his friends.

"You're just jealous your life in an oceanfront condo

doesn't come with the same excitement we Breeze Villagers get," Marney said. The words were thick as the pain medicines coursed through her system and she began to lose the ability to keep herself awake.

Lawrence paced tiny laps around the room, fussing. He tucked blanket corners under the mattresses, tidied cables, and straightened the magnetic dry-erase markers hanging by the whiteboard on the wall. Then he did another lap, straightening the same markers and re-tucking the blankets. On his third lap, Marney admonished him, and he sat, just taking in his friends' faces.

They sat in silence, entirely drained, and Virginia had begun to doze when the door swung open again, clattering into the wall.

"Mom!" Jack cried.

"I told you, visiting hours are—what are you two doing here? Visiting hours are over!" A new nurse, older than the one they'd had earlier and, judging by her expression, much more willing to kick out stubborn visitors, squawked at Lawrence and Dylan.

Jack tried to shove past her toward Virginia's bed, but the nurse, though she was a full foot shorter than him, bumped him with her hip and shoved him backward.

"Your mother is fine. I'll go over her chart with you, and you can see her at seven o'clock in the morning. But for now, you can't be here." She turned back to Lawrence and Dylan. "And neither can you. Out! Go on—get!"

Jack fumed but assessed the likelihood of changing the nurse's mind to be slim. With a promise to return at seven on the dot, he walked out, the nurse flicking the light off and slamming the door shut behind them all.

After a long moment of silence, blind in the new dark, Virginia said, "It doesn't make sense, does it? Bianca trying to set Loretta up? Why would she try to frame her best friend for murder?"

Marney's only answer was a long snore.

CHAPTER 33

After a fitful and interrupted night of sleep—by the nurse who turned the light on full blast to check her vitals and by the beeping and whirring of the machines monitoring those vitals—Virginia contemplated ripping the IV out of her arm and fleeing the premises before the clock could strike seven and visitors could arrive.

When a nurse came to check on them at a quarter before the hour, Virginia asked after Lucy and the others. She could see her pulse raise on the monitor beside her bed and then regulate when the nurse smiled and said, "All doing great. Your friend with the missing teeth is really something, isn't he?"

Marney's laughter was the first sign she was awake, and while Virginia threw her head back and laughed, she also had to wipe a tear from the corner of her eye.

"You want to go see them?" the nurse asked.

In the room Lucy shared with Patricia, her daughter was sitting up in bed. Her hair was somehow perfectly in place and her eyes were free of dark circles or any other sign that she'd had as bad a night's sleep as Virginia had. She typed furiously into her phone and looked around as if for her things.

"Mom!" she called out as soon as Virginia entered, pushing a hospital-provided walker. "I'm trying to figure out how I can get them to discharge me in the next five minutes. I need a shower and a coffee that doesn't taste like dirt before I can handle seeing Jack."

"I'm so happy to see you, too, sis."

Lucy's eyes went wide and fixed on the door behind Virginia, where she turned to see Jack striding through.

"I can't believe it." Jack's clothes were wrinkled, like he'd slept in them, and his hair stood up straight from his head. He ran his hand through it, tugging at the hairs as he exhaled in exasperation, and Virginia could picture him spending the entire night doing exactly that. "I tell you to keep far away from anything that could put our family in danger, and—"

Patricia smacked her hand on the mattress to draw their attention. "Jack Walker, you listen to me. I nearly died last night at the hands of the person who committed that murder in the art gallery. And it's possible that if your mother hadn't cared about figuring out who did it in order to prove your sister didn't, then I wouldn't have been in that situation. But because she did, because your mother *cared*, your sister won't go to jail for a crime she didn't commit, and a murderer won't walk free. Seaview is a better and safer place thanks to her."

Virginia couldn't have responded if she wanted to. Her throat stung, and she rolled her eyes upward to keep tears from flowing. Jack looked from Patricia to Virginia and Lucy, his mouth tight. Just as he opened his mouth to argue, Stephanie came into the room, Emily strapped to her chest, and said, "And we—and the whole town of Seaview, once they hear about it—are grateful for her persistence."

Upon seeing baby Emily's tiny curls sticking up from the baby sling, Lucy's eyes lit up, just as Virginia knew her own were.

"I'm so sorry," Stephanie said, wrapping Virginia in an awkward hug as she attempted not to crush the baby between them, then squeezing Lucy's hand. "I'm sorry I wasn't there for you both while you were going through all this."

Lucy's jaw dropped, incredulous. "You had a baby less than two months ago, and we weren't there for you afterward because I was arrested for murder. I don't think you have anything to apologize for!"

Stephanie sat on the edge of Lucy's bed, scooting in close like two girls at a slumber party. "Jack filled me in on the arrest and Virginia's subsequent refusal to let the process just play out in court—which, by the way, I wholeheartedly support—but I'm going to need to know how this all happened in the first place."

Lucy's cheeks flushed, and she cocked her head to the side as she weighed how to respond.

"Wrong place, wrong time," Virginia said before Lucy could answer. Someday, Lucy might decide to tell the others about Dax and the circumstances that had gotten her into this situation, but Virginia didn't want that time to be now, before Lucy had time to process her latest near-death experience and everything that had happened to her since discovering Ian's body.

"They got the actual murderer, though," Virginia continued.

"I'm just glad you're okay," Stephanie said.

"We'll be a lot more okay once they let us out of this joint," Patricia said, frowning. "I thought the coffee at Breeze Village was bad!"

* * *

VIRGINIA, Marney, and Patricia were a sight, shuffling down the hallway, pushing their walkers with IV poles like flags. Ronald had a private room, and they walked in to find him snoring loudly, the sound drowning out the cooking competition on the television. One leg was in a bright blue cast and propped on a pile of pillows. Patricia worked her way around the bed to reach his other leg and gave it a solid poke.

Ronald jolted awake, frowning, ready to fuss at whoever had disturbed him, then glowing with joy when he recognized his friends.

"I got shot!" he proudly declared with no lead-in.

"How many times did you think you could leap at a rogue gunman before it finally caught up to you?" Patricia demanded.

Marney told Ronald and Patricia what Dylan and Bill had explained the night before. She'd asked Dylan to get the police to Dax's apartment, and Bill had followed Virginia and then chased down Bianca and led the other officers straight to her. During the story, Dylan poked her head in and crooked a finger at Virginia.

"I wanted to talk with you and Lucy alone for a minute," Dylan said.

Virginia tried to read into her tone, but Dylan gave nothing away. The pair walked slowly down the hallway toward Lucy's room, otherwise empty while Patricia was with Ronald. By the time they slipped inside, Virginia couldn't take it anymore.

"Is she getting out? Getting away with it?" she demanded.

Dylan looked surprised, as if the question were ridiculous. "No. She confessed to it all. After officers brought her in, they got the confession on tape. It's official."

Virginia gripped the edge of Lucy's mattress, sinking down onto the surface in relief. She didn't realize she was crying until Lucy reached out for her hand and gave it a squeeze. When Virginia looked over at her, Lucy's face was wet, too.

"Bill said she was trying to frame Loretta for it all, but that doesn't make sense." Virginia looked up to Dylan, knowing that while Dylan shouldn't tell them anything—and probably shouldn't know anything herself, since she'd retired from the Force—in this case, she would.

Dylan held her eyes on Lucy's face, which flushed under the scrutiny. "Bianca was deeply unhappy in her marriage. And while she was feeling betrayed by her husband for dating someone else, her best friend started stepping out on her own husband. It sounds like this whole plan was supposed to teach Loretta a lesson on infidelity by setting her up to go down for murder, to punish her for doing the same thing to Ian that Bianca felt like Dax was doing to her."

"That's sick," Lucy whispered.

Virginia said, "But it was Lucy's belt in Dax's car, not Loretta's. Loretta grabbed it to borrow, thinking it was Bianca's. Then Bianca took it from Loretta's apartment to use in the crime."

As Virginia explained, Lucy's eyes grew wider.

"You knew about the belt?"

A flash of sympathy and perhaps guilt crossed Dylan's face, but Virginia only nodded.

"And you still wouldn't let up on the case?" Lucy asked. "You knew why the police thought I did it—that the murder weapon was something of mine—and you still wouldn't give up? You..." She trailed off, her voice growing more and more strangled.

"I believed you," Virginia said, her own voice choked. "I knew you didn't do it."

Dylan looked at the floor and fiddled with her hands.

After a moment, Lucy looked down at her lap and said, "I haven't gone to visit Dax. And he hasn't come to see me."

While Virginia still wanted to take another good swing at Dax with her cane for getting Lucy involved in any of this mess, she also knew Lucy would have to make her own decisions about how she wanted to move forward.

"That might be because he was taken into police custody earlier this morning," Dylan said. When Lucy and Virginia both looked at her in confusion, she added, "Bianca's confession implicated him in a money laundering scheme."

Fear sapped the color from Virginia's face as she realized that Lucy was also involved, but Dylan held up a hand and put her at ease. "Dax fully confessed to his crimes—taking counterfeit money out of the gallery, buying furniture in cash with the fake bills, then restoring it and flipping it for real money—and insisted that Lucy had no knowledge or involvement in any of it."

Lucy laid back, staring at the ceiling. Whether she deserved it or not, Lucy was spared the consequences of her participation. Virginia thought she'd already suffered enough for walking into that gallery with the briefcase.

"It sounds like the whole gallery has been in an upheaval this morning. Thanks to Dax's confession, the printer was arrested and thousands of dollars in fake bills were seized. Police are still searching the premises, but when they arrived, the owner of the gallery freaked out and confessed to defrauding his buyers, thinking that's why they were there."

"Sounds like a busy day," Virginia said, happy her part in it all was over.

"*There* you are!" The tinny voice hit Virginia's ears at the same time as the powdery perfume hit her nostrils. Jan jingled into the room, her earlobes stretched down nearly to her shoulders under the weight of her earrings. The massive blue stones were encircled by flower petals of clear stones, and silver threads with beads at the ends hung from the center and brushed her blouse as she walked.

Jan plopped herself onto Lucy's mattress next to Virginia without any further greeting. Lucy raised her eyebrows but didn't say anything.

"We just had a new resident move into Harbor Vale, and he listens to police scanners day in, day out, and he knows I like to be kept in the know. Boy, I shocked him, rushing straight out of there without finishing my breakfast the moment he told me about the fire. When they said it involved a group of senior citizens, I knew it had to be you. And everything going on at that art gallery! Can you believe it? And to think, Breeze Village took you all on a field trip there just a few weeks ago." She shook her head in disbelief.

"I'll leave you to it," Dylan said and started to leave, but Virginia leapt up after her, grabbing for her IV stand as she swayed on her feet.

"Let me walk you out," Virginia insisted. "In case you forgot where Marney's and my room is."

In the hallway, she muttered to Dylan, "The car... Lucy's accident... You said Bianca was charged with that, too?"

Dylan nodded. "Everything they say about a woman scorned... Bianca really took it up a notch. When her attempt to punish Loretta by pinning her for her husband's murder failed, she set her sights on getting revenge on Lucy. Her plan wasn't working, so she lashed out and tried to cause as much pain as she could to the people she felt had wronged her. But she's not getting away with it. Like I said, her confession was recorded. She's done."

Virginia threw her arms around Dylan. "Thank you."

The clinking of jewelry preceded Jan's coming into the hallway. "Lucy got a phone call, and I need to check on Marney, too. What they were saying on the police scanners… It was unbelievable! They say police aren't allowed to lie to you to trick you into getting arrested. Do you think they can lie on the scanners? I just don't see how one little gallery…"

Jan talked all the way back to their room, but Virginia hardly heard it. When Lawrence arrived and asked if she could show him where the coffee vending machine was, she heartily agreed.

They were just about to leave when Jan's phone rang and she exclaimed, "It's Dorothea! She'll want to hear all about this. Say, I think she's been feeling a little lonely lately. Next time there's an investigation, do you think you could loop her in? It would mean a lot."

"Next time?" Lawrence and Marney demanded in unison.

"Of course," Virginia said, but Jan was already gone, her voice getting quieter as she jangled down the hall and into the elevator.

"You don't actually want the coffee from that vending machine," Virginia said when she was gone. "It's awful."

"I didn't really want it in the first place," Lawrence replied with a chuckle. "I just wanted to not be in the same room with Jan, but I didn't know of a more graceful way to leave the moment I arrived."

lick. Click.

Virginia blinked in time with the camera shutter despite a herculean effort to keep her eyes open against the setting sun.

"Now let's get one with both grandmas and baby." The bubbly high schooler Stephanie had hired for a family photo shoot was all business. She stood straight and waved Jack to the side, dismissing him. He opened his mouth to object, but Stephanie plopped baby Emily into her mother's arms and stepped aside, beaming at Sam and Virginia from behind the photographer, and Jack grudgingly followed her lead.

"Do you want to hold her for one?" Sam asked.

Virginia hesitated. She did, more than anything, but she didn't expect Sam to offer. And as she reached out to take her granddaughter into her arms, part of her still waited for Jack to object.

She'd been discharged from the hospital two weeks ago to the day, and she'd spent the majority of those days visiting Jack and Stephanie, soaking up as much time with the baby as she could and making herself useful cleaning bottles or doing dishes. She still found herself quietly competing with Sam in the role of grandmother—Who could stop Emily's crying or get her down for a nap more quickly?—but they were finding their rhythm.

And Lucy, all charges dropped and her name cleared, had found work for a larger marketing firm. It required her to travel to Atlanta half-time, but when she was in Seaview, she was enjoying being an aunt. And working with her newest client, the Benson-Barnes Art Gallery right there in Seaview. After a murder on site, the arrest of its owner for defrauding buyers by inflating the value of the art sold through the gallery, and the unfolding of a counterfeiting scheme being run out of the gallery, the new owner decided they could use a marketing profes-sional to re-launch the gallery with an updated image.

Virginia put a hand up to shield her eyes, squinting at the figure walking toward them across the sand.

"That's Bill!" she said, the joy inside her bubbling up at the sight of him. She passed Emily back to Sam as he grew nearer and waved.

"Where's tonight's date?" Stephanie asked.

"Luigi's."

I want to see your face light up looking at that pasta again, Bill had said when he'd cornered her after class to schedule a date. *Just don't sprint out of the restaurant mid-date again.*

She'd promised she wouldn't. It was the easiest promise of her life.

Bill wrapped Virginia in a hug before greeting the

family. She turned to wave goodbye just in time to see Stephanie speaking into the young photographer's ear and gesturing toward them. The photographer snapped a few candid photos of her and Bill.

As they walked, holding hands, back toward the worn wooden walkway across the dunes to the parking lot, Emily let out a wail behind them.

"Sounds like the photo shoot is over," Virginia quipped.

"Once the most beautiful subject leaves, what's the point in taking any more pictures?" Bill asked. Then he stopped walking, tugged her toward him, then bent his head and kissed her lightly for the first time. Virginia wouldn't have been surprised if someone told her she'd levitated off the sand. Sensations fell away—everything except the warmth of his arms around her and his lips pressing into hers. When he pulled away, she giggled like a schoolgirl, her cheeks flushing.

"Don't do that again," she warned, "or we'll be late. Luigi said he'd save us the best table in the house. We can't let that go to waste."

* * *

If you enjoyed this book, please consider leaving a review. It helps me tremendously.

For the latest information on my upcoming releases, find me online at katemacleanbooks.com

* * *

ACKNOWLEDGMENTS

This book would not be in your hands right now were it not for the weekly writing sessions through Shut Up & Write. Thank you to the Shut Up & Write organization for bringing write-ins to folks worldwide, and thank you to my crew who show up every week and write with me.

I must also acknowledge the profound impact Sarra Cannon and her HeartBreathings Writing Community have had on me. Thank you for your relentless support.

A special thanks to my editor, Tracy Mooring Liebchen, for your hawkish eyes. This book is what it is thanks to you.

I have friends and family who routinely ask me how the writing is going and cheer me on. I am blessed to be surrounded by such encouraging souls. But chief among them is my husband, Ken. Thank you for believing in me. Thank you for ensuring I eat a real meal before my write-ins. Thank you for clapping when I could really use some applause. Thank you for it all.

ABOUT THE AUTHOR

A Georgia peach, Kate Maclean grew up in historic Savannah and spent much of her childhood reading Nancy Drew and Hercule Poirot mysteries on her backyard swing.

This lifelong lover of mysteries and crime dramas now lives outside Washington, D.C., with her husband. This is her fourth book.

www.ingramcontent.com/pod-product-compliance
Lightning Source LLC
Chambersburg PA
CBHW031848310726
48972CB00005B/1460